THEATRE
INSIDE
OUT

THEATRE
INSIDE
OUT

Kenneth Hurren

W. H. ALLEN · LONDON
A Howard & Wyndham Company
1977

*Printed and bound in Great Britain by
Butler & Tanner Ltd, Frome and London
for the publishers W. H. Allen & Co. Ltd,
44 Hill Street, London W1X 8LB*

ISBN 0 491 02170 4

CONTENTS

ACKNOWLEDGMENTS

Some of the material in this book is drawn from articles previously published in *The Spectator*, *The Telegraph Magazine*, *Drama*, *Signature* and *What's On IN LONDON*, to the editors of all of which I am indebted for permission to incorporate it.

The number of people who have talked to me about various aspects of the theatre is legion. I am grateful to them all, and especially to Ian Albery, Ray Cooney, Peter Cotes, Peter Hall, Marvin Liebman, Peter Plouviez and Martin Schute. In acknowledging their help I do not, of course, suggest that they are likely to endorse the conclusions I have drawn or the opinions I have expressed.

K.H.

OVERTURE FOR   I
BEGINNERS

You are interested in the theatre, or you would not have got as far as even picking up this book. The chances are that you *like* the theatre. We begin on that common ground. I like it too—even after going to the theatre *and* writing about what I see for what sometimes seems like a hundred years. I may have to sit through a dozen ghastly plays to every one that is tolerable. I probably watch a hundred that vary from the well-meaningly inadequate to the active public nuisance. But expectation continues to triumph over experience—or, if not expectation, at least hope, the hope of the one exceptional production that instantly nullifies the disappointments.

There is drama so stimulating to the intellect and the senses as to make me feel that I would rather be sitting in a theatre than anywhere else on earth. And there are musicals so effervescent with seductive razzmatazz that I think they would make *anyone* a little infatuated with show business. These things happen; not often, but sometimes; and as long as they keep happening, or promise to keep happening, the theatre is not likely to lose its fascination for *me*. You, too?

Nevertheless—all interest, liking, fascination apart—I shall assume that you don't really know much about it; and even perhaps as little as I did myself when I began making the initial inquiries and adding up a few researched facts that led to my writing this book. It is a bit of a love-child, romantically conceived, born out of ignorance. I was really most embarrassingly naïve. I believed almost everything I read in the papers, accepted the clichés and did not question the received mythology.

Thus, since an agent was invariably refered to as 'Mister Ten Per Cent', I thought that agents always took ten per cent of an actor's money; never more, never less. I not only thought of all bachelor actors as homosexuals but of all married actors as heterosexual. (No, honestly, do stop laughing.) I thought the people I saw described as the owners of theatres actually did own them. I thought actors earned more money than stagehands. I thought the principal object of press agents was to get their clients' names into the papers. I did not actually believe that the Government's theatrical subventions (via the Arts Council) went only to people and organisations with valuable contributions to make to the cultural health of the nation. But I *was* astonished by the scores of potty little groups, of which I had never heard, which were being subsidised. And in the commercial theatre, I thought impresarios were men who backed their own judgment, gambled with their own money and only made money with successful shows. If you have shared any or all of these misconceptions, there will be news for you in the ensuing pages.

The book is concerned in the main, if not quite exclusively, with the *London* theatre. Except for the Royal Shakespeare Theatre at Stratford-upon-Avon, which is inseparable from London (and, indeed, has a London branch at the Aldwych), references to the provincial theatre—or 'regional' theatre, which is now the preferred term—are only peripheral. This is not to say that I regard it as of negligible interest or concern. But—I might as well make a few enemies at the outset—it has importance to me only to the extent that its interests and influences are linked with or reflected in London. However much a theatre in a provincial town may be important to the cultural life of that town, to the creative people who work in it (playwrights, directors, designers, actors) it is important chiefly as somewhere to work while they are trying to get to London—notwithstanding enthusiastic, even fanatical, exceptions to this rule. Most of the commercial theatres in the provinces have closed down through lack of audiences, so the theatres that remain out there almost all owe their existence to subsidy. Provincial theatres are necessary as training grounds and testing grounds; but provincial people in general, I find, are only interested in the theatre when they come to London.

I cannot altogether blame them for this, since the general standard of provincial production is not such as to woo them persuasively from their television sets. Nearly everything that is

2

worth seeing in the provinces ultimately turns up in London. This is a fast, generalised and possibly tendentious dismissal of the provincial theatre. So if you believe that the soul of the dramatic art or the glamour of show business resides in your local civic theatre, struggling rep or decaying touring house, you'd best stop reading before you have that haemorrhage.

As well as being primarily about the London theatre, these pages are also primarily about today—give or take a year or two. The history of the theatre and of drama, nationally and internationally, is not included; references to the past are made only in the case of matters that have specific relevance to aspects of the present, and to put into useful perspective such things as the eventual coming to pass of a National Theatre and attitudes generally to the subsidy of the arts. There is no shortage on library shelves of historical treatises about the theatre and theatres, or of learned criticism of dramatic literature: and for detailed accounts of the development of drama, the changes in the status and techniques of actors, the technical advances in stage presentation, the improvements in working conditions and the rises and falls in the fortunes of theatres and theatre people over the centuries, I direct your studies elsewhere.

I make some reference to other sections of the entertainment business—to television and the cinema—but only to the extent that they are related to what happens in the theatre, and in recognition that a great deal of cross-fertilisation necessarily goes on in the way of ideas and talents. Most actors and many directors tend to work in all media. Entrepreneurs involve themselves often in show business as a whole rather than in only one manifestation of it. And the unions concerned with the theatre have overlapping interests with those concerned with television and the cinema (indeed they are usually the same unions). Nevertheless, the theatre is the focal point.

It is, these days, a minority interest compared with those other media of mass entertainment. In Britain, on any given night, at least 150 times as many people will be watching a single television programme as will be present at every live theatrical performance in the country. And a play in a West End theatre could play to capacity audiences for a couple of generations without being seen by nearly as many people as would view it in a single performance

3

on television. Such statistics are, however, misleading in respect of the theatre's importance for both participants and audiences. For example, the theatre employs twice as many actors—though, on the whole, at a lower rate of remuneration—than the cinema and television put together; it is also where actors tend to establish their reputations, and certainly where writers make theirs. The 'man in the street' who may rarely or never go to the theatre but watches a great deal of television would be more likely to be able to name half a dozen dramatists who write plays for the stage than even one who writes only, or mainly, for television. And those audiences who watch a televised play in their millions would still, I have no doubt, regard a visit to see a play in a theatre as a more important and memorable *occasion*.

The theatre somehow *is* 'an occasion'—still. It also somehow retains an aura of 'glamour' and 'romance'—and not only for audiences. I have known some tough operators in the theatre— hard, and not necessarily boiled—who are hooked on it for precisely that reason. When they listen to their heads and their accountants rather than their hearts and their press agents, they know that it is rarely glamorous or romantic. They will always believe, though, that it *can* be both. They are stage-struck.

That is, of course, an opinion. You may have noticed one or two already. The information and enlightenment in these pages is freely interspersed with arguable views on one thing and another. Information unadorned is dull, so, while hoping not to seem too much at the mercy of my prejudices, I cannot break the habit of employing facts to support opinions and opinions to illuminate facts.

The theatre, I suspect, is as much in love with itself as so many on the outside looking in are in love with the theatre; and I do not seek to face a charge of alienation of affections from either party; only to dispel an illusion or two. We shall, perhaps, find some happy plateau between the cloudland of innocence and the slough of disenchantment.

4

ALL THOSE 2
OLD BUILDINGS

I wouldn't bet much on the long-term future of the Palace Theatre. It has one of the most imposing, or at least most noticeable, frontages of any theatre in the West End of London, dominating Cambridge Circus on an island site at the point where Shaftesbury Avenue is intersected by Charing Cross Road. It stands, in a word, at the heart of London's theatreland. All somehow seems right with the theatre world when the Palace is flourishing—as it usually is. But that will not save it.

At the time of writing it is the London home of the musical, or rock oratorio, *Jesus Christ Superstar*, which may not be everyone's chalice but is unquestionably the most strikingly original development in the musical theatre since the second world war. Only a handful of London theatres are big enough to accommodate a show of these dimensions, either in physical or in economic terms. But the Palace may not be among them much longer. Its freehold is marked in the books of the property development company, Stock Conversion and Investment Trust, as 'held for development'.

Turning from one of London's largest theatres (the Palace seats about 1,400) to one of the smallest, the nearby Arts Theatre Club (capacity: 339), a similar pessimism must attend its prospects for survival. The great days of the Arts are past. Its most distinguished period—under the direction of the late Alec Clunes —was between 1942 and 1953. At that time it was described, with no more than a touch of hyperbole, as 'a pocket National Theatre'; and it had brief periods of worthy activity in the late 1950s and in the early 1960s, the latter as an 'experimental' branch of the Royal Shakespeare Company.

Latterly, apart from providing a home for the Unicorn Child-

5

ren's Theatre of the late Caryl Jenner, and accommodating an occasional transfer from the 'fringe', like the Tom Stoppard double-bill *Dirty Linen*, the Arts has given us nothing of much consequence. This is partly because the end of censorship in the public theatre in 1968 removed a large part of the theatre clubs' *raison d'être*, and partly also because too short a lease has been available to encourage any management of the Clunes calibre to take it over with a definable policy and a long-term view to the restoration of its fortunes. This is unfortunate since there are many plays which deserve to be seen in the West End but which would be 'lost' in one of the larger theatres. Only the Ambassadors (capacity: 453) and the Fortune (capacity: 464) approach the intimacy of the Arts, the freehold of which is owned by Knightsbridge Comprehensive Property Investments.

We can, just as a fun exercise, trace a tenuous connection between the Arts and the Palace. It is at once both complicated, because of the number of small links in the chain, and simple because virtually the whole of London's theatreland is covered by a series of interlocking networks of ownership.

Knightsbridge Comprehensive Property Investments, which is, as I said, the freehold owner of the Arts is, in fact, a subsidiary of the English Property Corporation. This Company was formerly known as Star Holdings and also owns the freehold of the New London Theatre, opened in 1973 on the site of the former Winter Garden Theatre.

The chairman of the English Property Corporation, the late Sir Brian Mountain, was also chairman of Eagle Star Insurance Company, which owns 19 per cent of EPC. Eagle Star also owns 23 per cent of another company called Grovewood Securities. And this company owns the freehold of the Cambridge Theatre, acquired in 1969 for close to half a million pounds from London Entertainments Ltd, a company controlled by Sir Emile Littler, who also happens to be a director of Eagle Star.

Now, the New London Theatre, the freehold of which comes, as I said, under the same umbrella as the Arts, has an issued capital of fifty £1 'A' shares and fifty £1 'B' shares, the former owned by the freeholders themselves, the English Property Corporation, and the latter by EMI. The directors of EMI are headed by Lord Delfont, who effectively operates the theatre and who will be generally thought to be the owner of it. Lord Delfont also heads a company called Bernard Delfont and another called the Bernard Delfont Organisation. They have the same directors, two others of whom are also New London directors. *All* the shares in these companies are owned by the Grade Organisation (which, again, has the same directors but do not, as you might suppose, include Lord Grade, although he is a brother of Lord Delfont's). And *all* the shares in the Grade Organisation and its subsidiaries are owned by EMI (chairman, Lord Delfont). As you can see from even this small segment of its operations, EMI is pretty big beans in show business. As far as London theatres are concerned, Lord Delfont is chairman of the Mermaid Theatre Trust, while EMI also owns the lease of the Prince of Wales (from the freeholders, Land Securities Investment Trust), the lease of the Comedy (from the freeholders, Chesterfield Properties) and half the lease of the Palace—which is where this chapter came in.

The other half of the Palace lease is held by Sir Emile Littler's company, London Entertainments, which used to own the freehold, but sold it for half a million in 1960 to the Stock Conversion and Investment Trust, subsequently leasing it back and then splitting the lease with EMI. It is unlikely that that lease runs much beyond 1980, hence that ominous notation, 'held for development' in the accounts of SC&IT.

Sir Emile Littler, it is amusing to reflect, was knighted in 1973 for his services to the theatre. It is true that he had had a long and active career in the theatre, mainly in the world of pantomime, and that he was engaged in a great many worthy and charitable ventures. Nevertheless, it is also true that his most striking service to the theatre in the 1960s was to sell off his two West End theatre freeholds—those of the Palace and the Cambridge—to property development companies. Even if pushed for the odd million or so he might, it may be thought, have been a little choosier about the buyers, since property developers in the context of planning and redevelopment generally in the West End area, offer the most direct threat to the survival of the theatre.

This need not be so. A little give and take among property men, theatre men and planning authorities, backed up by some tight legislation, and all of us with the future of the theatre at heart would feel a great deal cheerier. But we would need that tight

7

legislation, for it seems too trustingly ingenuous to leave everything to 'gentlemen's agreements' when it's hard to be certain who are the 'gentlemen'.

At present we have such operations as the 'Save London's Theatres' campaign more or less forced to take up illogical positions in sheer desperation. Theatre people who try to sustain an argument that none of the West End's present theatres should be pulled down are King Canutes on a certain loser. No one could view with equanimity the prospective demolition of, say, the Theatre Royal, Haymarket, or the Theatre Royal, Drury Lane. If such a thing were ever threatened, I think I'd be out there behind the protest banners—however raggle-taggle a crowd of marchers came along to man the defences and however dubious some of their motives might be suspected to be. The Haymarket and Drury Lane cases are, however, rather exceptional. And, while I have a personal fondness for old theatres, only a cloud-cuckoo would insist dreamily that *none* of them should be swept away. The tide of 'progress' will not be held back, however much we may sometimes be at odds with the kind of 'progress' we get. And, as the face of London changes, for better or for worse, several of the old theatres are going to be pulled down. To declare otherwise is to be unrealistic to the point of absurdity.

In 1973 the Arts Council of Great Britain commissioned Sir James Richards to undertake a survey of, and present a report upon, the planning and redevelopment schemes relevant to the West End of London with especial reference to their likely effect on the theatre. Sir James's subsequently published Report went, it seemed to me, considerably beyond those strict terms of reference. No one would expect the Arts Council—which is a deeply interested party, and exists to *be* so interested—either to want or to welcome a report that did not look at the situation from its own point of view and stress the manifest danger to the theatre of the unbridled horses of property development running loose in the West End.

I could not feel, though, that either the Richards Report or the various press commentators who supported it did their cases much good by the selective and tendentious use of plain facts. The Report told us, for instance, that 'the vulnerability in our time of the buildings used by the commercial theatre is summed up in the

8

list that follows'. And what is the list that follows? Is it, perhaps, a list of theatres lost and theatres built since the second world war? That would seem to be the natural period to take, at the lengthiest, when speaking of theatres that are both of our time and 'vulnerable in our time'. Sir James evidently felt, however, that the 'vulnerability' case would not look persuasive enough on that basis, so he chose quite arbitrarily to take his theatres from a period beginning in 1936 and was thus able to include among the losses a couple of theatres (the Alhambra and Daly's) that had succumbed to the cinema boom of the 1930s, plus others that were destroyed not by property developers (ostensibly his primary concern) but by wartime bombing. On the other hand, he did not feel impelled to include among the 'gains' either the Royal Court (which was a cinema in 1936 and did not become a live theatre again until 1952) or the London Casino (which was a cabaret-restaurant, similar to the present Talk of the Town, in 1936, but which, since the war, has been used alternately as both cinema and theatre).

If, in fact, Sir James's list had been of theatres lost *since the war*, there would not have been nineteen but only ten names on it. And even they include two which are not in the West End at all but at Hammersmith. The others would have been the Hippodrome (now the Talk of the Town theatre–restaurant), Playhouse (which has been a BBC studio, but may possibly become a live theatre again), Saville (converted to cinemas), St James's (demolished), Scala (which was rarely used for professional performances, apart from *Peter Pan* at Christmas), Stoll, Windmill (since reclaimed for live shows, admittedly of a not-too-elevating character) and Winter Garden. These are counter-balanced by those that have opened during the same period: the Jeannetta Cochrane, May Fair, Mermaid, National (in course of building at the time of the Report, but now open and incorporating *three* theatres), New London (on the site of the Winter Garden), Prince Charles (also equipped as a cinema and used as such at the time of writing), Round House, Royalty (on the site of the Stoll), Shaw and Young Vic. Additionally, the former cinema, the Cameo Poly, is now the Regent Theatre and, at least as long as *The Rocky Horror Show* keeps running, a former Chelsea cinema is the Kings Road Theatre. Some of the new theatres are certainly smaller than

9

the lost ones. But taking also into account a number of lively 'fringe' theatres—plus the Royal Court, Casino and the rebuilt Queen's—it would be difficult to argue that London's theatrical activity had appreciably diminished—in terms of either stages or audience accommodation—since the war.

I draw attention to this manipulation of facts not to minimise the vulnerability of theatre buildings in an age of architectural change and property development, but simply to get some of the more spurious 'evidence' out of the argument. The case for more realistic vigilance is powerful enough. But what must also be seen is that it is not in *every* instance that the loss of a particular theatre need be regarded as a disaster.

'None of the existing London theatres should be allowed to disappear,' was the hard-line conclusion of the Richards Report. If *that* were to be accepted by all the various authorities concerned, we could break up the meeting and forget the whole thing. But it is, of course, nonsense. The Report, indeed, recognises it as fairly dreamy because one or two other ideas—far more sensible ones—are put forward.

Thus: (1) 'The practice of permitting the demolition of a theatre building on condition that a new theatre is incorporated in whatever building replaces it is not satisfactory': (2) 'No building . . . should be allowed to be demolished until the design for the building that is to replace it has been given planning permission'; and (3) 'A new theatre, properly equipped, would be so expensive to build that, unless it was subsidised, no manager could afford to run it and only the rich could patronise it.'

The second and third points there are essentially what gives validity to the first point, and that one is vital. For the fact that I would concede that many London theatres will have to come down in the course of the next couple of decades does not mean that I think London can really do with any fewer theatres. That there is a demand for theatres on the part of producing managements is clear enough from the fact that no theatre is ever 'dark' for long. It usually only happens after a quick and unexpected flop, or perhaps when it has a future commitment making it less than worthwhile for a management to go in for a limited interim period. I doubt, however, whether managements are universally happy with all the existing theatres and their amenities.

10

One of the theatres the threat to which has occasioned howls of outrage from the save-them-all-regardless contingent is the Shaftesbury, formerly the Princes. The freehold had been bought by a company called Prinmar, owned jointly by the companies of Sir Charles Clore and by EMI, whose representative on the board was, as you may guess, Lord Delfont. Prinmar's balance sheet as of June 1972 valued the freehold at £363,084. Early in 1973 they sold it for one and a half million pounds to Peureula Investments, a property development company that had previously been acquiring other sites in the same general area with a view to substantial redevelopment—backed by the Keyser Ullmann merchant bank. This was a nice piece of business for Delfont and it could conceivably be contended that he had a powerful financial reason for his view that the Shaftesbury—with all its pillars and gallery seats—was an out-moded theatre and should be replaced by something better. Nevertheless, Lord Delfont had a valid point. Pillars *do* block the customers' view, and not many theatregoers in these more egalitarian times are keen to sit up in 'the gods': the gallery seats are always the last to be sold these days. Delfont's own (leased) Prince of Wales Theatre is far better off in that respect. Its seating is all in stalls or dress circle, so let's hope he sees it that way if he ever gets a hefty offer from Land Securities to buy off the remaining period of his lease on it.

Lord Delfont's views on the live theatre have sometimes seemed to be fairly adjustable according to circumstances. The old Saville Theatre in upper Shaftesbury Avenue always struck me as the most pleasant and spacious of the more modern theatres (it was built in 1931), and housed many lavish spectacular musicals and straight plays, both before and after Delfont was happy to acquire the freehold in 1961. 'We were terribly hampered with that theatre, which had a dreadful stage,' he said later, having turned it into the ABC 1 and 2 cinema complex.

The writing for that move might have been seen to be on the wall. For, shortly before taking the freehold of the Saville, Delfont had taken a lease of the new Royalty Theatre—which had been incorporated in the office block that replaced the old Stoll Theatre —setting advantageous terms from the developers, with whom he had a friendly relationship. In his programme-note introduction to the first production at the Royalty he wrote enthusiastically of

11

his determination that the theatre should house only live entertainment. Nevertheless, inside a year, it became a cinema under the aegis of M-G-M and was not reclaimed to the live theatre again for more than ten years. It remains to be seen what happens there in the future. Also to be watched is the New London which Lord Delfont insists will never be turned into a cinema—despite the thoughtful provision of all the accoutrements of a cinema in its design and equipment.

It is obviously impossible, of course, to compel theatres to operate *as* theatres at a loss (commercial theatres, that is; subsidised theatres, by definition, operate at a loss). Yet that would almost certainly be the case if the true economic rents were levied for theatres on newly developed sites. If the developer is required to put a satisfactory new theatre into an office block that has replaced a demolished theatre, the operation could cost him one and a half or two million pounds; yet no theatre management could pay an annual rental of £150,000 or £200,000. On the present scale of seat prices, he could not get close to recouping such a rent, and to raise the seat prices to the appropriate figure would mean emptying the theatre.

There is a *logical* case for higher seat prices, which have always lagged far behind inflationary trends, for they are now barely eight times what they were a hundred years ago. But theatregoers are unlikely to appreciate that logic and, except for the well-heeled elite, would simply stop theatregoing. Three elements will therefore be necessary in any legislation which is *genuinely* designed to ensure the survival of theatres in London, and which goes further than the well-meaning Theatres Trust Act 1976.

First: let us have drawn up by experts appointed by the Minister for the Environment a list of those few London theatres (and there are *only* a few) of real historical and/or architectural value, and let it be laid down by law that such 'listed' theatres (unlike the present 'listed' buildings) are *absolutely sacrosanct*, their future not subject in any way to discussions between property developers and planners and governmental or local governmental authorities, or to any 'deals', corrupt or otherwise.

Second: in regard to the rest, let us have it again laid down by law—without any mealy-mouthed clauses to provide loopholes—that whenever planning permission is given for the demolition of a theatre, an essential part of such permission must be a directive that the new building on the site must incorporate a new theatre, the design of which should be approved by some suitable body (perhaps a committee drawn from members of the Arts Council, the Society of West End Theatre Managers and Actors' Equity). In addition it should be stipulated that this new theatre shall stage only live theatrical entertainment for a statutory period of, say, 20 years. If exceptional circumstances should arise—as, for instance, an unforeseen decline in public interest in the theatre within such a period—amending legislation could be brought before Parliament.

Third: the rent of the new theatre should also be the subject of tight control, and should be determined by what is considered by a suitable authority to be an economic rent for the theatre without regard to building cost; which would inevitably mean, as far as the property developer is concerned, that the theatre rent would be to some extent subsidised by the other tenancies of the whole building.

These three conditions may seem difficult to come by. But, unless and until they are brought about, we shall not be spared the unseemly bickering and controversy that is provoked whenever the possibility of the redevelopment of a theatre site is mooted, leading, on the one hand, to insubstantial tongue-in-cheek 'guarantees' about the future from prospective developers, and, on the other, to palpably ridiculous claims from their opponents about the threatened building being historically irreplaceable, of sublime architectural merit and even of vital national importance.

We have before us, as an incentive to have done with the present situation in which all the muscle is in the money, the example of the long-drawn-out dispute over the Criterion Theatre in Piccadilly Circus. It is not to be denied—except, no doubt, by the 'Save Piccadilly' protest movement—that the Circus is a squalid and repellent urban vulgarity; nor would it be denied that most of the squalor was to the north side of it. Why, therefore, it came to pass that the south side—where the Criterion is, and which seems generally to be part of the empire of Trust Houses Forte Ltd— was marked down for the first steps in the redevelopment plans is doubtless an interesting if unelevating story, but not one that essentially concerns us here. Our theatrical concern begins only with the fact that Trust Houses Forte from which the Criterion Theatre has a sub-lease somehow got the jump on Stock Conversion and Investment Trust, which owns the Trocadero site, and Land Securities Investment Trust, which owns the Monico site, both over there on the north side.

This was too bad for the Criterion, which is one of four West End theatres controlled by the companies of Sir Donald Albery and his family, as highly respected as any management in the business. (The other three theatres are the Albery and Wyndhams, both leased from the Salisbury Estates, and the Piccadilly, of which they own a sizeable share of the freehold.) The Verity buildings on the south side of the Circus, of which the Criterion forms a modest and mostly subterranean part, were, as the entertaining phrase goes, 'listed' buildings; and that may well have accounted for the fact that Westminster City Council in 1972 felt that the frontages, at least, of these buildings should be retained.

The development scheme they approved in 1975, however, entailed the destruction of a considerable part of the younger (Frank) Verity's building over the theatre, and also the loss of several thousand square feet of the theatre's interior. Nevertheless, cheerful 'guarantees' were given that the theatre could carry on during the destruction and disruption—although no one came up with a practical suggestion as to how a theatre could operate in any tolerable way at the centre of a building site. There were further undertakings from the freeholders, the Crown Estates Commissioners (which also seem to have weighed with the Minister for the Environment who turned down applications for a public inquiry), that they would see to it that the Criterion, whatever else happened to it, would continue to be used for 'legitimate' drama. The Commissioners could only be, at best, well-meaning about that.

As it happens, the bottom has lately fallen out of the property market and the plans for the Criterion, at the time of writing, are not being proceeded with. This is, however, fortuitous, and any changes in the property business world would renew the threat to the Criterion—and, of course, to other theatres which are, or may come, within the control of property development companies.

Relatively few of them are actually *owned* by such companies— so far. And I have already mentioned most of them: the Arts,

Cambridge, Comedy, New London, Palace, Prince of Wales and Shaftesbury. To these can be added the Adelphi, and probably the Royal Court. The latter freehold seems to be held by Cadogan Estates, considerable parts of which were bought up in 1973 by our old and ubiquitous friends, the English Property Corporation, and the Earl of Cadogan became a director of that company. There may be others, for there seem to be cases in which, for mysterious reasons, the identity of freeholders is kept secret. In yet other instances, freeholds are owned by charitable trusts or individual landowners, any of whom, when present leases expire, could be tempted by property development schemes.

There are, on the other hand, many that are generally regarded in the business as being 'safe', because they are owned either by local authorities (eg the Garrick, Lyric and Young Vic by the Greater London Council; the Mermaid by the City of London; the Shaw by the Borough of Camden) or by theatrical or show business interests (the Aldwych, Duchess and Fortune by the companies of D A Abrahams and family, who also lease the Garrick from the GLC; the Vaudeville by Peter Saunders; the Phoenix by Gerald and Veronica Flint-Shipman; the Duke of York's by Ray Cooney; Apollo, Coliseum, Palladium, Royalty and Victoria Palace by Lord Grade's ATV or its subsidiaries, which also leases the Theatre Royal, Drury Lane, the Globe, Her Majesty's and Queen's) or by the Crown (the Theatre Royal, Haymarket and Her Majesty's).

In my more pessimistic moments, though, the only ones I think of as being really safe are the May Fair and the Savoy. They are both part of hotels, which I don't guess anyone is going to want to pull down and redevelop; but I suppose it is possible I could even be wrong about that.

BE AN 3
ANGEL

'Angels', a term that will henceforth be used without the inverted commas, are people who give money to producers to help them to put on theatrical entertainments. They are backers. That is to say, they are gamblers. But, guided by the instinct for respectability that causes some bookmakers to describe themselves as turf accountants, they prefer to be known as 'investors'.

Most people who are not in show business tend to believe, without really thinking about it, that the man named at the top of the posters as presenting a show is in fact the man with the money at risk. Not so. The chances are that he has no money in it at all. Why, indeed, should he? The arrangement is that, with nothing at risk except his reputation and office expenses, he will take 40 per cent of the profits (if any), anyway. Only 60 per cent will be distributed among those who take the financial risk.

No one seems unhappy with this ostensibly iniquitous arrangement. It is not likely to be changed as long as the angels come winging in to participate as they do, even though the general pressures of the inflationary economic situation mean that money has become as tight in this investment area, as it is in most others. At the same time, rising production costs mean that *more* money has somehow to be raised. Nevertheless, despite heart-rending bleats from production managements that the commercial theatre is no longer commercially viable, plays continue to get put on, successfully and unsuccessfully, and the demand of managements for theatres has not much diminished. The angels are still there. After all, if they put their money in the right productions (that's the trick, of course) they can still make a richer killing than in most investment operations. The odds against their seeing any profit at all may be variously estimated at between five and eight to one. But when the

17

winners turn up the return can run as high as thirty to one—in rare instances even more.

The possibility of such lavish dividends keeps the cash coming in. It used to be a game only for the very rich. The legendary C B Cochran, for instance, got the backing for his extravagant between-the-wars shows from the multi-millionaire, Solly Joel. Nowadays anyone with a little spare capital can play. I've met angels who were industrialists, secretaries, stockbrokers, farmers, journalists, engineers, retired service officers. Some are participants in syndicates, at once spreading their bets and getting the benefit of the judgment of the experts running the syndicate. This is not a guarantee of success; it may only ensure that the angel is not alone in disaster.

Readers of newspaper 'Personal' columns and 'Business Opportunities' might have noticed, just a year or two ago, an advertisement announcing the formation of a show-backing syndicate appropriately called Little Angels, which aimed at involving people with smaller amounts of cash to invest than would ordinarily be considered by the bigger managements. It attracted two hundred hopeful punters who put up a total of £6,500 in amounts as modest as £25. The money was split between two productions. Unfortunately both were flops.

Curiously enough, both these productions starred actors who had acquired a sizeable fan public though a popular television and radio series, *Dr Finlay's Casebook*: Bill Simpson and Andrew Cruickshank. Although such casting is unquestionably a theoretical success ingredient, it is not in itself a guarantee. Simpson's show, a slim little musical called *Romance*, was roundly panned by the critics, some of whom wondered in passing who on earth had been found to venture money in so inept an enterprise. Actually it was presented by the man who had promoted the Little Angels scheme, Charles Ross, in association with Henry Sherwood. Ross directed it; he also wrote the songs. The show closed at the end of its first week.

While the Little Angels could conceivably have felt aggrieved at Charles Ross's singular faith in himself, they could not but contemplate the prospect of the second recipient of their funds more happily. The Cruickshank play, *The Douglas Cause*, was by William Douglas Home who had written several previous hits as

18

well as having two of them running at that time. This one, however, which followed *Romance* into the Duke of York's, broke the sequence. Even stables in form have losers. *The Douglas Cause* ran only a few weeks. Once again the Little Angels thus lost their investment. They would not necessarily be discouraged from further dabbling, though: once bitten, play-backers don't necessarily stay bitten. And although, as in the case of horse-players, an initial win is the best encouragement to go on, it obviously isn't *essential*.

Typical of the Little Angels, and perhaps typical of the more modest angels generally, was a recently retired Yorkshire business-man. A few years previously, he had invested in a couple of revues staged by Charles Ross and had not done badly. He is a man who had always been attracted by the theatre and had written a number of one-act plays that had been performed by amateur companies. 'The theatre is not a business in which I'd put any really substan-tial sum,' he said, after the double Duke of York's débâcle, 'but if I'm going to gamble I prefer something in which I have a real interest, and I'd probably do it again.'

There are a few well-established syndicates in the angel busin-ess, one of them run by a film producer named Martin Schute, who would agree with the consensus view that the theatre is a gamble which is getting riskier. He used to limit his own invest-ment in any production to £125, and, despite inflation, has actually reduced it now to £100; he advises his syndicate members to be similarly cautious. The members grew from an initial half-dozen friends to as many as 50, but the members have dropped back to about 20. Schute's general procedure is to contract for a stake of £1,000 or £1,500 in a production on their behalf, then to circulate details to all of them and subsequently allot shares in the stake on a first-come-first-served basis. The first success in which they participated was Frank Marcus's play, *The Killing of Sister George*. One of the syndicate members had seen it during a Bristol try-out, recommended it to Schute as one with an even chance so the syndicate invested in it when Michael Codron decided to bring *Sister George* to London. Thanks to that success-ful gamble and their leading money-spinner so far, *There's a Girl in My Soup*, there has never been a time when the syndicate as a whole has been in the red. Some individual members though—

19

disregarding the standard advice to spread the bets and making just one or two unlucky investments—have been losers. Their 1971 investment in the long-running *No Sex Please, We're British*, was still putting money in the kitty over five years later. It came along after one year, 1969, when they took an all-round beating. That year they were into three flops in a single week and went down £4,500—unexpectedly, too.

Unexpectedly? That may seem a strange word, but a singular thing about Schute's angels—and about a great many others, too —is that their losses aren't *always* unexpected. Most of the time, while they are prepared to lose, they don't *expect* to lose; but there are other occasions when they'd be rather surprised not to. Their interest in, and regard for, the theatre goes further than the principle of greed that motivates the generality of gamblers. They recognise that it is sometimes necessary to back plays that, in the commercial sense, are forlorn hopes, simply because they are worth doing and involve talents on which the theatre's future depends. There is realism in their altruism, since their attitude is a sort of acknowledgment of the fact that if this kind of thing is left entirely to the state-subsidised theatres there will be, on the one hand, a tendency for the theatre to encourage only a certain kind of talent and, on the other, a possibility that the commercial theatre could be swallowed up by a monopoly in which the state, through its subsidies, is the principal shareholder.

It would, of course, be just as misleading to suggest that such 'realistic altruism' is the primary motive of angels as it would be to classify them as greedy gamblers. The latter appellation would seem to be ruled out of court simply on the grounds of the odds against, although the gambling man is not, by definition, deterred by any risk factor, so long as his interest is properly ignited in his chosen field of gambling—whether it is the stock market or the racecourse or the theatre. So what ignites that interest in the theatrical gamble? You may find angels talking about the art of the drama, how deeply they care about its future and the worthwhile nature of the theatre in the cultural life of the community. Well you can put most of that talk with the applesauce. What pulls the angels in is the 'glamour' of show business.

I know at least one man who knows angels from both sides of the production table: he has been one himself and has also used

20

them, a man who began by investing in other people's shows, discovered the way the dice were loaded and formed his own theatrical management. Marvin Liebman is an American who came to London in the 1960s with the resolve to get into the theatre. In the US he had been a public relations man working mainly for politicians and political causes and had no experience of the theatre —'although American politics is a branch of show business, not to mention vice versa'. Nevertheless he had always been attracted by it and, at 45, decided to change his whole way of life and do something about a lifelong hankering.

'I had no talent,' he readily admitted. 'I had written a couple of plays as a young man. But they weren't any good. It had to be a financial interest. I chose London because the deal looked better. There are more theatres and more plays. And there is still a middle ground between the smash hit and the dire failure. Also London has, anyway, become something of a haven for middle-aged Americans a bit disenchanted by the quality of life at home, much as Paris was in the 1920s.'

Liebman not only had money of his own to invest but he was on good terms with wealthy people in the States who were as enthusiastic about the theatre as himself. He looked around London and decided to approach impresario John Gale, later to become President of the Society of West End Theatre Managers. It was a canny enough choice, for anyone who had put £100 into each of the eight plays presented by Gale in the previous four years would have profited to the tune of at least £3,200 even though three of the eight were total losses. It was Liebman's bad luck, as it happened, to buy in to one of Gale's failures. However, in return for his own investment and the money he could attract from his American friends, he was allowed to 'sit in' on the production and see how the wheels of management went round.

After that, he backed two further London flops fairly heavily, which used up all the money he was prepared to gamble as an angel. Henceforth he would confine himself to management, while retaining the support of his distant angels in the States. Altogether he took them into five straight losers. But the sixth venture, presented in partnership with John Gale, proved a winner. It was *Abelard and Heloise*, which may not have been a work to engrave itself on the roll of Distinguished Drama of Our

Time, but it had Keith Michell and Diana Rigg in its title-roles and both of them took all their clothes off, which was a rare occurrence in that distant day and an item of intelligence not altogether kept secret in the pre-production publicity build-up. It recovered its costs inside three months, ran for nearly two years and wound up £90,000 on the right side of the book, recovering the faithful angels all their previous losses.

Liebman's angels were mostly men who became rich from industry, oil and real estate and were looking for an involvement in something more glamorous. The prospectus he sent them on a production naturally pointed out its merits as he saw them, but also included a paragraph such as this:

> *As always, I emphasise the great risk in investing in a theatrical enterprise. Only a very few make a substantial profit; and only a limited percentage of all plays presented, either in London or New York, recoup their investment. If you are willing to take the gamble, I will more than welcome your participation . . .*

'I would never approach a man who couldn't afford to lose,' he told me once. 'These people understood the facts and the risks, but mostly they still wanted to come in. With some of them it may have been the idea of participating in something of artistic merit. Mainly I think it was just the glamour of the theatre that was the irresistible attraction. Remember they could afford to lose the money. And, in any case, I didn't ask them individually for a lot. I would normally split the required capital into, say, twenty units of £750 and most of these people I'm talking about would only take half a unit, which was less than a thousand dollars. Considering that the US Internal Revenue man would have taken most of that, their theatrical hobby—tax-deductible in America—was really costing them very little.

'For my part I did everything possible to give them a feeling of being really *involved* in the theatre. Apart from financial reports, I sent them regular 'gossip bulletins', clippings, production photographs and programmes. Sooner or later nearly all of them came to London on vacation or business. Then, as well as getting them seats for the show—"their" show—I made sure they were given the proper VIP treatment at the theatre, and I'd probably

22

be able to arrange a little dinner party with the stars of the show they'd invested in. So, though they hoped it would be a success, they didn't cry if the luck ran the other way.'

Marvin Liebman himself, however, was never happy about picking duds and came to feel that British theatrical taste was eluding him too often. He was particularly discouraged when London didn't go for an award-winning American play called *The Effect of Gamma Rays on Man-In-The-Moon Marigolds* (which may be an intriguing title but, let's face it, not an instant 'come on'). Anyway, he went back to the US in 1975.

There are, nevertheless, other Americans who have come to London to get into play management and investment. Some of them take just a single flyer, lose and leave. Others stick with the game for a while or for keeps. One of the most recent stickers is Dodie Cushingham, an ex-actress from Seattle who had always been happier, she says, with the business and creative people in the theatre than merely with the actors. She decided that management was to be for her and chose London 'because there is more theatre, the costs are lower than on Broadway and the unions at least give you an even break'.

She had a play in her bag when she came. It was not a very good play and she has since abandoned it. But it was by a well-known yesteryear writer and she felt it was at least a means of introduction to the scene. Mrs Cushingham talked to Tennents about it. They weren't much interested. But they were quite interested in the fact that she could put up substantial capital (a little of her own, the rest from American friends keen to invest) for a thriller they were promoting called *The Pay Off*. This one was by William Fairchild and had a good cast headed by Dulcie Gray, Nigel Patrick and Peter Sallis. It did very well out of town, but received only so-so notices in London. After three months or so at the Comedy, Tennents—under pressure from the theatre's management, who had other plays wanting to come in—felt they had no option but to close it.

Mrs Cushingham, displaying rather more faith in the play than was perhaps justified, was not ready to accept defeat. She was, indeed, so unready that she formed her own management, booked the off-the-track Westminster Theatre and talked the cast into transferring there with it. This had meant a lot more money-raising, but that is something for which she seems to have a knack. The ending, because this is real-life and not a backstage movie musical, was downbeat: *The Pay Off* staggered along for a few more months. But it was a loser all the way and this is the point at which those with faint hearts would have given up. Mrs Cushingham didn't. She got busy again raising money among her circle of angels—'nearly all American business people,' she says, 'although some of them are living in London'—for further ventures. She backed Anthony Chardet in a terrible flop called *Norman, Is That You?* and then Henry Sherwood, who was bringing *Kennedy's Children* in from the 'fringe' (the Kings Head, Islington) to the Arts. The latter didn't do badly, but it's hard to make any money, even with a hit, in a club theatre as small as the Arts. Her angels still weren't hitting any jackpots, but she and they were sufficiently encouraged to go on.

The association with Henry Sherwood in *Kennedy's Children* brought her into contact with his old partner, Charles Ross and, of course, the Little Angels. Together they went into *Roger's Last Stand*, starring Leslie Phillips. This was an appalling comedy, but no worse than some that have run for years. Although it got a murderous set of reviews, Phillips recalled his previous experience with *The Man Most Likely To*, which moved from almost certain disaster to tumultuous success, and there was a general decision to take the initial losses in the hope that *Roger's Last Stand* would do the same.

It didn't. But, at the time of writing, it's out on tour, overseas options are being taken up and there seems to be an outside chance that Dodie Cushingham's backers will see some of their money back on this one. She herself, eager to get into solo management, moved into a Bury Street office and took on a business manager. When I last saw her she had found a play she believed in and had her fingers crossed that she could find a really top-flight director to share her enthusiasm. This is a perennial situation of managements. If you are seeing her name on playbills you will know at least that the money is still coming in from the angels. Some of it will even be going back—sometimes with interest.

A lot has to happen, though, before any angel does see his money again, let alone show a profit on a theatrical investment. We look a little more closely at some discouraging figures in the next chapter

24

on the commercial managements. Meanwhile it can be said that it is perfectly possible for a play (not a hit, hardly even a success) to run for months, returning a modest weekly profit, before an investor even recovers his stake—although backers do retrieve their initial investment before the management begins taking *its* 40 per cent of the profits.

The situation is still sunnier for angels in London than it is in New York, however. There, the producing management with the money at risk not only takes 50 per cent rather than British 40 per cent of any profits, but takes one per cent of each week's gross takings as well, plus, generally, a fatter office fee than the London counterpart. That, taken together with the more encouraging US tax laws, accounts for there being so much American money invested in the West End theatre. This is really what keeps London's commercial managements afloat and cheerful. In other respects their outlook—with more and more of the best talents being siphoned off into the bigger subsidised theatres—is not all roses.

PROUD TO 4
PRESENT

You might never guess it from reading the loftier prints, but of London's 40 or so principal theatres, only six—the Aldwych, the Mermaid, the Old Vic, the National, the Royal Court and the Shaw—have subsidised companies or are themselves subsidised. You can make that eight if you count the National as three theatres. The rest have productions presented by private-enterprise managements. Commercial managements. The London theatre is essentially the commercial theatre—scorn the fact though they may in the arts columns of *The Times* and *The Guardian*. It is a place of business, where profits and losses are made: that is to say, where most of the people make losses, but some of the people make profits. So is there a future in the commercial West End theatre? Ask me if there's a future in casinos.

Of course, it can be tough. It is getting harder, as noted, to compete with the heavily subsidised houses in recruiting talent. Everything is getting more expensive. Inflation tends to attack outgoings more violently than incomings. Theatre rents are going up. Production costs are going up. It's a high, high risk to put on a show these days. But when you really get one up there—like, say, *Jesus Christ Superstar*, or *The Mousetrap*, or *No Sex Please—We're British*, or *Oh! Calcutta!* or *Otherwise Engaged* or *The Rocky Horror Show*—the music sounds so sweet that you don't ever want to stop dancing. Except to retire. Rich.

Money has a great attraction for a lot of people. It may easily be the second most popular interest in the western world. And so long as the commercial theatre offers the prospect of carrying the stuff home in sackfuls—even if only once in 20 shots, once in 50 shots—there will still be a commercial theatre. When I hear people saying that the West End theatre will be finished in two

27

years—five years, whatever—I wonder where they live. Every time a show gets assassinated in the morning-after-the-first-night press, the telephone of the theatre's lessee begins ringing before he's even brushed his teeth and adjusted his hairpiece—asking please, please, we're wowing them in Brighton, and Manchester was better still, so please, please, can't we be the next one in?

And the next one in may be similarly assassinated. But they'll still keep coming: probably at five-weekly intervals, though it could be less. The 'five weeks' has to do with the arrangements for tenure made between the lessee (or owner) of the theatre and the management putting on the show. Because the theatre is rented for, say, £2,000 a week *or* 20 per cent (more usually now 22½ per cent) of the box-office takings *whichever is the greater*, and because the man controlling the theatre is exceedingly interested in that 'greater', there is an agreed minimum takings figure at which notice can be given at any time after the first two full weeks. Since almost nothing opens on a Monday, the first week usually doesn't count. And two weeks' notice from the end of the third week means a five-week run. Shows can close in quicker time than that, of course: it can be cheaper for the production management to pay the rent and close immediately than to shoulder additional overheads that would never be recovered at the box-office; and the theatre management can, and often does, let the production management off the rent if there is another show waiting to come in that seems to have better prospects of getting above the figure at which his percentage begins to operate.

Other considerations enter into the question from the production management's standpoint. Knowing, for instance, when to close a flop is one of the tricks of successful management. As well as the calculation of whether the continuance of a doomed run will increase or diminish the overall loss, there is the question of the subsidiary rights: the management staging the London production of a play has various contractual percentages to come (such as 33⅓ per cent of subsequent repertory production rights, and 20 per cent of television and film rights) *if* the play runs for at least three weeks. Although it may seem unlikely that a play that can only stagger to a three-week London run will ever be done anywhere else, this is by no means the rule. The film rights of stage flops are often sold, doubtless because they can be bought more cheaply than stage successes. 'Doctoring' by screenwriters can work wonders.

Beyond this, there is the matter of the management fee of from £150 to £400 a week, according to the steadiness of the manager's nerve as he puts it into the accounts. This is no small consideration for a small-time manager with a flop on his hands. It is, in fact, his only income from the production since he has, of course, no hope of reaching the point at which the investors have recovered their stakes and he can begin taking his 40 per cent of the profits.

Instructive, here, to look at a handful of figures to see what has to happen before the backers see their money back, let alone show a profit. Production costs, which always varied enormously, have been soaring in the 1970s. It is difficult to imagine a musical being launched now on a budget of less than £100,000 and a quarter of a million looks like becoming commonplace. Even a straight play can call for a budget of £45,000 or £50,000. You could say that £20,000 is nowadays just about the rock-bottom capitalisation figure. Of this latter amount, perhaps £14,000 would go in production costs before the play reached the West End stage, leaving £6,000 in reserve in case the play failed to meet its weekly running costs—and the backers would, incidentally, be committed to a 20 or 25 per cent 'overcall' at the discretion of the management if that £6,000 were used up.

We can look first at the production expenses of a modest production, figures being given for two plays—one in 1972, the other in 1977—to show the extent of inflation in this area during the last five years: see the table on pages 30 and 31.

The seeming discrepancies between the takings and the weekly profit or loss are due, it will be seen, to the percentages being paid to the author, director and theatre. It is also possible that the designer has a percentage agreement (only one or even a half per cent, but nevertheless a percentage), and more often than not these days the star or stars will have percentage arrangements. It would not be unusual for as much as 40 per cent of the gross to be taken out in this way. A profit at the end of the day is not easy to come by.

Without access to the books, it is virtually impossible for anyone to know whether a production is actually profitable or not.

Production Expenses

	1972	1977
Capitalisation	£15,000	£35,000
Scenery, building and painting	£2,500	£4,000
Furniture, set dressings, etc	500	1,500
Wardrobe	200	1,250
Properties	150	500
Fees		
Management	500	1,000
Director	750	1,000
Designer	400	750
Lighting	200	300
Rehearsal expenses		
Cast:	—	2,000
Understudies, 3 × 14 × 5 weeks	210	750
Company manager, 1 × 42 × 5 weeks	210	375
Deputy stage Managers: 1 × 28 × 5 weeks	140	250
1 × 25 × 5 weeks	125	225
NHI and SET	100	1,000
Rehearsal room for 25 days	250	400
Travelling expenses	150	350
Advertising and publicity		
Newspaper advertising	1,500	2,500
Printing	250	1,000
Press agent, fees and expenses	150	400
Signwriting	125	500
Photographs	150	275
Miscellaneous		
'Get in'—London	500	1,200
Scripts	50	125
Pre-production expenses	200	1,000
Total	£9,310	£22,650

We can now look at the weekly costs in the West End:

Weekly Running Costs in the West End

	1972	1977
Percentages based on box-office takings of	£2,500	£6,000
Cast and stage management	£855	£1,900
Author (5% of first £3,000; 10% over £3,000)	125	450
Director (2½%)	62.50	150
Designer	15	35
Hire charges	75	300
Advertising and printing	180	350
Press agent	25	40
Management fee	125	200
Accountant's fee	10.50	30
National Insurance	120	350
Theatre rent (against 20% of gross)	800	1,400
Theatre contra	900	1,600
Miscellaneous	50	300
Total	£3,403	£7,105

1972

On takings of £2,500 the weekly loss is therefore	£903
On takings of £3,000 the weekly loss is	£427
On takings of £3,500 the weekly loss is	£17.50
On takings of £4,000 the weekly profit is	£434.50
On takings of £5,000 the weekly profit is	£984.50
On takings of £6,000 the weekly profit is	£1,494.50

1977—The profit begins to appear on takings of £7,500 when it is about £8.

Even a long run can be a losing run. There was the notorious case of the musical *Robert and Elizabeth*, which clocked up over 900 performances at the Lyric on Shaftesbury Avenue in the 1960s but wound up in the red, because the theatre, though seating nearly 950, was too small to cover the expenses without being filled almost to capacity. *A Little Night Music* ran for a year at the Adelphi in 1975/76 and just about broke even. *Very Good Eddie*, an endearingly artless little musical spoof, ran at a loss for a year at the Piccadilly in 1976/77 because the loss was not as great as it would be if the theatre had gone 'dark'. This last was a special case, since the presenting management, the Alberys, are also owners of the theatre and the decision is all their own. The only way in which they might have cut the loss would have been not only to close the show but also to sack the house staff—which the Alberys would certainly be reluctant to do, for they are a management priding themselves on friendly relations with the workers in their theatres, many of whom have served them for over 20 years. Even so, the Piccadilly is one of the few theatres that does not have a queue of shows waiting to come in, and thus presents a problem: it seats 1,150 people, and lacks the intimacy that small cast straight plays look for, while not being big enough to be any management's first choice of venue for an expensive musical.

The Alberys bought the freehold of the Piccadilly from Norwich Union Assurance for £170,000 in 1971—or, rather, Piccadilly Theatre Ltd did, and Piccadilly Theatre Ltd is 83 per cent owned by Donmar Productions, which is owned by Wyndham Theatres (in which the Alberys have controlling interests) and other Albery associates. The price, for a theatre they had already leased, looked cheap at the time and a year later the freehold was valued at £379,174 in the company's fixed assets. At the end of 1972, the company was carrying forward a profit of about £100,000. But since then things have been getting stickier.

H M Tennent Ltd have been negotiating with the Alberys for one or two of their theatres, and I doubt if they would be reluctant to let the Piccadilly go. The Criterion, too, is a persistent headache—partly because of the threat hanging over it,* but also because, despite its prime position in Piccadilly Circus, it is not the most popular theatre with production managements. Only 410 of its 600-odd seats are not affected by the slim pillars that abound in the auditorium, and when intending patrons are told at the box-office about those pillars (as honesty dictates they *have* to be) they tend to shy away. With these disadvantages the Criterion's running costs are as high as those of Wyndham's (another Albery theatre, with 750 good seats) and not much less than the Albery itself (with 870 seats). Clearly the Criterion is not the family's favourite house.

That is not to say that it is unprofitable and a production management like Tennents is obviously interested in owning the leases

* See page 14.

32

of theatres, because it does cut out all the hassle of negotiating terms for getting their productions into somebody else's theatre, which can be a hard-bargaining business—even for them. Tennents, after all, are tough hands at the game, long established and with a certain amount of muscle to exert through interlocking directorships and shareholdings, though not as much, of course, as in the heyday of the late Hugh Beaumont, Prince Littler and Stewart Cruikshank. The joint managing directors of H M Tennent nowadays are Helen Montague and Arthur Cantor, the latter handling the American end of the firm's interests. In London, Miss Montague—an ebullient Australian who, with those H M initials, might almost have been predestined for the job—is head-girl in London. Under her direction the company has been making a bit of a comeback in production and, at any given time, will probably be in direct control of four of five West End productions, with investment interests in others.

Major producing managements in the West End today are those of Michael Codron, Michael White, Eddie Kulukundis, Duncan Weldon, John Gale, Ray Cooney, Bernard Delfont and the king of the sex shows, Paul Raymond. Any of these is likely to be responsible for four or five concurrent productions. Only the last three are also into theatre ownership or lesseeship. Only the last, Raymond, uses exclusively his own money. Kulukundis is *almost* in that remarkable category: wealthy from his family's business as shipping brokers, he has displayed a fanatical interest in the theatre for most of his life. In fact the shows he first presented when he got into production eight or nine years ago were mounted entirely with his own money. Which, most of the time, he lost. Still a heavy personal investor, he may still be, on balance, a loser and pick some terrible duds. But he is getting shrewder.

Codron's route into management was different. Never prepared to play the angel, he worked initially for the late Jack Hylton, which was a good place to learn that there's no need to gamble with your own money when a good living, to say the least, is to be had from the management fees and the management's rake-off of 40 per cent of the profits. He kicked off by taking the option (for £100) on a comedy called *Ring for Catty*, about which Hylton himself was uncertain. Codron raised the wind among the angel contacts he'd made, put the play on and watched the money roll

33

in. He has always been a good picker. Those who have invested with him—though they have not always seen their money back—have never been able to complain that he's let them in for a stinker. Even the ones that don't make money pick up compliments and the playwrights Codron has introduced to the West End over the years include Harold Pinter, Joe Orton, David Mercer, Frank Marcus, Simon Gray, Christopher Hampton and David Hare. Two of the five plays he had running in the spring of 1977 were the work of newcomers to the West End even though Codron worries that he has not been spotting as many new playwriting talents recently. He'll probably keep them coming though.

He'll have to if he is to survive. Even without getting into the high finance of musicals—the preserve, on the whole, of Delfont, Michael White and Harold Fielding—a management still has to raise between £20,000 and £50,000 to put on a straight play. The angels who provide it may be gamblers looking for the big winners and prepared to lose; in lieu of profits they may, for as long as they're able, make do with 'artistic satisfaction'; if they consistently get neither, they're not going to stick with the man who puts them in line to get the egg on their faces. The managements that fall by the wayside are the ones that take their backers into strings of financial losers, without either the compensation of artistic worthiness or the veneer of success.

That 'veneer' is a costly business, not necessarily for the manager but certainly for his investors. Yet it is astonishing how often the angels can be persuaded by a smooth, fast talker to cough beyond the 'overcall' to achieve it. The ploy of keeping a dud going until the damning reviews have been forgotten and the show has the outward appearance of success has very rarely worked. Moreover it is getting more expensive even to try to bring it off. But a management with an eye only to the short-term rewards of the office fees, and carefree with other people's money, can still get away with it. At least for a time. This is a shifty practice because it is done with other people's money and because it is also in the nature of a fraud on the public—if not exactly a criminal one. It entails bolstering the box-office returns by buying up tickets, and either giving or throwing them away, to keep the takings above the figure at which the theatre management is contractually able to enforce a closure on the production management. It is a hard thing to prove, but it is commonly believed that some managements in recent years have poured £1,000 a week or even more into a box-office.

There is a sense, of course, in which a manager could plead justification. He may genuinely believe, against all the odds of experience, that his play will succeed if he can only give it time to 'settle down'. He may also use the device simply in order to keep the tenure of a desirable theatre until he can bring in another of his productions with a better chance of success.

But let me not give the impression that these box-office shenanigans are all on one side. Theatre managements can be as unscrupulous as production managements, and a box-office can be 'killed' as well as 'fed'. The 'killing' happens in those cases in which a production is just ticking over at the minimum figure or just above it. The theatre management, restive at getting only the straight rent and none of the 20 or 22½ per cent gravy, has another play looking for lodgings—a play with the earmarks of being a great deal more lucrative than the one he's housing. So what happens? Things get pretty sloppy around the front of the house. Posters, with stars' names and reviewers' quotes, get torn and don't immediately get replaced. And strange words go out to the box-office manager: telephones don't get answered or are left off the hook, and intending patrons are given not altogether accurate information about the availability of seats. It's not the way to sell tickets, and tickets don't get sold, with the result that the hapless production management is nudged under the minimum and thus cannot avoid getting notice to quit.

Although this sort of thing cannot make pretty reading, the wonder is not that it goes on, rather that these and similarly sharp practices are not even more prevalent. Those who are ready to believe the worst of the capitalist system—the jungle of private enterprise, predatory, rapacious and ruthless—may take them simply as a confirmation of their cynical beliefs. The truth is, though, that a man who owns a theatre, or leases a theatre, while unquestionably less at risk than nearly everyone else in show business, is hardly employing his capital to the best advantage. He could even be accused of a certain amount of altruism, however reluctant it may be. To be getting only the straight rent is to be doing little more than break even; only at 20 or 22½ per cent of a raging hit is the game really profitable. And raging hits don't happen all that often. Theatre buildings are worth millions even in simple terms of bricks and mortar (considering what they would cost to build today), let alone as property sites in prime West End positions if they could be knocked down; and the return to be had from merely letting them is not nearly commensurate with the return on a building of similar cost and position let as flats or offices. That's the way theatre owners tend to look at their properties as businessmen; but it is not, of course, a realistic or valid attitude until they have permission in their pockets to demolish and redevelop, a matter dealt with in Chapter Two.

Getting back to the production managements, their biggest problem, next to finding plays that will be successful enough to take them up into that devoutly desired position where they are scooping 40 per cent of the gross, is in booking theatres to put them into. Suitable theatres. Unless they're actually in the theatre management business as well, they often have to put a play into production without any guarantee that a suitable theatre will be available for it when it's ready. Theatre lessees want to see the product first to assess its chances, estimate the value of their own percentage and weigh these things against their other options. Even if a production management is also a theatre management it can have this problem—and could decide in favour of keeping another producer's show, which has established itself in the profit area, rather than risk bringing in one of their own.

They may have a hard time explaining that sort of position to the investors in the show that's waiting out there in the cold. But investors—as observed in the previous chapter—are no great problem. They'll be queueing, anyway. Even at the door of a producer with a high flop ratio; so long as he has the occasional hit, the gamblers will be standing in line with their money—and their dreams.

THE 5
PETER PAN
CAPER

In the theatre, as on the racecourse, there are no certain winners, though for a long time it did seem that there was *one*: *Peter Pan* at Christmas.

Christmas is clearly a good time of year for a children's show. But they're not all, for that reason, automatic successes. Fingers have been known to get burnt—even at the London Palladium. And indeed impresario Harold Fielding did not have backers actually queuing to invest in *Hans Andersen* there—although, opening in December 1974, it ran far longer than any pantomime. Even pantomime is not the draw it was. Not so long ago the West End of London could support at least three or four lavishly staged pantos. But, in the 1974–75 season, there was only one—*Cinderella* at the London Casino—which Bernard Delfont must have regarded as a gilt-edged property, since it had no rivals and since it included such names as Twiggy, Harry H. Corbett and Wilfrid Brambell (television's 'Steptoe and Son'), Lenny the Lion, Nicky Henson and Roy Kinnear in the cast. But it was withdrawn prematurely carrying a six-figure loss. This was doubtless why, in the 1975–76 season, there were no West End pantos at all, although for 1976–77, the Palladium gave panto another whirl—with *Cinderella*, yet again.

There are a number of children's plays, some based on television series, others on well-loved books (*Toad of Toad Hall, Treasure Island, Winnie the Pooh*), which do well, but there are others that survive only one or two Christmas seasons of a few weeks. It is not until such shows become really established and can make use of the same sets and costumes year after year that they become really profitable investments. None, of course, has anything near the record of longevity achieved by *Peter Pan*, written by J M Barrie and first produced in 1904 to be staged in London every year since, with but three exceptions—the 1940–41 season, when the scenery and costumes had been destroyed in the Blitz; the 1970–71 season, of which more in a moment; and, to everyone's surprise, the 1976–77 season.

Generation after generation has grown up with this unique Barrie play, the fanciful tale of a little boy who himself didn't want to grow up. Many children see it year by year throughout childhood from six to sixteen (which ages are by no means the outer limits), comparing one Peter with another as maturer drama buffs compare performances of Hamlets. Every year there is a new batch of children to be introduced to it by their elder brothers and sisters, their parents or grandparents. The audiences may not be inexhaustible, but certainly there are enough customers to sustain *Peter Pan* through its relatively brief annual seasons. Five or six weeks in London, followed by a provincial tour of similar duration, have become standard over many years. And, since the same scenery and costumes serve for several years at a stretch, there is no mistaking its profitability.

What a charming success story it has been to be sure, despite all the lofty reviewers who, from time to time, insist on examining the play and its author's motives in Freudian terms. Children know nothing of this. They may be wrong, as some would say, but they do like the play. Further, its success is in a good cause— for Barrie, in his will, bequeathed the rights in *Peter Pan* to the Great Ormond Street Hospital for Sick Children. (The copyright runs in Britain till 1987, in the United States until 1984.) For some reason, Barrie asked that the amount of money the hospital received in royalties, etc should not be revealed. However, taking into account all the film, television and literary as well as theatre rights, the figure must by now be in the neighbourhood of a million pounds. It was Barrie's wish also that the play should be done as nearly as possible in accord with his own view of it (he himself personally supervised the production in London and the provinces for many years) and the hospital contracts with producing managements always stipulate that it should be done 'in a first-class manner in a suitable theatre'.

This leads us to the matter of how *Peter Pan* came not to be staged in London in the 1970–71 season.

The manner of the production and the suitability of the theatre in which it was staged had become major points of contention between the hospital and the Daniel Mayer Company (who then held the producing contract) prior to the 1969–70 season, when it was proposed to mount the play at the New Victoria, a vast auditorium more generally in use as a cinema. The hospital authorities felt that this would be in contravention of both the contract and the spirit of Barrie's Will (it was, to quote a spokesman for the Board of Governors, 'as unsuitable as putting on the Aldershot Tattoo at the Palladium'), and took the company to court. The judge agreed with the hospital view, but nevertheless allowed the production to go ahead in the special circumstances prevailing, which were that the theatre in which *Peter Pan* had been produced in London since the 1945–46 season, the Scala, was no longer available, being scheduled for demolition, and no other theatre was at that stage available either. After that, however, the Daniel Mayer Company's contract lapsed and *Peter Pan* was up, as they say, for grabs.

There then began a most unseemly scramble for that contract, of which I suspect the governors of the hospital (chairman: Mrs James Callaghan) knew nothing, or at least very little. It is not possible to discover precisely how many theatrical producers, managers and entrepreneurs of one sort or another actually made a formal application for the contract, but since the play was reputed to turn a profit of around £30,000 annually for the producing management, it can be taken for granted that there was no perceptible dragging of feet. On the other hand, it was clearly improper that the play should be regarded simply as a commercial money-spinner. With the hospital governors bearing a special responsibility to their benefactor as well as to his benefaction, it was unlikely that many of the applicants could be taken seriously on their past records. The governors were more or less bound to satisfy themselves not only of the financial capacity of an applicant actually to mount a 'first-class' production and of his access to a 'suitable' theatre in London, but also of his proper respect and affection for the play itself.

Clearly this limited the field—or should have done. There were those, indeed, who felt it limited it to one man. Mr Roger Lancelyn Green, for example, who would be generally regarded as our foremost authority on *Peter Pan* and who was the author of the definitive history of the play in performance, was quite positive. 'The future of the play,' he said, 'would be safest in the hands of Peter Cotes. He is quite clearly the ideal man to produce it—the only man, as far as I know, who has the expertise combined with the necessary knowledge and love of the play.' Others who knew Cotes shared this view. His enthusiasm for *Peter Pan* dated from his own appearances in it, first as a boy actor as one of the Darling children, then as one of the Lost Boys, and later as Starkey the pirate. Additionally, he was an experienced West End director and had his own production company.

Was Cotes, however, an applicant for the contract? Indeed, he was; that much had been urged upon him at an early stage and he had written to the Great Ormond Street Hospital where a Mr Gordon Piller, formerly House Governor, was designated 'Honorary Agent for *Peter Pan*'. Cotes's first letter to him was dated November 10, 1970, and there were two meetings of the two men in the following weeks—one at Cotes's office, the other at his club. Prior to these meetings, however, the producer-applicant's first intimation that his letter had been received came in a visit from a Mr Cyril Hicks, whom he had known some years previously as being associated with Bernard Delfont and who had evidently been asked by Piller to 'sound out' Cotes in regard to his detailed proposals. Hicks was also present at the two meetings of Cotes and Piller.

The significance of this—and it was to become even more significant later—was that Hicks was now acting as liaison man not only between Piller and Cotes, but between both and Tom Arnold Presentations, now presided over by Helen Arnold, widow of the theatre, circus and ice-show impresario.

Tom Arnold Presentations had had one previous connection with *Peter Pan* in that they had presented it *on ice* at the Empire Pool, Wembley, for the 1962–63 season. In the light of the hospital's later objections to the New Victoria cinema as a venue, it might be thought that there would have been even more strenuous objections to the Empire Pool and a manner of presentation that may well have had Barrie spinning in his grave; but as it happens there had mysteriously been no protests and Cotes had the impression that a particularly warm and friendly relationship existed between

Piller and the Tom Arnold office. He was therefore, if somewhat bewildered, not discouraged when Hicks arranged a meeting between him and Gerald Palmer, Mrs Arnold's director of productions, as a result of which Palmer suggested that TA Presentations associate themselves with him in his application, agreed to put at his disposal such costumes as were appropriate from those that had been used in the iced production and to arrange—through the provincial theatres they are associated with—the six-week tour that would follow a London season of the play.

Cotes included these facts in his formal application for the *Peter Pan* production rights, submitted to Piller through his solicitors, Goodman, Derrick and Company (Lord Goodman's firm) on January 26, 1971. At the same time he assured himself of the requisite financial backing needed to mount the production in a 'first-class' manner. Additionally, having learned that the only other applicant under serious consideration was the Savoy Theatre (which, of course, had the primary advantage of a 'suitable' theatre), he began negotiations for a six-week, matinée season the following Christmas at the London Coliseum. He also suggested more generous royalty terms than the hospital had hitherto agreed with commercial managements; but at no time, of course, either then or subsequently, did he think of offering any bribe to any individual.

The sequence of events from that point is very curious indeed, especially in regard to the availability of the London Coliseum—which is the home of the English National Opera (at that time still known as the Sadlers' Wells Opera), whose then managing director, the late Mr Stephen Arlen, Cotes met in February.

Arlen reacted favourably to the idea, but wrote (February 25) that he was 'a bit perturbed' because of the technical difficulties of mounting *Peter Pan* (with all its 'flying' wires) for matinées when there still had to be an opera production in the evenings. 'When we finally go into it all,' he wrote, 'it may not be practicable or it may only be practicable on such a restricted basis as to be impossible for you.'

In the light of this, it hardly seemed possible to take seriously a gossip column item that appeared in the same week disclosing that Mrs Helen Arnold was buying the stage rights of *Peter Pan* and planned to present it at the Coliseum at Christmas. (The dis-

41

position of the rights was not decided by the Hospital Governors *until June*.) Arlen wrote to Mrs Arnold (March 3) that while he had been 'having informal discussion with Peter Cotes on the subject, there are considerable doubts on its feasibility'. He went on: 'That it should, at this stage, appear in print is, to all intents and purposes, wholly unsatisfactory and extremely discourteous.' And, by March 23, Arlen had ruled out the Coliseum entirely, writing to Cotes: 'I am afraid we have had to go ahead with our plans for the opera, and these from the stage point of view, make it completely impossible for us to present anything other than our own work during that period . . . Naturally this does not preclude our considering *Peter Pan* for the future, but if there is any suggestion I must know at a very early stage as it clearly means that we have to organise ourselves with a very simple operatic repertoire and this we must know *at least twelve months ahead*.'

Again, therefore, it did not seem likely that there was any basis in fact for a news item appearing only two days later (March 25) in the *Daily Express*: '*Peter Pan* will be staged in modern dress in a £40,000 charity production at the London Coliseum this Christmas, the Great Ormond Street Children's Hospital said last night.' It can only have seemed to those involved that someone at the hospital, not knowing of Arlen's decision, had spoken 'out of turn' and got everything wrong. What was happening, though, was that the press was getting everything more or less right, despite the various letters being written and statements being made that suggested otherwise.

The *Daily Express* item was, in fact, extracted from a story put out by the Press Association, and the PA, in accord with journalistic tradition, did not disclose the source of their information. It is interesting, though, that the full text of their story referred to Tom Arnold Presentations as the production management, and to Peter Cotes as the director of the production. This would have been news to Cotes, who had at no time in his conversations with either Cyril Hicks or Gerald Palmer been informed that TAP were independent applicants for the *Peter Pan* rights, and at no time—either then or later—did they suggest an arrangement whereby *they* would 'present' and *he* would 'direct'. Nor had he gained any such impression from either Stephen Arlen or Gordon Piller. Because of the discrepancy between the published news item and the information in Arlen's letter to him, Cotes wrote again to Arlen at the end of March seeking enlightenment, while Goodman, Derrick and Company wrote similarly to Piller. There was no reply from Arlen, but Piller replied (March 29) to Goodman, Derrick and Company:

'The Hospital Governors are making a final decision about *Peter Pan* at their Board Meeting at the end of this month and we shall be in touch with you then.'

In view of the date, it was uncertain whether 'this month' referred to March or April, but no further news about the matter actually came until May 26 when Arlen was amazingly quoted by the *Daily Telegraph* as forecasting a Christmas matinée season of *Peter Pan* at the Coliseum. In response to Cotes's bewildered query, referring of course to his letter of March 23, Arlen replied (June 2):

'Thank you for your letter. Really, the never-ending confusions about *Peter Pan* are impossible. I would request you to get on to the hospital and discuss the whole matter with them. I can have no further part in it. I am merely trying to negotiate *Peter Pan* next Christmas, for the Coliseum, with the people who were originally associated with you, on the understanding that they had a contract. It is not for me to involve myself further.'

If only because of the last sentence (from the managing director of the lessees of the theatre involved) and because there could hardly be any greater 'confusion' than that occasioned by his own conflicting statements, this is surely an extraordinary letter. It would seem also to me the letter of a man both lacking in frankness and under considerable pressure of one kind or another. It may, indeed, seem so obvious, to anyone looking dispassionately at the *Peter Pan* caper up to this point, that 'the fix was in' (though by whom and for whom and with whom can only be conjectured) that it may be wondered why Peter Cotes, who was by now actively involved in another production, bothered any further. However, his naïve reluctance to accept that the individual had no chance against the big battalions in such a matter, and doubtless also because the managerial cut of a likely £30,000 a year is not to be lightly renounced by anyone, drove him on to the bitter end. (The end, of course, had already unofficially been reached; its full bitterness was yet to become apparent to him.)

He had had one or two conversations with Lord Goodman over the matter, although at Goodman, Derrick and Company it was being dealt with by a partner. Cotes felt, though, that his lordship—whose power in the land was legendary—might well be brought into the arena with advantage. On receipt of Arlen's latest letter he therefore wrote direct to Goodman at his private address:

'You will doubtless recall our discussing this property some weeks ago . . . At that time you assured me that Mrs Helen Arnold, with or without Mr Delfont, would produce the play at the London Coliseum only over your dead body.'

Goodman telephoned (June 7) to say that he would have a word with Stephen Arlen. He seemed in good health.

Cotes also wrote to the chairman of the Hospital Board, Mrs Audrey Callaghan (wife of future PM Mr James Callaghan), to whom he had a letter of introduction from a mutual friend, Mr Kenneth Robinson, the former Minister of Health and future Arts Council supremo. Mrs Callaghan, no doubt very properly, declined to see him on the question on the grounds that she had not personally seen *any* of the applicants for the contract. She wrote, interestingly, that, since the Board's knowledge of theatrical affairs was not great, they had decided 'to seek professional advice, which I believe to be of the highest order, to assess the applications'.

Mrs Callaghan's letter was dated June 21. She did not indicate that any decision had been reached at that time (it will be recalled that Mrs Arnold had been quoted as early as February as saying she had obtained the contract and would present the play at the Coliseum), but on June 29 a letter from the House Governor, Mr P W Dixon, informed Cotes that 'an agreement has now been engrossed but not yet signed between my Board of Governors and a major theatrical controller for the production of *Peter Pan* on the English stage for the next seven years'. And, on July 12, Dixon wrote further to say that 'on Wednesday of this week we shall be holding a press conference to break the news that the stage rights are to be awarded to Tom Arnold Presentations'. And so they did.

I am still intrigued to know precisely whose 'professional advice', which Mrs Callaghan believed to be 'of the highest order', the Board had sought. There was, of course, Mr Gordon Piller readily at hand, the former House Governor, the Honorary Agent for *Peter Pan* and certainly the hospital man most actively concerned with the play for some years past. He might, indeed, have been regarded as being 'professional' in this matter, although the context of Mrs Callaghan's use of the phrase suggested some person or persons within the theatrical profession. I know of no critic who was so approached. Mr Roger Lancelyn Green, the acknowledged authority, Barrie biographer and *Peter Pan* historian, was not approached either.

Mr Piller himself, and therefore the Board, doubtless had the advice of Mr Cyril Hicks, once associated with Bernard Delfont and later with the Tom Arnold office. Lord Delfont, as he now is, assuming he was not himself an applicant for the contract, is the sort of theatre man whose advice it would have been reasonable to seek. The Delfont and Tom Arnold organisations were both, however, subsidiaries of the Grade Organisation, which is owned by EMI, the chairman of which is Lord Delfont, the brother of Lord Grade. The freehold of the London Coliseum is owned by the Stoll Theatre Corporation, all the stock in which is owned by the Associated Broadcasting Development Company, which is a subsidiary of Lord Grade's Associated Television. Lord Goodman is on the Board of the English National Opera (formerly Sadler's Wells Opera), which leases the theatre. Lord Goodman's interests are, of course manifold, and it often seems that there can be no area of our national life in which he is not called upon to serve, whether as a diplomat in negotiations between the British and Rhodesian governments, or as mediator between unions and the government. His theatrical involvement is considerable, not only as a devoted theatregoer and operagoer and as a man whose advice is invariably sought in all matters relating to national arts and culture, but as a large shareholder in theatrical companies. In his professional capacity, he is the legal adviser to many important show business people and organisations, including the Grades and Delfont, whose holdings, subsidiaries and general ramifications are so extensive that he must find it a constant difficulty to ensure that he or his firm is not in some way representing opposing parties or conflicting interests in any given theatrical situation.

No doubt I digress. But the nature of the showbiz network may, in these particular instances, be relevant to the disposition of the *Peter Pan* contract by the governors of the Great Ormond Street Hospital, via Mr Gordon Piller, to Tom Arnold Presentations, and to the subsequent presentation of the play by that management at the Coliseum.

As to the 'professional advice' taken by the hospital in the matter, it seems quite clear that, although no decision was taken until June 1971, Mrs Helen Arnold was aware and confident of what it would be *four months earlier*. What seems also clear is that the Coliseum was, at the same time, earmarked for the presentation of *Peter Pan* the following Christmas and that the later, quite categorical, view of the managing director was overridden to bring it about; and that, further, the man who had first set in train negotiations for that theatre, and whose qualifications were ostensibly of the highest, was eventually squeezed out.

It is fair to go on from here to observe that, once having the official contract, Tom Arnold Presentations took some care by their lights to ensure that they should not come under criticism for the manner of the presentation. They engaged Dorothy Tutin to play Peter, and there could have been no better choice. They also brought Sir Robert Helpmann back from Australia to direct the production which, in commercial terms, was an unqualified success. Sir Robert said: 'I am going back to the original play. Barrie left very specific stage directions and is very clear about what he wants.'

There was room for dispute, however, about that. The *Daily Telegraph* reviewer, John Barber, in a special article written after the production had been playing for a month, took apart Helpmann's claim of fidelity to Barrie. 'This revival,' he wrote, 'follows neither the "original" nor the printed text . . . (Barrie) specified, for example, that the Darlings' house was in a "rather depressed street" and the nursery basically "a shabby little room". A 1904 photograph shows it pathetically plain and little . . . The Coliseum stage is the widest in London. So the nursery looks the size of the Hall of Mirrors at Versailles. It is separated from the audience by a gulf as wide as the Rhine . . . The play is further cut off by a false proscenium. The wistful original music by John Crook could not survive such conditions and has been abandoned in favour of ad-jingles, raucous and percussive . . . A big stage also dissipates

46

drama. The thrilling Mermaid Scene . . . becomes a dreamy ballet. The Lost Boys' encounters with the pirates and the wolves go for nothing. Poor Miss Tutin, begging us to save the dying Tink, might be a kitten mewing across the Grand Canyon . . .' and several hundred words more describing the loss of the play's subleties and its shortcomings when measured against Barrie's ideal production. 'Well, it makes money and the kids love it,' concluded Barber, 'but let no one imagine that this is not "a fine jewel in a tarnished setting" as W A Darlington characterised a vulgar revival.'

That was how the Tom Arnold Presentation—authorised by the Hospital Governors, in their wisdom and in their regard for the memory of their greatest benefactor, after 'professional advice' of 'the highest order'—appeared in the 1971–72 season. Dorothy Tutin again played Peter in the 1972–73 season and was succeeded the following year by another distinguished actress, Maggie Smith, once more at the Coliseum.

For the 1975–76 season the production was put on at the Palladium (owned by Moss Empires, which is owned by Stoll Investments, which is a subsidiary of ATV) and Peter was played by the pop singer, Lulu. This was getting about as far away as it is possible to get in the London theatre from the original productions supervised by Barrie at the Duke of York's, and it is hard to think that the governors of the Great Ormond Street Hospital for Sick Children felt much happier about it than they had about the production at the New Victoria, to which they had taken such exception six years previously. Worse, however, was to follow. In the 1976–77 season, for only the third time in the play's history, and without the excuses available on the other two occasions, there was *no production at all*.

Mrs Arnold's explanation was that there was no theatre *large enough* (my italics, of course) available for a production that she claimed cost £25,000 a year to refurbish. John Barber, commenting on this in the *Daily Telegraph*, said: 'What a misguided waste of money. Her capital should be put into mounting a more modest version that would be closer to Barrie's conception.' Not only would such a course have been more in keeping, as some may think, with the spirit of Barrie's bequest, but it would also, presumably, have solved the difficulty about the availability of a

47

theatre. As we have seen, Tom Arnold Presentations is a subsidiary of the Grade Organsiation, which is wholly owned by EMI, the chairman of which is Lord Delfont, who is clearly not a man altogether without influence in the matter of making theatres available. The idea of his being unable to help out Mrs Arnold with a theatre is rather as if Sir Charles Forte were unable to find a friend an hotel room.

What seemed to have happened, however, was that the one-time 'cert', *Peter Pan*, an annual profit-maker to the tune of £30,000, had become so elaborate that only a really enormous theatre could enable it to make a profit at all. Obviously everybody had been getting the sums wrong. The 'network' had failed to deliver, and the net result of the *Peter Pan* caper, at the end of the day, was that the Hospital Governors found they had given the property to a company which, in the sixth year of the seven-year contract, could not mount any London production.

It is not unusual, in the commercial theatre, for a scheduled production to be dropped when it becomes clear that it is not going to be profitable. Few can have imagined that *Peter Pan*, in London at Christmas, would ever fall into that unhappy category. Least of all, apparently, the governors of the Great Ormond Street Hospital for Sick Children.

IT'S 6
YOUR
MONEY

You may be interested to read in full the text of a statement issued to the press in February 1975 by the Theatre at New End, a small 'fringe' theatre in Hampstead:

> *Theatre at New End's administration has been unofficially informed by the Arts Council that their application for a grant has again been refused. It has today been announced by the Theatre's administrator that unless the Arts Council can reverse their decision New End must close at the end of this month.*
>
> *New End was built with private money at a cost of some £130,000. Spiralling building costs far exceeded the original budget and as a result the theatre was left without reserves. Previous requests for grants to Camden Council, the Greater London Arts Association and the Arts Council have been rejected but the Administration managed to keep open in the hope that the Arts Council would help the theatre for the new financial year.*
>
> *Fringe theatres because of their limited seating capacity have no hope of covering their running expenses but they fulfil a vital function in providing a venue in which young and experimental artists can work and be seen. New End is probably the best equipped fringe theatre in the country and it seems inconceivable that the Arts Council will make no contribution towards its survival.*

It is possible, especially if you are in agreement and sympathy with the last paragraph of that statement, that you would have been deeply touched by the plight of the Theatre at New End.

You may even have felt as indignant about it as they did. Your indignation might have been differently directed if you had actually seen any of the productions that contributed to New End's 'vital function'—for example a version of Strindberg's *The Father*, revised 'to meet the demands of our time', demands interpreted as requiring an amplified rock-music introduction, fairground decor and a sawdust ring as the playing area—but let it pass.

What struck me particularly about the response of the Theatre at New End to a fairly common predicament of the time was its sense of grievance, the belief that an artistic venture privately financed had some sort of claim upon public finance if the private finance ran out, and the continuing belief that such public finance *should* be forthcoming even though all previous requests for grants-in-aid had been rejected. There is a breathtaking arrogance here which is by no means uncommon among the arts community.

I may be unfair in picking on that little Hampstead place for a temerity it had merely absorbed from people who had been in the begging-bowl business far longer. There is, for example, Theatre Workshop, the Company founded by Joan Littlewood at the Theatre Royal at Stratford in East London, which must have done some dumb deals to come out a long-term commercial loser with such long-running West End transfers going for it as *The Hostage*, *Fings Ain't Wot They Used T' Be*, *A Taste of Honey* and *Oh! What a Lovely War!* together with all those film and other subsidiary rights spinning off from them.

In the financial year 1974–75, Miss Littlewood and her general manager, Gerry Raffles, were shocked to learn that their hand-out from the Arts Council was going up from £45,000 to £55,000. No, no. I don't mean that they were, as good socialists, appalled by the profligacy of a Labour government that didn't know which way to turn to meet its welfare-state commitments; I mean they didn't think it was *enough*—even though they had another £20,000 also coming to them from the Greater London Council and the Newham Borough Council. Raffles almost broke down and cried. He said he needed at least another £800 a week to run the theatre, and if he didn't get it he saw no option but to resign. (He didn't and he did.*) Anyone looking at the Theatre Royal, Stratford,

* It is a sad postscript, though irrelevant to this discussion, that Mr Raffles has since died.

could be forgiven for wondering how it was possible to lose a steady £1,500 a week there, let alone £2,300; but that wonderment would assume audiences of paying customers. If Theatre Workshop, existing to bring live theatre to East End audiences, was not getting those audiences, the losses became easier to understand, but in that event, why were they existing and being subsidised, anyway?

The answer to that is tied in with the whole 'the-state-owes-me-a-living' syndrome presently afflicting the arts in Britain, its institutions and its individuals. The attitude of Theatre Workshop may be extreme—an extremity fostered by the long years of fawning upon it by press commentators notoriously indulgent of the amateurish chaos of so much of its work. But it is reflected in some degree in the attitude of virtually every theatrical enterprise in the country that has ever been intoxicated by the whiff of government subvention. It is, moreover, an attitude that has communicated itself, understandably enough, to the arts community as a whole. Criticisms of the Arts Council are amusingly self-centred and merely underline the difficulties of the Council in deciding what is worthy and what is not. For, in the eyes of the 'artist', the mere fact of *being* an 'artist' is itself worthy—a principle that would disturb me less, and might indeed claim my support, if the description were not so frequently entirely self-adopted. To adapt an old aphorism, people are divided into the artists and the others, and it is the artists who decide which are which.

Thus we had, in 1974, a one hundred page cyclostyled Report issued by a group called 'Artists Now' and entitled *The Patronage of the Creative Artist*. Though the panel of five that conducted the investigation leading to the Report included two former members of the Arts Council's grants committees, their conclusions were in general an assault upon the fundamentals of the Council's approach. They shouldn't be doling out money to institutions (or, at least, not so much of it), said 'Artists Now' in effect; they should be doling it out to individual artists. The major complaint was that all the big money goes to theatres, orchestras and art galleries that put on only a trifling proportion of new work: in the year examined (1972/73) it appeared that only 43 plays out of 360 performed by the 40 theatres receiving the bulk of the Arts Council drama grant had been new ones. The conclusion drawn from this was not exactly that only 43 new plays were worthy of production but implied that there must have been hundreds more that were casually rejected!

'Artists Now' claimed that there are 1,000 to 1,500 dramatists in Britain today—by which I take it they mean that there are 1,000 to 1,500 people who *think* they are dramatists, or call themselves dramatists (it often seems many more to the professional 'readers' who have to sift through the rubbish that most of them write), and the same goes for the rest of their figures: 500 composers, 7,000 painters, etc.! And they were all said to be terribly, terribly sensitive people who are damaged to their souls when their work is rejected: the Arts Council should foster schemes to ensure that it is all performed, God help us (and them, for the pain and trauma of rejection in private are a great deal easier to bear than rejection in public).

Whatever might be assumed from the tenor of the foregoing, I am not, repeat not, taking up a stance opposed to state subsidy of either the theatre or the arts in general. I doubt whether such a point of view is intellectually or philosophically tenable, although there are still those about who hold the opinion that any artistic endeavour that cannot support itself should perish, that theatres that are unprofitable should close, that playwrights whose work does not attract the public in sufficiently large numbers should not be writing plays at all, other than for their own satisfaction in time spared from more useful work.

No one with a care for the cultural health of the community could go along wholly with that opinion . . . but I could easily get bogged down here in an extensive argument over the value of the arts. Anyone who cannot accept the assumptions, (a) that the world would be a poorer place without them, (b) that the question is not whether they should exist but how they shall exist, (c) that more than the immediately popular deserves to survive, and (d), given the preceding point, that some form of patronage is necessary, had best make his excuses and leave.

The arts have always depended for survival on a certain amount of patronage. In other ages the matter was attended to privately by the noble and wealthy. The arrangement served well enough, though it was, in truth, an arbitrary and whimsical business. Just

200 years ago, Samuel Johnson wrote to Lord Chesterfield: 'Is not a patron, my Lord, one who looks with unconcern on a man struggling for life in the water, and when he has reached ground encumbers him with help? The notice which you have been pleased to take of my labours had it been early had been kind; but it has been delayed till I am indifferent and cannot enjoy it; till I am known and do not want it.'

Chesterfield had praised the famous Dictionary on its publication though he had resisted Johnson's appeals for financial aid while it was being compiled. Thus the Dictionary itself defined a patron as 'commonly a wretch who supports with insolence and is paid with flattery'.

There may still be a little private patronage around; there are also the great trusts, such as the Gulbenkian and Ford Foundations; and there are industrial companies and even newspapers that will sometimes lend financial support to artistic enterprises. Nevertheless the sources of such patronage have been drying up throughout our century: there are no longer wealthy enough men who are also interested in the idea. And the firms big enough to find the spare cash for the purpose seem to prefer, on the whole, to sponsor horse races.

Although Mr Harold Lever (who was appointed in 1976 by the then Prime Minister, Harold Wilson, to look into the matter of financing the arts) would like to see a general cooperation of the Government, local government and private business in supporting the arts, since the second world war the patronage business has generally been taken over by the state, via the Arts Council. It is possible that this in itself has diverted the attention of the private patron from the arts; and many will think, too, that the new system is as arbitrary and whimsical as the old, and equally deserving of the Johnsonian epithets pertaining to 'insolence' and 'flattery'; nevertheless, it seems to be here to stay on a relatively permanent basis.

The cost to the taxpayers has steadily risen, often well beyond the general trend of inflation, although for a time, by force of economic circumstances, the two came into a closer conjunction. In the financial year 1954/55, the total of Arts Council grants to the arts was just under £800,000; twenty years later, in 1974/75, it was £21,300,000. Under pressure of persistent lobbying (as well, it may fairly be said, as inflation), the Government raised the grant for 1976/77 to something over £36,000,000, and the estimate for 1977/78 is over £41,000,000. The figure of 41 million pounds is not a great deal in the context of the entire national budget, but it will seem expensive enough to most people. The arts do not come high on the list of popular charitable causes— however enthusiastic minority appreciation may be.

In hard economic times nearly everybody—including artists, if they can take time out from their 'the state-owes-us-a-living' bleat to think about it—can bring to mind worthier causes for support from the public purse. It does not follow, though, and never has, that the money a government saves on one venture is devoted to a more desirable other. If the armament programme were abandoned the money so saved would not, I fear, be diverted to cancer research, as some might wish. Bursaries for playwrights would not, if dropped, be translated into higher old age pensions or subsidies to homes for retired donkeys. And, if the National Theatre had not been built, it is unlikely that a hospital would have been instead. So, while the case for even further increases in Arts Council funds cannot be validly argued (even by bringing in the argument that the whole principle of arts subsidies was established at a time of even greater national hardship, i.e. during the second world war), neither can it be said that much would be valuably gained in other spheres by decreasing them. The point primarily at issue is whether the available funds are going in the right directions and being made the best use of; specifically, for the purposes of this book, in the theatre.

To imagine that all of those funds are being devoted to creative artistic activity is to be sensationally naïve. For example, according to the Arts Council's published accounts for the year ended March 31, 1976 (the most recent available at the time of writing), while 'general expenditure on the arts' in Great Britain amounted to £27,346,367, the Council's 'general operating costs' were £1,537,762. If that seems a high administrative figure in relation to the total, consider also that the 27 million-odd pounds described as expenditure on the arts was itself going to hundreds of organisations, large and small, each of which doubtless had administrative costs in similar proportion—and the bigger the organisation the larger the proportion of the grant that goes into its administration. Perhaps it is all essential—without getting into all of them with a time-and-motion man and a cost accountant it is hard to say. But it did give the poet-playwright Ronald Duncan material for a provocative article in the *Telegraph Magazine* in which he weighed these figures against the profits and operating costs of a big industrial corporation—and reached the conclusion that in Britain today giving money away is more expensive to administer than making it.

As far as the theatre is concerned the big recipients of grants are, very properly, the National Theatre and the Royal Shakespeare Theatre (£1,931,500 and £915,000, respectively, in the 1975/76 accounts and going up), followed by the English Stage Company at the Royal Court (£196,738), then by some of the larger provincial theatres, and amounts ranging from £44,000 to £75 given to over 90 'fringe' and experimental groups (of which there were suddenly fifteen more than in the previous year).

The money is doled out by the Arts Council on the recommendations of its Drama Panel, a committee of 30-odd that is more or less self-perpetuating since the membership, by its replacement appointments, determines its future constitution. As if that were not disquieting enough, there is the further curious circumstance that several members of the panel are in some way connected with organisations in receipt of its grants. This is somewhat analogous to a situation in which a town council was largely conposed of builders and the like who were given civic contracts. In the case of the theatre it might well be difficult to get together a competent advisory committee composed entirely of individuals who could approach the matter of grants in a spirit of total disinterest—for there are relatively few workers in the theatre who are unlikely to be working sooner or later, if they are not already, for a state-subsidised theatre. But I should not have thought that the task was altogether impossible.

The principal beefers about the present set-up, naturally, are those who feel in some way discriminated against—either because they get no hand-out at all, or because what they get is not, in their view, enough. Obviously some of the 'fringe' groups can argue a case by comparison—the assessments of the panel of their value and needs are essentially matters of opinion. But, equally, there is an argument on the question of whether the 'fringe' has much value at all, whether it is, in fact, a valid part of the 'culture' that the nation, by comment consent, is committed to preserve and foster by public patronage. It is a question, perhaps, that deserves a brief, opinionated chapter of its own. And so, on quite another hand, do the affairs of the theatre's subsidised 'giants', the National Theatre and the Royal Shakespeare Company.*

The English Stage Company at London's Royal Court Theatre in Sloane Square, however, makes a natural entry into the discussion at this point, since it at once highlights the extent to which the money required for theatre subsidy has increased over the years and also leads directly to a consideration of the value of subsidy and some misconceptions about it. For the Royal Court has been the star turn, the brightest jewel in the crown that subsidy has placed on the brow of the British theatre these post-war years; and anyone who happens to express the merest unease about the extent to which the subsidised theatre has come to dominate the commercial theatre in the same period will be instantly asked whether the high international reputation of British theatre and British drama today would be imaginable but for the Royal Court. Let's look then.

In what many would regard as its most successful and influential years, the English Stage Company was subsidised by the Arts Council to the tune of £5,000 or, at the most, £8,000 a year. That was in the second half of the 1950s. The late George Devine, who was running the company as artistic director, could be said to have reinvigorated the English theatre by the encouragement he gave to new dramatists—some of them already well-known in other fields of literary endeavour (such as Angus Wilson, Nigel Dennis and Gwyn Thomas), but others, and more successfully, who were entirely unknown. The policy, though obviously worthwhile since it restored to the theatre some sadly needed intellectual sinew, was obviously chancy in the commercial sense. The enterprise might not have survived if those new dramatists had not happened to include one John Osborne, who sent along a work called *Look Back in Anger* in 1956.

Now, in the mid 1970s, the English Stage Company's subsidy

* The 'fringe' is discussed in Chapter 21, the National Theatre and the RSC in Chapters 7 & 8.

56

from the Arts Council is running at over £200,000 a year and deficits are being carried forward. Of course, these two decades have been generally inflationary in all areas. But perhaps not at the rate of 4,000 per cent! During this period, plays at the Royal Court, though none has made quite the impact of *Look Back in Anger*, have transferred regularly to West End theatres for extended runs. But despite the fact that considerably more money is also being taken at the Royal Court itself, the financial capacity of the house being now about £5,000 a week against the £340 it was at the start of the English Stage Company operation, the additional subsidy has been easily swallowed up. There is clearly a sort of Parkinson's Law operating in the subsidy area: the more you get, the more you use, and ultimately, the more you need.

Sometimes it almost seems as though failure is an essential qualification for subsidy. Actually to be seen to be making money is to be caught in an indecent act. This is not a situation that can arise at either the National Theatre or the Royal Shakespeare, any more than it can at the Royal Opera House, for no matter how well-attended the performances may be there is no way in which those expensive productions can break even in repertory; and even successful overseas tours or transfers to West End theatres (perhaps in association with commercial managements) merely help to reduce the deficit; overall profit is not possible.

This is not, however, necessarily the case elsewhere. It is not difficult to visualise a situation in which, say, the Royal Court—with absolutely everything going for it—could have two or three of its plays running commercially in the West End and another playing to capacity at the Sloane Square house, the entire operation being successful enough over the course of a year to take the English Stage Company into the black without recourse to the subsidy. This hasn't happened lately—notwithstanding such winners as *The Philanthropist* (the company's most successful single production), *The Changing Room* and *The Rocky Horror Show*—but it did happen, I think, back in 1957–58 when transfers and the sale of film and other subsidiary rights resulted in a situation in which that year's subsidy was added to profits, rather than set against losses.

If this were now to happen again, and happen as a regular thing, nice problems would arise for both the Arts Council (why should public money be presented to a company that could be clearly seen to be commercially viable?) and for the English Stage Company (should it stop producing plays that the public was going to support and make a serious effort to start losing money again?). The critical and public disenchantment with the Robert Kidd and Nicholas Wright regime culminating in the much publicised resignations early in 1977 of these joint Royal Court artistic directors and the appointment in their place of Stuart Burge may be relevant here.

I'm not sure how the Royal Court would handle too much success, but I have a notion how the Mermaid would. The Mermaid is the theatre in the City by Blackfriars Bridge, run by Sir Bernard Miles, which has grants from the Corporation of the City of London and from the Arts Council (the latter went up from £42,000 in 1974/75 to £97,000 in 1975/76). In July 1974 the Mermaid staged, as its contribution to the City of London Festival, a musical called *Cole*—a stuck-together compendium of Cole Porter songs which, for that reason alone, could hardly miss. For the rest of that year, up to mid-December, it played consistently close to the house capacity of £6,500 a week. Business fell somewhat when it was running in tandem with the Christmas show, *Treasure Island*. But it gradually built up again after that and was still playing to around £5,000 a week when Miles decided to close it in April 1975 to make way for a revival of *The Doctor's Dilemma*. He had generally resisted deals offered by commercial managers to take *Cole* into the West End, where it would probably have been good for another six months of life and profit to the Mermaid.

The implication here seems to be that *Cole* looked like being so profitable that—at a time when the Arts Council was hard-pressed to meet all its commitments—it might have endangered the Mermaid subsidy; yet if it transferred to the West End as several previous Mermaid productions have done, it could actually have subsidised the inevitable Mermaid loss-makers. I should have thought that would have been a highly desirable situation, particularly for the taxpayer and ratepayer. The Mermaid subsidy, in any case, is earned, I have always considered, because of its location, because it brought theatre back to the City of London for the first time in centuries, rather than because it contributes lavishly to the cultural life of the capital or the nation. Although Sir Bernard Miles would hardly agree, my view is that its classical revivals, while generally well-meaning, are rarely done with distinction. It does best with Shaw and notoriously badly with Shakespeare. Its successful new plays have been of a kind that the commercial theatre might have been just as likely to produce—with perhaps the exceptions of Peter Luke's *Hadrian VII*, originally produced at the Birmingham Repertory Theatre, and John Arden's *Left-Handed Liberty*, commissioned for a City of London Festival.

Having said that, I am bound also to say that it is an erroneous assumption, anyway, that the subsidised theatre has been responsible for everything that is worthy in the British theatre today—or, indeed, for most of it. While it has often seemed that the subsidised houses have, one way or another, hived off all the gifted directors and most of the distinguished actors, it is upon the quality of its dramatists that a healthy and developing theatrical art ultimately depends; and in this regard the subsidised theatre has a poor record of discovery. The English Stage Company might well be exempted from this judgment, although even that nursery of playwriting talent—now regarded, almost, as a shrine before which generations yet unborn will genuflect—is often given more credit than is wholly its due.

J W Lambert, who was then a member of the Arts Council and chairman of its Drama Panel, wrote for the *Sunday Times* (a newspaper of which he was literary editor) in the spring of 1975, an article much concerned about the indifference of the Government to the financial plight of the theatre and gloomily headed, 'Requiem for British Theatre':

> *Is it generally understood that the English Stage Company at the Royal Court, which has nurtured almost all those dramatists of the last twenty years whose plays are constantly being performed all over the world, and have made Britain's name paramount for playwrights of our time, is already compelled to compromise by playing for West End transfers and the like? It has already been practically driven to abandon, in its founder George Devine's phrase, 'the right to fail'—without which significant success is not to be expected.*

Now, with respecct to Mr Lambert, none of this is really true. It is, not to put too fine an edge upon it, hogwash. 'Almost all those dramatists of the past twenty years . . .' Well, y-e-s, there were John Osborne, Arnold Wesker and John Arden and there is Edward Bond; and there are David Storey and E A Whitehead (if you feel that these, too, are names to conjure with and make our national name paramount) and the West Indian, Mustapha Matura, who is probably on his way. I do not wish to make light of any of them. But the Royal Court, though it has staged plays by Joe Orton, say, did not 'nurture' him. He was in fact first put on in London by a commercial management. And though Christopher Hampton had a spell as the Court's resident dramatist and wrote *The Philanthropist* and *Savages*, it was a commercial management that first gave his earlier piece *When Did You Last See My Mother?* a proper production in London, after it had been seen at Oxford and in a Sunday night 'production without decor' at the Royal Court. As for Tom Stoppard, Peter Shaffer, Peter Nichols, Alan Ayckbourn, David Mercer and Harold Pinter (I'm just plucking names out of the air), none of these are Royal Court dramatists. For the most part commercial managements (in some instances following the lead of commercial *television*, down there in the despised basement of the arts) can take the credit for providing their initial encouragement. None of which is to denigrate the fine part played by the English Stage Company, merely to put it in some more accurate perspective.

As for the 'compromise' of 'playing for West End transfers and the like', no one at the Royal Court views that judgment very kindly. They have always been glad of those West End transfers, and they go back a long way—to *Look Back in Anger*, in fact—and I cannot think that *anything* that has transferred to the West End from the Royal Court would be regarded as any sort of compromise with their own standards. (There was just one play, perhaps, that might not have been staged but for the urgent need for a money-maker, but that was not due to the compulsions of 1975—it was back in 1959, it was Noël Coward's *Look After Lulu*.) Like any theatre, the Royal Court has had its share of failures (no fewer, proportionately, now than in the past), but I cannot think that it has ever welcomed them, whether or not it considered itself to have a 'right' to them.

60

In this matter of nurturing new writers, economic pressures on commercial managements are probably shifting the balance from them to the subsidised theatres. As much is indicated by the fact that those dramatists whom I've mentioned, while they may have gone in the first instance to the commercial managements, are now going to the subsidised ones.

I wish I could have the same confidence in the judgment of men who have their carefree 'right to fail' as I would repose in those who are looking primarily for success. There is, of course, an obvious need for that 'right to fail' commercially with something worthy—it is the phrase that justifies the whole principle of subsidy resting on the unfortunate truth that worthiness is no passport to instant popularity—but it has seemed sometimes, as subsidy has proliferated, that an attitude has developed that tends to translate the protective right into the positive duty. The fact that the worthy may sometimes fail has seemed to encourage the absurd notion that commercial failure is the proof of artistic worthiness, whereas it indicates as often as not—and probably more often than not—artistic failure, too.

Even in those 'bad old days' when the theatrical art was at the mercy of commerce, I doubt whether much in the way of genius went undiscovered. It is true that the rules of the market-place have always decreed that the bulk of theatrical fare is frivolous— because the public, generally, has a preference for frivolous entertainments. What has happened now is that, given the present economics of a business that was always a high-risk area, it has become even harder than it once was for good serious drama to compete commercially with good frivolities. Profit margins on even the latter are so cramped that they can no longer be relied upon to underwrite the losses on the former. Nevertheless, the best of the commercial managers always knew a good play when they saw one, and I suspect they still do. (Thinking back to the days when outlying theatre clubs were the equivalent of today's 'fringe', providing a platform for the works that the commercial managers had turned down; and slogging around them in a youthful enthusiasm for seeing everything that was happening I cannot remember seeing anything that did not, in fact, deserve its Shaftesbury Avenue rejection slips.) What I should like to see is the co-opting to subsidised companies—at suitable rates of remuneration—of commercial managers who have a proven eye for spotting a serious new talent, and who, while aware of this state-given 'right to fail', would not, because of it, renounce their belief in the virtue of success.

Such a move might also somewhat redress the political imbalance of the subsidised theatre that occasions such uneasiness among those who foresee all serious drama becoming the exclusive preserve of such theatres. For the fact has to be faced that the serious drama offered by the subsidised houses, as their direction is at present constituted, is fairly one-sided in a political and sociological sense. I may personally agree with the point of view they invariably project: I should sit very uneasily, not to say indignantly, through plays that were dramatised pleas for, say, keeping Britain white, reducing social services or restoring capital punishment. Even so, it would seem to me a dangerous pity if the only plays dealing with vital issues of the day that had any prospect of production were those of the persuasion that its adherents deem to be 'progressive'.

There is a further danger which should give pause to all those who feel that the theatre's greatest hope for the future lies in the extension of subsidy to the point where no theatre has any worries whatever about finance—perhaps even taking the whimsical view of Peter Brook, who has been quoted by Judith Cook* as saying:

> . . . *even with a big subsidy a company must always earn a large proportion of its money through the box-office. In a sense, total freedom doesn't exist even with a high subsidy; total freedom exists when the subsidy means that you need never work at all, and that was the ideal circumstance I wanted, that we could put ourselves in a position of total luxury where some unknown benefactor could set us up to sit and do absolutely nothing, recognising that once that situation was created there were the conditions of a research laboratory.*

The danger in this, whatever Brook may think, is that the security of subsidy does not, in fact, promote and encourage creativity but stultify it. The greatest achievements in the theatre, and indeed in the arts generally, have rarely grown out of the condi-

* *Directors' Theatre* by Judith Cook (Harrap, 1974).

tions that Brook would regard as 'ideal', from the mighty days of Ancient Greece down to the present day. They have come, rather, under the pressure of competition and in the nervous atmosphere of risk.

'Security, or even its distant prospect, is theatre's most pernicious enemy,' is an admonitory view that should be soberly heeded by advocates of more and more subsidy (a tenfold increase of Arts Council funds has been seriously suggested in one Labour Party discussion paper), for it is the view of an authority who knows what he is talking about. The words are those of John Russell Brown, Professor of English at Sussex University and formerly head of the drama department at Birmingham University, who noted in an article in *Theatre Quarterly* that 'long-established state theatres in other countries do show the inhibitions that can come through developing too much bureaucratic fat'. The professor is now an associate director of the National Theatre.

THE NATIONAL 7
THEATRE

Though its grant from the Arts Council still lags somewhat behind the annual subvention in support of the Royal Opera House, the National Theatre represents far and away the heaviest drama commitment of the British taxpayer. The building itself, on the South Bank of the Thames, cost around £16 million by the time it was finally ready in 1977. Such a sum was not really a lot compared with the cost of similar buildings elsewhere in Europe—especially in the light of the first estimate of £7½ million, all those inflationary years ago in 1966. Even before its building was complete in 1976 the company moved in from its temporary home at the Old Vic with an Arts Council subsidy of nearly £2 million soon to be supplemented by an extra £1 million largely to cover building delay costs—plus a GLC grant of something over £300,000.

It is doubtful whether the British public actually wanted it, or whether they would have sanctioned the outlay had the question been put to them in advance by referendum. As Bernard Shaw remarked in 1938, when an earlier National Theatre scheme was in the air, 'they never want anything of this sort, they never wanted the British Museum or the National Gallery or Westminster Abbey, but now they are there they are quite proud of them and feel that the place would be incomplete without them'. So it may be with the National Theatre, the building of which might be said to be the natural culmination of the nation's generally reluctant acceptance of the principle of state-subsidy of the theatre and other arts.

Even so, it was a longish haul. The first positive suggestion for the establishment of a national theatre had been put forward by a London publisher named Effingham Wilson in 1848, and it took

65

129 years to get from there to here, despite the nearby example of France where the Comédie Française had been established since 1680. The reason for Britain's tardiness in giving the theatre the fiscal blessing of the state was ascribed in part—by Kenneth Tynan in an address to the Royal Society of Arts in 1964—to 'the lasting damage inflicted on the theatre by the Puritans in the seventeenth century'.

> *After their moral lacerations* [he said], *acting came to be regarded as a form of clothed prostitution; and though Charles II subsidised actresses, he did not subsidise plays. Until Irving got his knighthood in 1895, acting remained a dubious profession, barely a stone's cast away from the brothel. And this mighty backlog of Puritan disapproval had to be dislodged before a British government could be persuaded to spend a penny of public money on an art so trivial.*

'God help the government that meddles with art,' the Liberal prime minister Lord Melbourne had said in the 1830s and British governments for a further hundred years and more were tacitly influenced by his warning. Not until around the turn of the present century, indeed, were really important voices heard ventilating the national theatre idea, but in the Edwardian era plans for, and objectives of, a national theatre were formulated in a book by the actor-manager-director-dramatist Harley Granville Barker and the critic William Archer. Their scheme was subsequently adopted by the movement to build a national memorial to William Shakespeare and a body called the Shakespeare Memorial National Theatre Committee was set up. As it turned out, this was probably not a helpful collaboration of interests as far as the national theatre idea was concerned, since the vital part of the Shakespearians' objective was achieved at Stratford-upon-Avon and some of the urgent steam went out of the larger scheme in consequence. Limited funds were raised in the 1920s and 1930s, as a result of which a site was acquired at South Kensington. But still there was no state money forthcoming; nor any public demand that it should be.

After the second world war—during which the value of the arts was offically recognised, and the principle of state-subsidy was

66

established in the grants and guarantees given to various artistic organisations through the Council for the Encouragement of Music and the Arts (CEMA)—a growing number of politicians were prepared to embrace the cause. It was not likely to win them many votes, but perhaps it wouldn't lose them many, either. In 1949, a National Theatre Bill actually passed through both Houses of Parliament without a division and the government of the day was thereby empowered to contribute up to £1 million towards the building and equipping of the theatre. What a paltry sum it seems now, and even then it was hardly enough to get anything usefully moving. A foundation stone laid by the Queen Mother in 1951 was regarded with rather more hope than confidence. Enthusiasts for the idea were really just running their flag up the pole to see if anyone saluted. Nobody did, although some seven years later an Arts Council report entitled *Housing the Arts in Great Britain* urged that a high priority should be accorded the building of the National Theatre. Four years after *that*, in 1962, a National Theatre Board was appointed by the Chancellor of the Exchequer, and then Lord Olivier (or Sir Laurence, as he then was) was appointed Director of the National Theatre. Of course, there wasn't a new theatre. But the enterprise had a Board and it had a Director, and soon it had a Company. Progress was being made, though at a rate more usually associated with the mills of God.

In October 1963, Olivier took his company of National Theatre players into what was to be their temporary home at the Old Vic and dreamed of taking them into the permanent theatre perhaps four or five years later. But by then the new building had not even been started. The years were flying by. Work actually began on the finally agreed South Bank site in the autumn of 1969 to the designs of the architect, Denys Lasdun. Olivier—as Director—got as far as the 'topping-out' ceremony. This little ritual and celebration is held when the top of a new building is reached by the builders and in this case Olivier performed it with Lord Cottesloe, chairman of the South Bank Theatre Board, in May 1973. In November of that year, after a six-month turn-over period, Peter Hall took over as Director. Ill-health might well have made Olivier's retirement inevitable, anyway, but the manner of his going did not notably become the Board who engineered it.

Although Olivier had, in fact, offered to resign in the summer of 1971, when the fortunes of the company were at their lowest ebb, apparently he was not taken seriously. Things went on as before and, as we shall see, he did succeed in restoring the NT's fortunes and reputation. But, behind the scenes, the chairman of the National Theatre Board, Sir Max (now Lord) Rayne, and Lord Goodman, then chairman of the Arts Council, began their discussions with Peter Hall. To say, as was said, that Olivier was 'consulted' in the matter was, at best, a half-truth. He was consulted eventually—when, indeed, the matter had been settled. But he was not consulted at the outset, nor given any reason to suppose that he would not be taking the company into the new building.

At the end of March 1972, the *Observer* blew the gaff; Peter Hall was 'on' for the National job. And it became clear, as the rest of the press followed the lead, that this was news to Olivier. 'No curtains for Larry,' said the *Guardian* headline; 'Olivier: "I will not be moved" ' read another in the *Evening Standard*; 'National Theatre denies report that Lord Olivier is to be replaced,' said the *Times*.

Olivier called a meeting of the company to assure its members that there was no question of his leaving until they moved into the South Bank complex. On April 13 the Board issued a statement confirming that. But a week later they issued another to say that Peter Hall was joining the company early in 1973 as Director-designate; and Olivier was on the way out.

The Olivier years had had ups and downs. The repertory was enormously varied and established from the first a pattern of presenting a balanced mixture of classics (some well-known, others relatively neglected), foreign plays of distinction and a fair number of works representative of the drama of our own century, including a smattering of specially commissioned new plays.

The first four years of the operation at the Old Vic were generally superb. There were the occaasional failures, but triumphs predominated—and it was my convinced view that the captaincy of Olivier himself was primarily responsible for that agreeable state of affairs. Confirmation of this is implicit in the fact that it was around the summer of 1967 that the rot of the second four years began to set in. At that time Olivier, stricken by cancer, was persuaded that the manifold responsibilities of administration, production and acting were beyond the resources of a man in indifferent health. Understandably, he began to shed some of the load. Unfortunately the unhappy truth was that no one proved capable of shouldering it in the same inspirational fashion.

It is highly likely, not to say inevitable, that many of the people most closely concerned with the Olivier years will produce 'histories' of the way the theatre was run and of the wrangles behind the scenes that ran concurrently with what we were seeing on the stage; but they will all present necessarily subjective versions. As it appeared to a detached observer, a revival of Chekhov's *Three Sisters*, which Olivier had in rehearsal in the summer of 1967, was arguably the high peak of the National's achievements up to that time. Following that production—with Olivier ill and no one able to take major decisions that would be accepted unquestioningly by everyone else—the record went into reverse. For the next four years, instead of only occasional failures, there were only occasional successes.

We had had a sweet run embracing such memorable productions as *Uncle Vanya*, *Saint Joan*, *Othello*, *The Master Builder*, *Hay Fever*, *The Royal Hunt of the Sun*, *Trelawny of the 'Wells'*, *A Flea in Her Ear*, *Black Comedy*, *The Dance of Death*, *Rosencrantz and Guildenstern are Dead* and the aforementioned *Three Sisters*. Now the lean years were upon us, and it is the ghastlier events that surge back to mind: those irksomely self-indulgent productions of Tyrone Guthrie (*Volpone* and *Tartuffe*) and Peter Brook (Seneca's *Oedipus*), the Brecht re-write of Marlowe's *Edward II*, banal and tedious on a scale monumental even for that Teutonic plague; a disreputable and vulgar reading of *The Way of the World*; a production of Webster's *The White Devil* absurdly tricked out with touches of bizarre eroticism—followed by woefully inadequate adaptations of Cervantes, Rostand and Dostoievsky.

It all seemed rather more than merely a run of 'bad luck' and undoubtedly some of the impetus went out of the drive for a proper National Theatre building, so that no progress whatever was made in that direction for the next two years. The complacent underlings of the National Theatre company, reasonably happy to be splashing around in an Arts Council grant that had risen from £130,000 in 1963/64 to £240,000 in 1967/68 to £375,000 in

69

1970/71, were not depressed, though. Like some unlucky airline company that puts a lavish new advertising campaign underway the day before its latest jet disintegrates over the ocean, they announced that shortly the company would be appearing not only at the Old Vic but at the New Theatre* as well. This arrangement they proposed to continue until the South Bank building was ready for them. The crash that instantly followed was the première of *Coriolanus*, a hydrid, or bastard, production (by Brecht out of Shakespeare by rape) which turned out to be as doleful an occasion as any in the four preceding, terrible years.

As if there were not numbers enough in the company at the time (there were four associate directors—three of them actually directors in the production sense—and not one but two literary consultants, a staff producer, four assistant producers and an acting complement of over eighty), alien assistance was enlisted for the *Coriolanus* disaster, in the persons of Manfred Wekwerth and Joachim Tenschert. These were a brace of Brecht disciples from East Berlin who were co-opted, I understand, primarily on the advice of the National's resident Brechtian enthusiast, one of the two literary managers, Kenneth Tynan. They evidently arrived with the notion that they were to reproduce their master's Marxist interpretation of the work. But other views had by now prevailed in the councils of the company, and that was no longer quite the idea: the unadulterated, unrevised Shakespeare text was to be used, but Brechtian methods were to be applied in its production. This was folly of a high order, as was divined almost instantly by Christopher Plummer, the actor who had been engaged for the title-role but who withdrew at an early stage of rehearsals. It was not a unique occurrence at the National in those disputatious days. Anthony Hopkins, who took over from Plummer, had himself previously escaped from the production of *The Idiot* by withdrawing after a disagreement with the director (in that instance, Anthony Quayle), but here he fell in loyally with the Wekwerth-Tenschert travesty and was not to be held wholly responsible for the interpretation imposed upon him. The production proved to be untenable in its premises and an unspeakable bore in performance.

I dwell upon this particular débacle because it seemed at the

* Since re-named the Albery.

time a sort of watershed. Work on the South Bank site had been in progress for some 18 months, and whatever may have been the feelings in the company and its boardroom, outside opinion was that something drastic would have to be done if that building was ever to be occupied by a company worthy of the name of National Theatre. *Coriolanus* looked very much like the end of the road, and the company's announcement about taking the tenancy of a *second* theatre so that productions 'can be seen by nearly 15,000 people each week' was optimism to the point of inanity. In the event, it quickly became apparent that the company was *not* going to stay at the New until its new building became available. In fact, after a deadly run of four productions there—*The Rules of the Game, Amphitryon 38, Tyger* and *Danton's Death*, only the first of which, directed by Olivier and starring Paul Scofield and Joan Plowright, had any success at the box-office—the decision was taken to cut losses and close-off the operation early in 1972, after little more than six months. As it fortunately happened, however, this was the dark hour before a new dawn. Just around the corner was the sensationally successful production of O'Neill's *Long Day's Journey Into Night*, which not only brought a semblance of respectability to the overall figures at the New but later had a sell-out season at the Old Vic.

Those who think that it is money that is the vital factor in a theatrical operation—with the implication that the higher the subsidy the greater the prospect of success—will find some figures on the respective production costs of the disastrous *Coriolanus* and the triumphant *Long Day's Journey* illuminating. Of course, the former with a cast of over 30 as against a cast of only five in the latter, was more expensive to run. But *leaving aside* the question of the players' salaries, *Coriolanus* still cost nearly £17,000 to mount (including a lavish allowance for the hotels of the German directors in addition to their substantial fees) whereas the O'Neill play cost just over £6,000, the direction being handled by Michael Blakemore as part of his salaried duties as an associate director,

The production of *Long Day's Journey* was superb in every respect: the four-hour play itself, largely autobiographical and not 'good drama' in any formal sense, is nevertheless extraordinarily moving. It was certainly directed and acted magnificently. Every part was flawlessly taken. But the really stunning achieve-

71

ment was the performance of Olivier himself. Recovered, at least temporarily, from his illness, he was able again to lift and inspire the company as he had done in the early days with his Othello. This was the turning of the tide. Things looked up again for the National and for the remainder of his period at the helm failures again became the exceptions in a splendid run of successes: Tom Stoppard's *Jumpers*, the British première of Hecht and MacArthur's *The Front Page*, a sparkling new adaptation of *The Misanthrope* by the poet Tony Harrison, Peter Shaffer's new play *Equus*, which was to have a further triumph in New York, and *Saturday Sunday Monday*, which went on to have a commercial run in the West End. But by this time, as related, Olivier's regime as Director of the National Theatre was running out and the continuing delays in the completion date of the new building put his dream of leading the company into its permanent home out of reach. Though Olivier is widely believed to have pressed the claims of Michael Blakemore as his successor, conceivably in partnership with Joan Plowright (Lady Olivier), it was, of course, Peter Hall who inherited the dream and the headache.

The early part of Hall's term as Director followed a pattern that was the reverse of Olivier's experience: the indifferent productions came first, the successes later. For about a year after taking over, very little went right for him: the revivals were undistinguished (they included a misguided 'straight' version of Beaumarchais's *The Marriage of Figaro* and an almost incredibly tawdry treatment of Wedekind's *Spring Awakening*) and the new plays were dismally below the quality essential to a National Theatre. Even Peter Nichols (responsible for a previous success, *The National Health*) came unexpectedly to grief with *The Freeway*. Standards of production and performance fell to an abysmally low level.

It is possible, indeed likely, that Hall's absorption in administrative matters and his worries over the tiresomely unstable availability date of the new building were largely responsible for the woebegone state of the company as it appeared on the stage. Hall had first been told that the new building would be ready in 1974. It wasn't. In the spring of that year, though, the word from the site was confident enough for him to make plans to open at any time between February and April of 1975. Again the date was put back; plays were rescheduled; actors, engaged for an expanded company in anticipation of a three-theatre complex, had to be sacked. At this point, Hall turned almost his full attention to the business of pulling things together on the stage of the Old Vic. As in the case of Olivier—the influence of the man of action in command was decisive.

At the beginning of 1975 Peter Hall embarked on a series of productions, many of them directed personally by himself, that wholly restored the reputation of the National Theatre. There was one dud—an inexplicable revival of W S Gilbert's *Engaged*, a piffling comedy interesting only because it was shamelessly plagiarised by Oscar Wilde in *The Importance of Being Earnest*. Everything else, though not every play or every production was quite to everyone's taste (a clear impossibility), was done to the highest standard. By the time a new date was given for the move into the new National Theatre on South Bank—this time the firm one of March 1976—there was reasonable confidence that the company would be worthy of the prestige attaching to its name.

Whatever may be said of our National Theatre as a *building*— and, although personally I like it rather more than most of the contemporary buildings that clash with the traditional edifices of the London skyline—there can be no denying its functional excellence. The actors of the company, who had become accustomed to the cramped backstage conditions at the Old Vic and to rehearsing in a leaky old hut down the road, now splash around delightedly in rehearsal rooms that are big enough to allow them to work in the actual stage sets; just as the workshops are big enough to allow the construction and painting of scenery appropriate to the size of the stages. Writing of working in theatres, Robert Morley has said:*

> *In the 40 years I have been sitting around in dressing rooms I don't believe I have ever sat in a new armchair. I have never used a lavatory which hadn't been designed half a century before, or looked into a mirror that wasn't lit by a naked bulb. I have never seen a carpet in a corridor or a picture on a wall. The higher you climb in most theatres the more sparse the*

* In *Theatre 72*, edited by Sheridan Morley (Hutchinson).

furniture becomes . . . To strip an average theatre of its furni-
ture and fittings, most self-respecting junk men would demand
a fee.

If or when Robert Morley works at the National Theatre, he
will have an entirely different experience. There the dressing
rooms—49 of them to accommodate up to 150 performers in
singles, doubles and multiples—are spacious and air-conditioned
and each has a sound-relay system that can be tuned-in to what is
going on on any of the three stages. There is no climbing to speak
of: there are lifts—to the dressing rooms and to the stages.

These stages are, of course, the *raison d'être* of the place, and
everything in it is directed towards them—to getting people and
things on and off them, and to changing the sets of one production
for those of another with a minimum of delay*. Soundproofed
doors separate the acting areas from the backstage assembly spaces
where scenery is moved on motorised wagons. Lighting installa-
tions have computer-operated control systems. The proscenium
of the Lyttelton can be adjusted in height and width, and the
level and rake of the stage are similarly adjustable.

But the technical wonder of the National is the stage of the
Olivier Theatre, built on a drum-revolve 40 feet in diameter and
45 feet high, split into halves which are on lifts that can bring up
complete stage sets and return them to workshop level below.
The lifts operate separately, and either or both can be going up or
down while the stage is independently and silently revolving at
speeds variable between five revolutions a minute and the crippled
snail's pace of one every two hours. It is hard to think of circumstances in which either of these unlikely extremes would be useful.
But ingenious playwrights can make extraordinary demands when
they put their minds to it. And directors are notoriously fond of
new mechancial toys.

As far as the plays are concerned, the original idea—when the
company was first formed under Olivier in 1962—was that every
successful production, after doing its stint in repertory, should be
put into cold storage, as it were, so that the theatre would build
up a permanent repertoire. Thus any play could be brought out
at any time and performed after a minimal brush-up rehearsal

* See page 101.

74

period. This idea never materialised at the Old Vic, where, despite that theatre's Annexe the shortage of storage space for scenery and costumes alone made it impractical. It is not likely to be revived under Peter Hall, who is generally opposed to having any sort of permanent repertoire and is additionally opposed to having a permanent company. In the Olivier period, some actors remained with the company for years, and there were one or two who saw out the entire eleven-year stretch. With Peter Hall, actors are getting much briefer contracts because, he says:

> I fear security is not natural to the creative actor. He only wants it if he can reject it. Most actors don't like it. They must be encouraged to go away, and what we're trying to do is to have a system that allows them to come and go as part of a regular pattern, The basis is that they're with us for eight months at a time. Then they go away for eight months, and then come back for a further eight months. Everyone can therefore plan their lives to a degree. And plays, without becoming permanent, should have a longer life because, after a gap out of the repertory, we should be able to revive them with very nearly the same casts.

Much of this is tendentious, specious and just not true. After the initial stimulation of precariousness, for example, actors *do* like security. Those who don't are those who have no need of it: they are in great demand and they earn big money in fees and percentages when they're working. Naturally they don't want to be contracted to work more than they need to. They are the stars, and Peter Hall knows perfectly well that he cannot get the big stars on long contracts—not when he can afford to pay them only half of the four-figure weekly sums they can get in the commercial West End, to say nothing of the highly-paid film work they would have to forgo. So he 'encourages' them to go away for eight-month spells? They don't need much encouragement. On the other hand, the 'supporting' and small-part players—the solid adaptable backbone of the company—do. No lavish film and telvision offers are coming *their* way. After eight months of regular work they don't want to go, and indeed—despite the 'basis' and 'regular pattern' of Peter Hall's system—some of them stay. All this system essentially amounts to is that after eight months the actors who haven't quite come up to expectations, or for whom there seem to be no suitable parts, can be dispensed with without either humiliation for them or embarrassment for the management. There are always mistakes in picking actors for a company, and the larger the company the more mistakes there are likely to be; in announcing that he would not have a 'permanent' company and that basic contracts would be for only eight-month periods. Peter Hall was ensuring that those mistakes could be corrected with a minimum of fuss. He had learned that from his years with the Royal Shakespeare Company when he used to put his actors under three-year contracts in the 1960s.

His adaptability in such respects is part of the shrewdness and thoroughness with which he handles his job. He has the biggest and most important theatre job in Britain at a salary of something over £20,000 a year, and he likes having it. Without being a dictator, he is very much the boss; his associate directors and other advisers have their say, but the final decision will always be Peter Hall's. If it comes to it, he is prepared to overrule them all when he makes it—though he is by no means obstinate and is constantly prepared to question and re-examine principles. It is doubtful whether there is anyone else who combines in such high degree a devotion to the art of the theatre and practical experience of it with a flair for administration. Further, he revels in that combination, differing from the majority of people concerned in the artistic aspects of the theatre (and notably from his predecessor at the National, Lord Olivier) in that he enjoys the administrative chores quite as much. Forced to choose between the two, he confesses that he does not know how he would resolve the dilemma. Frustration would chafe him if the responsibilities of running the theatre precluded his getting down among the actors and personally directing many of its plays. He says, however, 'unless I work on the management and administration side as well, I cannot be entirely happy as a director'.

He is more of a realist than most directors of subsidised enterprises. The decision not to have a 'permanent' company is part of that realism, for he regards a permanent company as an ideal— but an ideal which, like democracy, is festooned with impracticalities and cannot, therefore, be regarded as a dogma. I doubt

76

ROYAL, ER, 8
SHAKESPEARE?

It's probably a vain hope, but I coquette now and then with the wishful idea that somebody, quite soon, will somehow discover positive proof that William Shakespeare, author of many well-known plays, was not at all the same fellow as one of similar name born and buried at Stratford-upon-Avon. Other people, of course, have and have had the same thought. They feel, as Henry James put it, 'sort of haunted by the conviction that the divine William is the biggest and most successful fraud ever practised on a patient world', and would like to see an end of it. Their motives are various, ranging from a simple belief that the historical record should be tidied up, to the impish thought that it would be rather fun to see the whole Shakespeare industry of Stratford come tumbling about the heads of its citizens.

My own motives—though I freely concede they have embraced all such notions—are essentially, nowadays, somewhat differently based. Why I should like the shrine of authorship to be moved elsewhere is that I should like to see the productions at the Royal Shakespeare Theatre at Stratford and be free to like them or not as their merits demand. Instead I feel that—because of where they are, and because they are attended by people who come to see 'Shakespeare at the source'—the people putting them on bear a special responsibility and owe a decent respect to the work of the man whose genius has brought them their livings. It may be that setting *A Midsummer Night's Dream* in a gymnasium or *Romeo and Juliet* in a shipyard, or exploring *Twelfth Night* in terms of some psychiatric theory, or 'improving' *King John* by substituting material from other sources on the grounds that Shakespeare himself had pretty well botched the job, are ideas that I should not easily tolerate anywhere; but their implementation at Stratford somewhow adds an extra dimension of pain to such experiences.

There is, of course, a further reason why the works of Shakespeare should not be regarded by the Stratford people as vehicles for their little eccentricities, precious experiments and bizarre theories of 'interpretation'. Although a commercial one it is nonetheless valid—if the sordid may be allowed to impinge for a moment upon the rarefied lives of artists who have been largely relieved by the state of the necessity to heed the Johnsonian dictum that 'they that live to please must please to live'.

The Royal Shakespeare Company, operating both at Stratford and at the Aldwych in London, has, over the years, it is fair to say, contributed a great deal more, proportionately, to its running costs than other subsidised companies. While the National Theatre is expected to meet only half its costs from box-office and other receipts, the RSC has consistently, in recent years, met around four-fifths of *its* costs. It was unquestionably assisted in this, it is also fair to say, by its rather special position as a focal beneficiary of the British tourist trade. Nevertheless, since 1974, the RSC has been grappling with a financial crisis.

In part this has been due to the general inflationary situation—but not in whole. It is due also to a falling-off of audiences at Stratford which, by 1974, had plummeted well below the 90 per cent capacity (virtually a full house at every evening performance, and even an 85 per cent house or better at midweek matinées) to which the management had become accustomed and on which its financial calculations were based.

The company may well claim that there were other factors than the nature and quality of its productions to account for this; but in my view the fall-off was due to the word getting around, both in this country and abroad, that the Stratford productions were more likely to outrage than to please those who revere Shakespeare —and people who revere Shakespeare are the people upon whom this particular theatre greatly depends.

Regular theatregoers in capital cities and university towns, it could be argued, have seen Shakespeare's plays in performance often enough to indulge and even welcome some fashionable director's 're-interpretations'—however wayward. But this is hardly the case with the tourist pilgrims who have flocked to Stratford in the past, but have done rather less flocking of late. It is significant, perhaps, that when the Royal Shakespeare Theatre mounted a special Centenary Appeal which, in 1975 and 1976, raised about £150,000 to renew the theatre's heating and ventilation plant (which was outside the scope of subsidy and could not be done out of normal receipts), the proportion raised from patrons of the company's actual performances was minute—a matter of some £4,000 from 200,000 playgoers, or an average of 2p per head, which seems to be derisory and perhaps a comment by the customers on what they thought of the performances.

There seems to me a positive relationship between the things Stratford directors have been doing with Shakespeare and the response of audiences. It could be said, for example, that the most deplorable assault upon Shakespeare seen there lately was the version of *King John*, adapted and directed by John Barton. He is the last man, as a general rule, to take a cavalier attitude towards Shakespeare's texts. In this instance, he decided, however, that the work was so 'immature' and had such 'areas of uncertainty' that he felt justified in filling it out with bits from two other sixteenth-century plays on the same subject (Bale's *Kynge Johan* and the anonymous *The Troublesome Raigne of King John*), plus a certain amount of vivacious pastiche of his own.

What he seemed to be offering was a sardonic comedy in which he was less concerned with the historical context than with implied comment on our contemporary political and economic situation. Everything he did with the play was in some sense justifiable—but it is *not* justifiable in a theatre occupying the special place of the Royal Shakespeare at Stratford-upon-Avon. The reviews, whether favourable or unfavourable (and they were a mixture), were explicit about what Barton had done with the play. The box-office was stricken by disaster: at one particular performance, traumatic for the company, there were no more than 350 people in the house, barely a quarter of capacity.

Peter Hall, now Director of the National Theatre, as we have seen in the last chapter, was the Director of the RSC from 1960 to 1968 (although its present name did not come into use until 1961, when the Shakespeare Memorial Theatre at Stratford was re-named the Royal Shakespeare Theatre). Hall's impact was tremendous—and beneficial. He revivified the theatre at Stratford, cajoled its Board of Governors along paths not previously trod, extended the operation from the home base in Warwickshire to a London showcase at the Aldwych. And, when running into financial difficulties, he persuaded the Arts Council to include the RSC in its programme of subsidies with a basic grant of £40,000 in 1963, which had snowballed to £915,000 for 1975/76.

From the start he had been resolved to make the company, despite its name, far more than a Shakespearian repertory company: other classical revivals were mounted at the Aldwych and new plays were commissioned both for the Aldwych and for the experimental seasons the RSC staged. The 'studio' work at the Place in London and the Other Place at Stratford had its beginnings in the seasons Hall inaugurated in 1962 at the Arts Theatre Club. Opponents of the National Theatre idea in the early 1960s based their main argument on the fact that the RSC was serving precisely that function and that the NT was therefore unnecessary.

No one could deny that Peter Hall was good for the Royal Shakespeare Company; and if, in his days there, he was not quite so good for the national exchequer, he was compensatorily good for the national balance of payments—for he instituted foreign tours and the filming of productions which brought in valuable hard currency, a policy continued so successfully that the RSC's overseas tours regularly bring hundreds of thousands of dollars annually into the United Kingdom.

Despite all that might be said in favour of his RSC days, however, it could also be maintained that it was Peter Hall who essentially— and with the active collaboration and connivance of the other directors who worked with him—set Stratford on the wrong track in the vital matter of Shakespearian interpretation. At the time, the RSC did not suffer, for it took some time for the awful truth to dawn that the stage at Stratford-upon-Avon was no longer a place where Shakespeare was treated with reverence or even respect. The effect has been cumulative and Trevor Nunn, who succeeded Hall in 1968 and continued along similar lines, is suffering for it now.

Ironically, Hall himself has revised his attitude to Shakespeare quite spectacularly in the interim. He has admitted that, at Stratford, though a great deal of time was spent in analysing texts, he and his directors really showed scant respect for them; they made cuts 'for very arbitrary reasons' and the attitude they adopted he now regards as 'extraordinary'. In 1976 Hall was saying, relative to his National Theatre plans that 'I don't want to give a falsely modern relevance to Shakespeare, by setting it in modern dress or in a particularly modern period. For the little it illuminates, it obscures or warps a great deal more.'

This is certainly not quite the man who, at Stratford in 1965, had directed what was mysteriously described as 'a *Hamlet* for our time' with the Prince of Denmark in a long, woolly, college-student's scarf, and whose leading actor, David Warner, was later quoted in the *Times* as saying dashingly: 'How the hell do I know what being princely is? You can be a prince and you can pick your nose, because the prince has the freedom to do whatever he wants. My first objective is to make people who are bored with Shakespeare try and understand. If I cut under the verse, give the wrong inflections or pause in the wrong place or mess up the iambic pentameters, I don't care.'

The Hall-Warner *Hamlet* had been enthusiastically received; most of the Shakespearian 're-interpretations' in those days were. Especially favoured were those of Peter Brook who, at Stratford as long ago as 1962, had directed Paul Scofield in a production of *King Lear* which, because it substituted a 'recognisable man' for the majestic mythological protagonist, was widely acclaimed as being a 'revelation'. It may well have been, though it certainly no longer concerned the sort of man that Shakespeare had, or would have, written that sort of play about.

Brook went on, eight years later, to direct his famous—or notorious—*A Midsummer Night's Dream*, which can by no means be called a commercial failure. It was, on the contrary, a sensation, a box-office smash. I suspect, however, that it was the sensation-seekers rather than the Shakespeare-lovers who made it so. More illuminating, I think, than any of its reviews, was a straight news report from New York where the production went (as it went elsewhere in the world) to repeat its success in England. The report is taken from the *Daily Telegraph* and read:

> *Members of the Royal Shakespeare Company prevented panic when fire broke out on the stage of the Billy Rose Theatre on Saturday night by carrying on as though nothing had happened.*

Flames and smoke enveloped the stark white setting of A
Midsummer Night's Dream *towards the end of the play.
Many theatregoers at the capacity-filled Broadway theatre*
thought at first that the fire was one of the unorthodox
stage effects . . .

I emphasise the last 13 words, though you may not need that to
catch the point. Here I shall back the detached eye of the reporter
against, metaphorically speaking, the detached retina of so many
of the reviewers who verged on the ecstatic in greeting this 're-
interpretation' of Shakespeare. For who can doubt the accuracy
of this report of an instinctive reaction on the part of 'many
theatregoers'? Or the logical basis for such a reaction? They had
already seen Bottom transformed not into an ass but into Mickey
Mouse, and Titania's fairy attendants into a strapping working-
party in dungarees, and the Athenian wood itself survive only as a
few coils of dangling wire. A smoky conflagration in the last act
can hardly have struck them as untoward. Indeed, in a production
that was said to 'highlight a cruel and violent side to the play which
years of schoolroom performances with Mendelssohn accompani-
ment have obscured', a forest fire, in which all these dreadful
people perished, might well have seemed the right climax; even
to have a kind of inevitability.

That this production, with all its absurdities, should have been
so enormously successful at the box-office, merely encouraged the
RSC to continue, all too frequently and with dire consequences,
along the path of 're-interpretation', if never quite to the same
degree of outrageousness. The effect is of a snare, in which they
seem to be sitting biting a leg off.

It need not be necessarily so, and it is not always so: the conception of 'The Romans', putting together Shakespeare's four
disparate Roman plays (*Julius Caesar*, *Antony and Cleopatra*,
Coriolanus and *Titus Andronicus*), did not offend. But later productions of the historical plays, *Henry IV Parts 1 and 2* and *Henry
V*, in epic sequence, veered again into 're-interpretation' and
would not seem to many scholars to accord with the spirit and
intention of Shakespeare. In the 1976 season, a production of
Much Ado About Nothing, set in India in the days of the Raj, did
the text no damage and worked devilishly well; and a musical

84

treatment of *The Comedy of Errors* set mostly in a market square of contemporary Greece, with Zorba-ish dances padding out the action, was undeniably a sprightly entertainment. But—at *Stratford*? The RSC plays a perilous game here, and unless it returns sternly, as a matter of high policy, to non-gimmicky productions of Shakespeare, it will find it more and more difficult to make ends meet at headquarters.

As to the non-Shakespearian parts of the company's activities, it might be seriously questioned at this time whether they can any longer be justified. This is not because they are bad—on the contrary, they are often very good—but simply because they do not seem altogether appropriate to an organisation with the name, Royal Shakespeare Company. There are two sides to this question. On the one hand, the argument once used (unsuccessfully) against the National Theatre idea, the argument that such an institution was unnecessary since its job was substantially being done by the RSC can now be turned against the RSC itself: that is to say, now that the National Theatre is in operation and has three separate theatres available for classical and modern repertories of British and foreign drama, as well as for experimental work, can there be any point in the RSC continuing to perform these functions and being subsidised to do so? The RSC performs them very well; on the balance of the last few years, it has not had as good a record as the National with new plays. But one like Tom Stoppard's *Travesties* can and does make up (commercially as well as artistically) for an awful lot of duds. There is no reason to suppose, however, that if the RSC were not in this particular branch of the business its work would not be done equally well by the National. And while it might be contended that there is no more reason why the Royal Shakespeare Company should be confined to Shakespeare than that the Comédie Française should be confined to Molière, the fact is that, although it is known as *La Maison de Molière*, the name of the Comédie Française does not include the name of Molière in its title, and the name of the Royal Shakespeare Company does imply for most people that Shakespeare is what they perform.

The contrary argument, however, is a telling one and at present is seen as the more persuasive. It has two main threads. One is that the National and the Royal Shakespeare—both being national companies of wide prestige and attracting major talents, and both devoting themselves to many different kinds of drama—are in direct, if friendly, competition. Under the stimulus of that competition, the argument goes, they are both likely to do better work than either would do if given a monopoly. In this context it is also true to say, though this seems like mere coincidence, that they have been, in recent years, rather on a seesaw. The consequence of the friendly rivalry has therefore been that when the quality and reputation of one of them have been in the doldrums, those of the other have been in the ascendant. From these points of view the co-existence of the two companies doing similar work looks desirable.

The other thread of the contrary argument against confining the RSC to its Shakespearian function has to do with the actors. The present Director of the RSC, Trevor Nunn argues that 'no actor should be confined to playing only Shakespeare, because all too quickly he starts to play Shakespeare badly'. Even if this proposition seems dubious to some of us, it is likely that the RSC would find it a great deal more difficult to attract the superior acting talents if they were to be confined to Shakespeare. Especially would this be the case if they were to be confined to Stratford as well. Trevor Nunn has also pointed out the possibly unpalatable truth that

> *Television has become the staple provider for actors who expect to work in all media in any given year. To work exclusively in the theatre is, financially, an unattainable luxury. Long seasons at Stratford deprive actors of their life-line in television, while increasing their financial and domestic burdens; since they usually have to maintain a London home while working in Stratford. or uproot families and interrupt children's education, or pay for commuting. The major inducement for actors to work in Stratford is their certain knowledge that their best work can be seen in London, and that their Shakespeare performances will be stimulated by work in new plays. For established actors, working in Stratford is now a sacrifice. The Aldwych makes the sacrifice worthwhile.*

There may be elements of exaggeration in all this, since it is taken from an open letter addressed by Nunn to the Minister for the Arts, and published in the *Sunday Times*, at a time when the RSC had a heavy campaign going for an additional subsidy to sustain the Aldwych operation. Nevertheless the facts are basically incontrovertible in regard to most actors. The RSC has a good case for maintaining its role as a second 'National Theatre' and not simply a 'Shakespeare theatre' if only because, if existing exclusively in the latter capacity it is doubtful if it would exist at all; and if we assume that the writing on the wall will be heeded— that the company will turn from its more eccentric 're-interpretations' of Shakespeare—there is no one who would want to see it perish.

It is also desirable that the company should keep a London base—which has been the Aldwych Theatre since 1962 but in due course will be the new theatre in the Barbican complex—because that makes good economic sense. No one would have guessed as much from the bleat the RSC put up in 1975 and 1976 when the pressure campaign for a bigger subsidy was at its height and when the chairman of the Arts Council, the newly ennobled Lord Gibson, was persuaded to argue in his maiden speech in the House of Lords that if the Arts Council didn't get enough extra money to be able to shove a further £200,000 in the direction of the RSC the likelihood was that the company would have to withdraw from the Aldwych. This was seized upon and headlined in all newspapers whose arts policies were sympathetic to increased subsidy. But it was fatuous nonsense, The Aldwych was not *costing* the RSC money, it was *making* it money—or, if it wasn't, there was something grotesquely wrong with the way the company's affairs were being administered.

It would, in fact, be obvious to a child that to have two theatres rather than one in which to display a production allows the opportunity to recover more of the costs of that production. So it has been the case that the successful productions at Stratford in one year have been taken to play at the Aldwych the following year. It does not, to be sure, take an impossible degree of organisation and ingenuity to arrange the repertory and the casting to deploy the full payroll strength of the company six nights a week at one or other of the two theatres—if the company is seriously concerned to help itself to the maximum in a hazardous economic situation.

Stratford's Shakespearian productions, with their huge casts, are necessarily expensive (though not necessarily as expensive as 'The Romans', the set for which is said to have cost a quarter of a million pounds), and those costs must be undertaken—as must the salaries of the contract players be met—whether or not the London revenue is there to help defray them.

Nothing was said of this, either by Lord Gibson or in the plaintive appeals of the RSC itself. Yet it is hard to believe that the Aldwych—mounting no new productions of its own, but simply giving London playgoers an opportunity to see the best of the Stratford work and running these in repertory with the company's successful and relatively small-cast non-Shakespearian productions—could not show some profit, or at least no loss. It was absurd for the chairman of the RSC, Kenneth Cork, to say (as he was quoted by the London *Evening Standard* as saying in May 1975) that 'it is not the RSC's job to keep commercially successful plays running indefinitely'. Isn't it, indeed? If they are not producing worthy plays for people—as many people as possible—to see, what the hell *are* they doing?

OVERLAPPING 9
SECTORS

When is the subsidised theatre *not* the subsidised theatre? A good question. And to rephrase it: when is the commercial theatre the subsidised theatre? You may think that the terms 'subsidised' and 'commercial' in the theatrical context are opposites, mutually contradictory. Not necessarily so. The theatre is part of a mixed economy, and sometimes that economy gets so mixed as to produce a blend in which the component parts are inseparable; and not mutually contradictory, but mutually beneficial.

Next time you're in a theatre—in or out of London—that is commonly, and accurately, regarded as subsidised, take a careful look at the programme. You'll always find a line that reads, 'The ——— Theatre acknowledges assistance from the Arts Council of Great Britain', or similar words to the same effect. But up there above the title on the first page, you may find some other lines that read, 'The ——— Theatre, in association with "X", presents . . .' and 'X' will be the name of a commercial production management: say, Michael Codron or Eddie Kulukundis, Michael White or Donald Albery. The theatre you are in might be, say, the Royal Court or the Mermaid, the Nottingham Playhouse or the Bristol Old Vic. And the play you see may, later, turn up in the West End—when the billing will be slightly amended so that the commercial manager's name comes first, with the 'in association with' bringing in the name of the subsidised house where the production first saw the light of day.

How's this, then? What is a theatre with those lofty and public-spirited ideals, so eloquently pleaded at the bar of the Arts Council when the begging bowls are out, doing in having this close truck with the avowed money-makers? And by what clever trick are the commercial boys able to cut themselves in for a slice of the state's hand-out? Purists look askance at such goings-on. Dedicated supporters of state patronage in the names of art and culture can be pretty sniffy about the people who are into those things for the profit; and taxpayers confronted with a situation in which their money seems to be subsidising commercial impresarios are apt to take a touch of umbrage.

These objectors may have a point. But the system, as noted, is mutually beneficial. If a commercial manager can arrange with a subsidised theatre to put on a play on which he holds the option, he is going to get it mounted for considerably less than he would have to spend if he were doing it on his own and going to the expensive wear and tear of a pre-London tour. He will further have the opportunity to see how it goes before deciding whether to bring it into the West End. So he's happy with the deal, and playgoers should be happy with it, too: if the practice were more widespread we might be spared some of those turkeys that can always be spotted with ten minutes of curtain-rise and should clearly have been spotted at some earlier stage.

As for the subsidised theatre and *its* patrons, the infusion of commercial money is going to result in a much better production than could be offered by a management on a tight subsidised budget: so they, also, should be happy. And if the production does come into the West End and is a success, everybody will be happier still—especially the subsidised theatre which, as these things are usually contracted, will be in for half of the management profit, but will not be liable for any loss. It's a neat arrangement for all parties, and objections can be only idealistic, hardly realistic.

Similarly, I may say, in the case of Royal Shakespeare Company and National Theatre productions that come into the West End *without* any prior agreements. RSC productions, such as *London Assurance* and *Travesties*, have been presented in the West End under the 'godfather' management of Eddie Kulukundis and the RSC has benefited handsomely. NT productions, when they come into commercial houses, do so under the direct management of the 'National' itself—as in the cases, for instance, of *No Man's Land* and *Equus*, and the NT has benefited even more handsomely. There is, of course, the question of whether Peter Hall, say, as director of *No Man's Land* should also have benefited handsomely to the tune of a four per cent director's percentage for a job he did on the public payroll; but that is an unrelated digression.

Where I really begin to feel dubious about the mixing of commercial and subsidised interests is in the direct employment of Arts Council money in the commercial theatre—as envisaged in the Theatre Investment Fund. You've probably heard of it, for it is a scheme that has been in the air ever since the idea was mooted in the Arts Council Report on *The Theatre Today* back in 1970. 'In the air' is not, perhaps, the right phrase, in view of the time it has taken to get the thing off the ground. Even at the time of writing, here in 1977, it is still only a theoretical operation. But, with the ubiquitous Lord Goodman as chairman and with former Old Vic Company man Patrick Ide as managing director it does seem on the brink of activity. A quarter of a million pounds is in the kitty for starters, £100,000 kicked in by the Arts Council, the balance from other sources.

The idea is to invest in productions set up by commercial managements who are, for some reason, unable to raise the requisite backing capital from their regular angels. The Arts Council, it seems, does not regard its contribution to the TIF as being a subsidy in the ordinary sense of the word, but quite specifically as an investment. The Council claims actually to anticipate making a profit on the investment, the profit to be taken back into the Fund and thereafter re-invested.

This is cloud-cuckoo stuff. The Arts Council is a babe in the wood in the theatre of profit. Neither the Council itself nor its advisers are accustomed to judging drama by any sort of commercial criteria. It might also be said that, on the one hand, just to suppose that the Council is right in its belief that the investments will be successful, these are not, in fact, the ventures that have a legitimate claim on public monies. On the other hand, if the investments are *not* successful and the money is lost, they will amount quite plainly to state subvention—of a kind which many will think should be handed direct to an officially subsidised management whose record, for good or ill, has already been assessed and approved by the Council's panel.

I worry, too, about those 'other sources'—presumably private investors—on which the TIF is relying, and who have so recklessly thrown in their lot with a scheme in which the state has, in effect, a 40 per cent holding. Why are they not making direct investments with the managements whose judgment of plays they can trust, or with one or other of the backing syndicates that have a fairly good record of investing in success? Perhaps they are quite simply prepared to throw their money down the drain in what they deem to be a worthy cause; in which case they cannot have been paying attention when the Arts Council was talking about its expectations of profit.

My cynical view is that there really are no such expectations, and that the suggestion that they are held is only window-dressing for public consumption to disguise the fact that another bundle of public money is on the loose. It is a trifling amount, of course, in the context of today's government expenditure. And it may be a desirable thing to devote this modest bit of patronage to commercial managers who have, on the whole, a better record in the discovery and encouragement of new talent than has the officially subsidised theatre. But are these, in fact, the managers who will be *looking* for the TIF subsidies? I think it more likely that it will be the failures who will be on the scrounge. It is a part of the mixing of economies on which I confess unease.

NOBODY WORKS 10
UNLESS . . .

The professional theatre—commercial and subsidised, London and provincial—is a closed shop. No actor (a term which please take, unless otherwise stated, to mean 'actress' as well) can be employed without his being a member of Equity—the British Actors' Equity Association. No stagehand or technician or anyone else of the backstage personnel can be given a job without his being a member of NATTKE—the National Association of Theatre, Television and Kine Employees. No one can be employed as a musician without being a member of the Musicians' Union.

This is the union network, with which managements have to deal. The managements themselves—as in the case of employers in other fields—are less tightly organised. But anyone who is not a member of the Society of West End Theatre Managers and who wants to put on a London show finds it a little tougher to do so than the established members. Apart from the difficulties he may have in getting into a theatre (theatre owners and lessees and the SWETM being fairly cosily clannish), the non-member manager will be required by Equity to put money on deposit covering two weeks' salaries of actors and stage management before rehearsals begin.

The three unions don't see eye to eye on everything. But they do get together in the Federation of Theatre Unions in some endeavour to keep their disagreements behind closed doors. On the whole, there's not a lot of give and take, each of them being naturally keen to protect and consolidate its own share of the loot. Even so; there is a sort of tacit understanding that, if one union succeeds independently in securing a better deal for its members in the way of minimum rates, then the others won't use that as a

93

basis on which instantly to move in to maintain previous differentials.

They also get together in the Confederation of Entertainment Unions, which brings in the Association of Cinematograph, Television and Allied Technicians. Although this is a union not directly involved in the theatre, it will be obvious that conditions in film and television studios can have their repercussions, even if indirectly, in the theatre.

The theatre set-up that Peter Plouviez, General Secretary of Equity, would regard as ideal from the point of view of his union would be one in which actors were no longer treated and regarded as 'casual' labour. He is not, in fact, optimistic that any such state of affairs could be brought about. Nevertheless, he doesn't believe it an altogether impossible aim, thinks that a certain amount of progress could be made towards it even now. And he is fond of drawing an analogy with the position of dockers, whose labour is no longer classified as 'casual' even though the work is necessarily dependent, like that of actors, on a number of variables—in the dockers' case a variable number of ships and cargoes.

In Plouviez's view it would be theoretically possible for all professional actors to be paid a lowish basic retaining fee, and to evolve for them a rotating pattern of employment in films, television and London and provincial theatre. I'm afraid, though, that this would require his members to come to terms with an unacceptable measure of direction of labour—'unacceptable', that is, to the majority of actors I know. Even so, it falls a long way short of the nationalisation of the entire entertainments industry as envisaged and promoted by the extreme left-wing of Equity and the entertainments branch of the All Trades Unions Alliance. This group is more or less identifiable with the Workers Revolutionary Party and shares the same address, although its most well-publicised campaigner, the dear but dotty Vanessa Redgrave, doesn't live there.

Similarly unacceptable, I should say, would be the restraints put upon the freedom of managements—in both the commercial and subsidised areas—in the matter of the players they employed. Perhaps we (and they) should all get used to it. But I doubt whether we shall have to, since it would be basic to such a scheme that the 'pool' of professional actors, like the pool of dockers, be stabilised

94

at a realistic level in relation to the number of jobs available. And Equity is a long way short of achieving any such balance, since it is generally without the plans and practical means to enforce it.

Peter Plouviez knows, of course, that the hopes he cherishes are up against the psychology of the actor and his long-time-a-dying view of his profession as a 'game of chance'. But hell, it *is* a game of chance, and some very revolutionary things are going to have to happen before the generality of actors get to regard having a job as a matter of right rather than a matter of luck. The average number of weeks in a year that a male actor is in employment is about 17 or 18; that's all the work there is to go round (this being all the entertainment the public is prepared to pay for, or the state to subsidise). And for a woman the number of employed weeks is considerably fewer, it being one of those depressing things for them that there are more actresses than actors, but fewer parts for women.

Those who believe in their talent take a little comfort in early adversity from the further belief that 'the cream will always rise to the top'. But, sooner or later disillusion sets in, because anyone who knows the profession and can look at it detachedly is perfectly well aware that there is nothing inevitable about *that* process. This is not to say that what rises to the top is not cream; usually it is. Certainly what *stays* at the top is cream: no actor unworthy of major parts in the theatre will get them and *keep* getting them. It is also true, though, that many worthy actors, for one reason or another, never even get those opportunities. The Plouviez 'pool of actors' and 'rotating opportunities' would straighten out this situation and get rid of the 'game of chance'. Even so, it's a moot question whether that alone would make the plan desirable, even if it were practical.

Equity at the end of 1976 had a membership in full benefit of something over 23,000 and it's a rising membership: in 1970 it was 17,000. The annual intake of new members is about 2,500— (excluding the temporary memberships of visiting artists from overseas, but including variety performers). The rising membership, taken together with a decreasing number of jobs, is Equity's major practical worry. The Council of Equity (the official policy-making body, elected by the membership and largely composed of fairly well-known players, these being the candidates the rank-and-file tend to vote for) have not been keen on 'controlled entry' to the profession. But, without it, without some sort of rules that are liable to exclude the unexpected natural talent, they would have a tough job even *trying* to keep the numbers down. And that they *have* to do, with the leading drama schools alone churning out hundreds of new hopefuls annually into a profession that can provide a decent living for less than a third of the existing Equity membership. Hence the 'casting agreements' which have been made with the employers' organisations.

Equity is at its stickiest in the matter of unfledged newcomers coming in 'at the top', and this, of course, is where the members' interest might very well clash with the public interest. The regulations in this regard, agreed with the Society of West End Theatre Managers, mean that no one can walk into a part in the West End of London without having 40 weeks of professional experience (which can be in films, television or theatre) and thus be a full, as opposed to provisional, member of Equity.

Clearly this knocks out the 'casting couch' starlet who could once be given a lead in a London show because lover-boy had bought her into it. Okay. But where does it leave the really outstanding new talent, the untrained 'natural' or the drama-school leaver who is exactly right for Ophelia or Juliet or whatever? Most of the time, I fear, it will leave her out in the cold—at least for that statutory 40 weeks, during which the producer who has spotted her will have to wait while she works, if she can, in out-of-town productions or perhaps in television—provided she can get through the net of the limited quota of new entrants to this medium. She's the innocent victim of well-meaning rules that are good for, and endorsed by, the majority of the profession.

It seems hard, but on the whole I would not want seriously to argue with those rules. For one thing, a bit of apprenticeship never did anyone any harm. And, while 40 weeks may seem interminable to the young and eager aspirant—in the context of a whole career it isn't much of a delay. Certainly, no experience is ever a waste of time. For another thing, I frankly doubt whether the theatre actually does lose any great talents this way, and slightly more modest talents, exposed to premature stardom and publicity and criticism, might easily be irreparably damaged. That did happen under the old free-for-all system: I can think of many a young player—whose present privacy and obscurity I need not invade—who dropped from the limelight, instantly and permanently, after what had seemed an auspicious career-beginning in the West End.

One of the luckier ones in the days before this particular agreement was reached between Equity and the theatre managements was Judi Dench. In 1957 she walked right out the Central School of Speech and Drama to play Ophelia in *Hamlet* with the Old Vic Company: good for her, but at that time she really wasn't as good as all that; there were experienced actresses, as young-*looking* if not actually as young, who could have done it better and probably had every right to resent the luck of the fledgling. Miss Dench herself got a great deal better later on, mostly because she stayed with the Old Vic Company for another three years (something that would hardly have been possible if her chance had come with an independent management in a one-off production).

To come back to my general approval of this Equity rule, it has the further circumstance in its favour that, in the really exceptional case, there is an 'out'. If a producer says, 'I must have X or there's no show, and I don't give a damn whether or not he (or she) is a full Equity member or not,' Equity will not like it. And will argue about it. If the producer is still adamant, the case will go for decision to the London Theatre Council—a joint body with its members drawn from both the Equity Council and the Society of West End Theatre Managers—where the arguments from each side will be considered. The rules do not, after all, have legal weight and if the case for X is genuinely irrefutable, the artist will get the part.

In practice, bearing out my previous points, there aren't many occasions when there is a possibility of the rules being breached in this way. When they do occur it is usually fortuitously, as in the case, for instance, of Nicky Guadagni, who played Miranda to Paul Scofield's Prospero in *The Tempest* at Wyndham's in 1975. This was a production that had begun life at the Leeds Playhouse where Miss Guadagni, a provisional Equity member only a few weeks out of drama school, was quite legitimately given the role. When the transfer to the West End was mooted, while the 40-week rule certainly required that she should be replaced by someone with the statutory experience and the production would hardly have been abandoned if it had not been waived, the injustice of denying to Miss Guadagni the West End opportunity that her performance at Leeds had earned her was appreciated by Equity. No objection was pursued.

In fact, though, this was a case which itself would seem to support the propitiousness of the rule. For Miss Guadagni, who may very well develop into an actress of real distinction and was certainly treated with benign and tactful gentleness by the London critics, was not, to be quite frank about it, 'ready' for the West End. Nor, for that matter, was the production as a whole. But the presence of Scofield ensured packed houses, money was made, and in these hard times such benefits are not to be sneezed at.

As well as the headache of an overcrowded profession, Equity has another which it shares with the other theatre unions—brought on by the twin circumstances that, while they have an obligation to their members to seek and press for a more attractive wage structure, they are also aware that the survival of the theatre generally, and specific theatres particularly, could be threatened by rising costs. Their position, ostensibly, is much the same as that of some of the industrial unions which are not infrequently accused, not without justification, of wanting to kill the goose that lays the golden eggs. The difference is, perhaps, that minimum rates of pay in the theatre, except for some NATTKE workers, could never be called 'golden eggs'—as they might be in, for instance, certain sections of the printing industry. As far as actors are concerned, they don't have much opportunity of working, and the vast majority of them when they do work, don't work for much.

In November 1974, Equity negotiations succeeded in raising the weekly minimum paid in the West End theatre to £30, a sum increased by 1977 to £44.50 but still nobody's fortune. It succeeded too, in extending this minimum to rehearsal periods—a logical enough development, since an actor is probably working harder when rehearsing than in performance, though this had never previously been recognised. (And there are managements, set in the old ways, who don't want to recognise it financially and pay up with ill grace, arguing with their own logic that, after all, *they* don't begin taking the money with which to pay until the rehearsals are over and the show is on.)

Additional payments of a few pounds a week have also been

negotiated from time to time for companies on tour. None of the sums involved is sensational. Even so, it all places a strain on the smaller theatres and the less affluent managements, which find themselves forced to cut down on the numbers of their 'labour force' with the result that, although actors are getting more, even fewer of them are getting it.

There is also the point that Equity can negotiate only over *minimum* rates. It cannot reasonably concern itself as well with the grading of actors and the finer shades of differential payment. These are matters mostly for agents to negotiate; but an agent can't put on much pressure unless he has a highly desirable leading player to negotiate for. The position being reached in practical terms is that managements—over the agents' barrel where the stars are concerned, and paying higher minimum rates at the other end of the scale—have less money to offer the middle group of actors. These are the majority and the ones who are feeling the squeeze.

More civilised and more aware of the dangerous economic facts of life than most unions, Equity has gone so far as to exempt particularly hard-pressed little theatres in the provinces from paying the agreed minimums.

Good thinking; but the exemptions are rare and temporary. So the Equity dilemma remains. The union has got to get its members something near a living wage, but it doesn't want to put theatres out of business. Its officials will point out that in the period when most of Britain's provincial theatres closed down, Equity was not by any standards an active trade union, and the minimum weekly wage for an actor was £7. This, however, is whistling in the dark while playing with statistics, for it seems obvious that some managements and some theatres in the commercial sector will have to put up the shutters because to put up seat prices instead, to pay the rising salaries, would be more than the traffic will bear.

This is tough for Equity. It has come a long way since its formation in 1929 (initially as a sort of professional guild, rather than a trade union) and its skirmishes in the 1930s with the big battalions of the commercial theatre which it usually won. The legendary individualist, C B Cochran, tried to buck the trend to the 'closed shop' contract but when the game was at the big table he had to accept that the actors' refusal to work for him was a higher card than his refusal to employ them.

Even the most rabid union-bashers would concede that its record, in the trade union context, has been consistently responsible. It has kept clear of party politics, and its high-talking minority of left-wing activists, who want its organisation restructured to their own blueprint, is inevitably defeated when the membership votes in strength. Nevertheless, in the present time of economic crisis and in its own cleft stick, Equity can only put its hopeful trust in the dictum of Mr Clive Jenkins of the ASTMS that managements that have to pay more become more efficient—even though the cost of that efficiency, in itself, could include the loss of some actors' employment.

For the public on the outside, a disturbing feature of the situation is that, as more theatres get into financial difficulties, it seems likely that there will be louder calls for more subsidy—calls so anguished and persistent that the government might well mount just such a rescue operation. However one might regard that—and there is a limit to the taxpayer's sympathy, to say nothing of his capacity, in the matter—there is the undoubted fact that the theatre unions are inclined to press harder any company that is in receipt of a subsidy. The 1974/75 dispute of NATTKE workers with the English National Opera at the London Coliseum, and the 'unofficial' 1976 and 1977 NATTKE strikes at the National Theatre, provide illuminating demonstrations of the point.

The NATTKE people at the Coliseum are, in financial terms, the élite of their trade. Their take-home pay is far in excess of that of their fellow union workers in any other London theatre. In the Coliseum itself, at the time of the dispute, they had a comfortable edge over both the Musicians' Union members in the orchestra and the Equity members in the opera chorus. The 76 members of the chorus were costing the ENO some £190,000 a year, the 90 players in the orchestra were costing £270,000 a year. But the 81 people of the backstage staff cost £320,000 a year, NATTKE having negotiated some cute overtime contracts whereby a man who worked for five *minutes* (if they were after midnight) got paid for five *hours*.

There is no point in recounting here the boring details of the absurdly trivial dispute between the NATTKE men and the ENO

100

management, or in making any judgments over the rights and wrongs involved at different stages of it. The point is simply that it is hard to imagine that any union men, unless insane, would have pushed it to the extent of causing the closure of the theatre with a consequent loss of over £100,000 at the box-office if they had been dealing with a commercial management. For a commercial management, as they well would know, would have no option but to go out of business and put the entire NATTKE complement on the breadline. But the English National Opera, subsidised by the Arts Council (which is at least one of the reasons why it came to be paying its stagehands so lavishly in the first place), was plainly not going out of business. Somehow or other, whatever happened, the taxpayer would foot the bill.

Precisely similar thinking seemed to account for the strike at the National Theatre in 1976, which, though not so prolonged, nevertheless cost the theatre £11,000 in box-office takings for five cancelled performances in the Lyttelton auditorium and two at the Young Vic (which the company was using pending the opening of its experimental Cottesloe Theatre in the South Bank building).

The union stage staff had been edgy about things at the National Theatre ever since it became apparent that one of the advantages of the way the new building had been planned, and the technical resources it could command, was that the changes of the sets of one production to that of another—a perennial problem of theatres with several plays in repertory—were going to be far more easily and quickly accomplished. An advantage to the theatre; but not an advantage to the union men, who had become happily accustomed to lavish overtime working at the Old Vic.

When the strike came it was not, in fact, related to this particular point, but over the question of working on rehearsals in the Olivier Theatre (which was not then open), while performances were going on in the Lyttelton, for what seemed inadequate rewards—though some of the union men were taking home upwards of £200 a week. Their strike was 'unofficial', in that they did not have the official support of NATTKE, any more than did the Coliseum strikers. But, whether a stoppage is effected by official or unofficial action on the part of union men, the resultant loss of revenue for the management is the same. And the attitude of some backstage workers towards subsidised managements is a major problem with which the latter have to deal. Roger Wraight, the West End officer of NATTKE, is also painfully aware of it, knowing that the unrealistic demands of this special section of the membership can lead only to discontent, acrimony and division among the membership as a whole. 'Subsidised theatres,' he said ruefully, 'seem to attract a certain sort of person. They think money grows on trees.'

Clearly the National Theatre's labour troubles are not yet over; indeed, it is my guess that they will proliferate and that there will be repercussions backstage in other subsidised theatres where the men feel that the existence of the theatre is regarded as so important that it becomes an ace in their own hand when they go to the bargaining table with management. Such success as they may there achieve could then have repercussions in the commercial theatre. It is just possible that the NATTKE membership as a whole will come to accept as a permanent fact of life a double standard of employment, whereby the workers in the leading subsidised theatres are the élite and those in the commercial houses are hoi polloi. It does not, however, seem likely.

'I WANT
TO GO ON
THE STAGE . . .'

There can seem very little in these pages that would positively encourage anyone to go on the stage. But it always has been a tough profession and those who are stage-struck tend not to consider practicalities, let alone to be daunted by them. Youngsters with their hearts set on becoming actors and actresses are rarely interested in the theatre as a business, in the monopolistic power structures of the commercial sector and the economic controversies that afflict the subsidised sector. Nor do they pause to consider the grim unemployment record in the profession and the clear reality that there are a thousand broken dreams to every fairytale success.

There is, of course, no truth in the drivel about certain divinely chosen and endowed people having a compulsion to 'act' that will *not* be denied. It is simply that these people are at their happiest when escaping into the make-believe of characters other than themselves, and/or are so infatuated by the limelight, the applause and the glamour of theatrical success that they come to believe even themselves—sometimes to the point of madness—that 'acting' is their inescapable destiny. To these have been added, in this particular generation, great numbers of young people who merely pretend to be so motivated because they see the theatre—especially the 'fringe' theatre—as a sort of extension of 'play school' combining a maximum of self-expression with a minimum of self-discipline in a marvellously carefree way of life. Don't, therefore, weep *too* much for the hordes of unemployed in the acting profession: a lot of them are virtually unemployable, having no talent and little training, or vice versa.

With some, at least, of these considerations in mind, the representatives of three theatrical organisations—Peter Cheeseman of the Council of Regional Theatre, Peter Plouviez of Actors'

lity, and Raphael Jago of the Conference of Drama Schools—
together in 1972 and addressed a bold request to the trustees
the Calouste Gulbenkian Foundation.

'We are all greatly concerned,' they said, 'at the haphazard way
in which so many train for and enter the acting profession. The
recent severe increase in unemployment coupled with the multi-
plication of training establishments has led to a critical situation
and we all feel that a national inquiry is now needed.'

They might, of course, have set up such an inquiry themselves
but guessed—no doubt rightly—that their findings, whatever they
might be, would be generally regarded with some suspicion of
partiality. Moreover they had little hope of persuading the
Government—through the Arts Council or some other agency—to
undertake the job, since the Government might find itself thus
committed in some way to do something about the findings—again
whatever they might be. They turned, then, to the Gulbenkian
Foundation, a trust established in 1956 for purposes that are
'charitable, artistic, educational and scientific', and found sympathetic ears. The Foundation eventually set up a committee of
inquiry to get at the facts and make recommendations. The committee's Report, *Going on the Stage*, was published by the Foundation in September 1975 (£1).

There were some sound recommendations in the Report, and
perhaps some of them will be acted upon. But they are tricked out
with so much tendentious twaddle, mixing disturbing facts with
woolly-headed opinions, that the chances of the document's being
taken seriously as a whole are correspondingly reduced.

My guess is that the Foundation more or less wasted its money,
that the committee members wasted their time, and that Messrs
John Mortimer QC, Michael Elliott and Oscar Lewenstein, who all
resigned from the committee (the first-named after nine months,
the other two after a year), were being pretty smart. By their
resignations these three were relieved, at least, of the need to
associate their names with a Report which, in a preliminary survey
of the situation they were to consider, came up with this astonishing set of facts, opinions and non-sequiturs under the heading,
'Changes in the Theatre':

Perhaps the most significant change of all has been the

104

development during the last five to ten years of fringe theatre. Approximately 25 per cent of working actors are now engaged in this area, operating largely outside the conventional framework of theatre buildings and taking their work directly to people who have previously had little interest in the established theatre.

The result of these changes is that, within a few years of completing their training, young actors will find that they have had to adapt to the different demands of working in at least several, and perhaps all, of the following situations—television, radio, films, repertory theatre, the West End, theatre-in-the-round, theatre in pubs, in the street, in clubs, theatre-in-education. And the roles that they have had to play may have embraced not only classics and new plays of a conventional sort, but also theatre of the absurd, of cruelty, of alienation, mime and improvisation. We live in an age where the opportunities, which the theatre offers to those who work in it, are more diverse and more challenging than ever before.

The consequence has been an emphasis upon acting as a career and as a profession, with an accompanying emphasis upon preparation for it and the determination to create conditions within the acting profession which are not notably worse than, although in the nature of the case they are necessarily different from, the working conditions which prevail in other professions. This is a central fact of our Enquiry . . .

It will be clear to any detached observer that any committee that saw *that* as a central *fact*, in the context of the build-up given to it in the first two paragraphs quoted, was not too securely hooked into reality. The committee did, in consequence, burble its way around the situation without ever getting properly to grips with it. These paragraphs are absurdly 'loaded'. Suppose they were to be rewritten thus:

A change of apparent significance in the last decade has been the development of what is called fringe theatre; at times as many as a quarter of working actors have been employed in this area, although the evidence suggests that the phase is now on the wane. They have been taking their work to people who

105

have previously had little interest in the theatre; and its quality, fortunately or unfortunately, has not been such that any significant new interest in the theatre has thereby been stimulated.

Trained actors take part in these activities largely because they are unable to gain employment in properly established theatres, either commercial or subsidised, or in other branches of the profession—television, radio and films—that are able to offer them a proper reward for their skills. In so doing they have the advantage of continuing to practise their profession at times when they would otherwise be unemployed. At the same time they suffer the disadvantage of having to work with untrained actors, with directors similarly untrained, on poorly written scripts and in conditions bearing no relation to those obtaining in professional theatre companies, thus running the risk of the gradual erosion of their own professional skills and techniques.

In this situation it is important that those entering the profession with serious intent should be protected from the direct influence of those who are 'actors' or 'directors' only because they have so styled themselves and whose 'work' is often no more than an arrogant or idle self-indulgence. The emphasis on acting as a career and as a profession needs to be separated from this area. The central fact of this Enquiry is that there are too many actors.

Of course, this too is 'loaded', but it is considerably more realistic. It is certainly important that actors should be well and properly trained. But there are too many of them, and there are too many of them doing things which may well be fun for them but which are of no consequence whatever to the nation and community as a whole. It is ludicrous to imply that the vast number of fringe shows of one kind or another should be maintained simply to provide 'challenging opportunities' and work for actors. If it were to happen that we had too many doctors, the answer to that situation would not be to ensure that more people were sick but to train fewer doctors. The simple logic of applying this procedure to actors seems not to have occurred to the doubtless worthy people on the Gulbenkian committee.

106

They were 'satisfied that substantial unemployment exists, though it is probably not as great as some figures have led people to suppose'. That, in fact, is only true if, in so far as figures are available at all (and most of them are based on Equity surveys and questionnaires which do not purport to be comprehensive), the statistics relating to actors trained at the leading drama schools are separated from the statistics as a whole: that is, by excluding fairly arbitrarily all those actors who did not go to those schools and may be (though not necessarily are) untrained or inadequately trained. Even those figures can be misleading, though. They would show that a high percentage of the actors trained at the top schools (over 80 per cent, in fact) obtain acting jobs within a few months of leaving—which looks pretty good on paper, until it is realised that the jobs they get may not last long and may be the only ones they get in the course of a year or so. The Equity estimate is that no more than a quarter of the membership is actually employed on anything at any given time—and that *doesn't* look so good on paper, even allowing that some of the employment will be in high-fee television or film work which can keep actors surviving through some months of subsequent joblessness.

The Gulbenkian Report went on hopefully to recommend 'that the Department of Employment and the Office of Population Censuses and Surveys should regularly inquire into unemployment in the acting and other artistic professions, which gives rise to serious problems both to those engaged in them and to those who benefit from their work'. The last few words there are deeply irrelevant and characteristic of the committee's woolly attitude and its attempt to extend the significance of its investigation of conditions in a small, specific area into some general national problem.

What on earth was the 'serious problem' about unemployed actors for 'those who benefit from their work' (ie audiences)? Was it that audiences are inadequately supplied with entertainment? Plainly not, for it can be taken for granted that where an audience, or potential audience, exists there will always be someone ready to provide what they will pay for. What seems unhappily to be implied is that entertainments of one sort or another should be cobbled up to provide work for the acting workforce, even though no one wants it enough to pay to see it. That is to assume an extension of subsidy to the point where all actors are employed all the time on entertainments which will always be available for people to attend, regardless of whether they want to or not.

For there was nothing in the recommendations of this Report that is directed towards a reduction in the numbers of drama students and thus of the numbers of people in the acting market who are expecting to make a living:

> *We consider that the present support for drama training from public funds is both uneconomic and inadequate . . .*
>
> *We believe that the most likely way in which drama schools will obtain the additional financial support they need is by establishing links with local authorities . . .*
>
> *We recommend that a National Council for Drama Training should be established . . . (which) would discuss with local education authorities and the Department of Education and Science how support can best be organised for the drama schools which it recognises . . . Four major London drama schools seem permanently guaranteed and we hope that a further four will be recognised and supported in a variety of different ways, which might include direct subsidy from central government . . .*
>
> *We recommend that the DES should issue guidance to local authorities to the effect that students obtaining places at NCDT recognised drama schools should be given grants as a matter of course . . .*
>
> *We recommend that grants should be automatically available, as a matter of policy, for graduates who are accepted by recognised drama schools offering post-graduate courses of up to two years . . .*

All this is well-meaning enough to the extent that it would emphasise the advantages and increase the influence of the 'recognised' drama schools, which we can assume to be the best, by ensuring that they are adequately supported from government and local government funds; and additionally that the best potential actors—that is to say, those who have the apparent talent to gain admission to such schools—are given the same right to grants that is enjoyed by students going to universities. This would not essentially change the present position, except that the grants which are now 'discretionary' (and thus do lead to certain anomalies because of the varying attitudes of different local authorities) would become mandatory.

The Report's expectation that, as a result, we would see 'the non-recognised schools begin to diminish in number and importance following the concentration of public support in the recognised sector' would obviously be justified, simply because students would plainly prefer to have their training paid for from public funds. If more were taken into the 'recognised' schools there would be fewer left-overs for the others (of which, taking the loosest definition of a drama school, there are probably well over one hundred in the country). But there is no basis for believing that the total numbers would be reduced. The Report went on, certainly, to recommend that Equity, in granting membership, should favour the students emerging from the 'recognised' drama schools; but certainly not that all others should be *excluded*. And, indeed, it specifically and rightly noted that 'although the vast majority of entrants into the profession will have completed a course at a recognised drama school, we believe that it is highly desirable that it should still be possible to enter the profession without formal training'.

So where would this leave us? It would bring us, on my reading, to a point at which—*unless further subsidies of theatres, theatre companies and miscellaneous theatrical enterprises were forthcoming*, in addition to the further subsidies envisaged for the training of actors—even the present arguable *percentage* of students from the top drama schools who obtain jobs soon after leaving would sharply decline. If there were *more students* emerging from the top schools, and if only the *same number of jobs* were available, this much is obvious.

In the economic and inflationary condition of Britain in the 1970s, with the realistic sections of the major political parties in general agreement on the necessity to curtail public expenditure, only if a government were to go berserk could we envisage a significant extension of subsidy in this area. It is therefore unlikely that the situation confronting the aspiring actor will improve. It would not make it any easier to make a living as an actor, even if the logical and most desirable recommendations of the Gulbenkian

Report were to be implemented in some form—that is if, without increase in the total grants expenditure, the standardisation of the grants policies of all local authorities were introduced so that potential students are not at an advantage or disadvantage according to their place of residence, and also if restriction of such subsidised training were limited to the properly approved drama schools. On the contrary—it might very well, indeed, increase the disgruntlement of those young actors who, having properly trained talents, were still unable to find employment regularly enough to give them a decent annual income. For this is the situation in other areas, sociology, for example, in which the number of employment opportunities are substantially fewer than the number of graduates.

The disgruntlement is, and would be, unreasonable, of course. The situation is clear and should be considered realistically before the training is embarked upon. That this often fails to happen is because, as the Gulbenkian committee did recognise

> *. . . once the desire to go on the stage has been conceived, the would-be actor is not easily diverted . . . Acting is, theoretically at least, a very attractive job compared with the means by which most workers have to earn their living. The well-publicised and often exaggerated earnings of a very small number of star performers give an added incentive to the young person who believes he has talent and is prepared to 'chance his arm'. For others, the attraction is that of following an artistic career, which may have been stimulated by the greater interest in the arts that goes with rising standards of education. Whatever the reason, the fact that for most performers the reality is not fame and fortune but bare subsistence is not so off-putting as might be the case elsewhere. Failure is a statistical probability and thus no personal reflection upon those who suffer it.*

Except, it might be added, upon the state of their heads if—in the light of the plain facts and probabilities—they did not bargain for it. Let us honestly concede, though, that the logical converse of the present situation is that all would-be actors would reach the rational decision that the odds against success were so great that

110

they would be foolish to take the risk. They would embark on the harder studies required in accountancy or law or medicine, or settle for the disagreeableness of being dustmen or the humdrum unglamorousness of being shopgirls or filing clerks. As a result of such sensible decisions, so far from there being too many actors, there would be none at all.

This is not an hypothesis that need be seriously considered. There is, in fact, no persuasive evidence that the numbers of young people who want to become actors, and who make some effort to fulfil that ambition, will perceptibly diminish. It can only be hoped, not that the area of subsidised theatre will be wilfully expanded simply to provide employment for all of them, but rather that those who do not succeed in what is unarguably an over-crowded and highly competitive market will abandon their doomed aspirations and move into some other activity—just as, presumably, sociologists and butlers, historians and chauffeurs, psychologists and gardeners, if unable to find employment in the fields of their first preference, turn to something else. This would be sensible. It is also sensible for anyone wishing to embark on any profession to try to obtain the best possible training for it. In the case of acting that means trying to get a place at one of the top drama schools, which can be taken generally to be those that are members of the Conference of Drama Schools.

Most of the CDS establishments are in London: the Royal Academy of Dramatic Art, the London Academy of Music and Dramatic Art, the Central School of Speech and Drama, the Guildhall School of Music and Drama, the Webber Douglas Academy of Dramatic Art, the Drama Centre and the East 15 Acting School. The others are the Rose Bruford College of Speech and Drama (at Sidcup, Kent), the Guildford School of Acting and Drama Dance Education, the Birmingham School of Speech Training and Dramatic Art, the Bristol Old Vic Theatre School, the Manchester Polytechnic School of Theatre, the Arts Educational Trust Schools, the Royal Scottish Academy of Music and Drama and the Welsh College of Music and Drama.

The range of fees is between £450 and £750 annually at the time of writing (1977). But most of the British students are there on grants from local education authorities. These, as noted, are not mandatory (because degrees or their equivalent are not awarded)

111

but 'discretionary'. Although most local education authorities *do* come across with the grants, at least in regard to the CDS schools and a few others besides, it is, of course, high time that the policy throughout the country became standardised.

Getting in is a matter of taking an audition—which can be a quick 15-minute affair, or a whole gruelling day or even a weekend. Only about one out of every dozen applicants is taken. That's the overall average: in the case of male applicants, the success figure is nearer one in six, while among female applicants it is only one in 25 or so. Girls had best get used at this early stage to the reality that things are a whole lot tougher for them—not only are there far more girls than boys who want to get into acting, but there are far fewer parts for girls anyway.

Not even all of the aspirants who successfully get through the auditions to ensure a grant and enrolment actually survive the training period in these top schools. Some drop out of their own accord. Others just fail to come up to expectations and are asked to leave. Not more than 350 students will embark on the course in any one year. And the number successfully completing the three-year course will vary between 200 and 300. These are, as it were, the cream, the ones most likely to succeed. Of these the sunniest statistics say only one in five fails to get an acting job and an Equity card within a few months of graduation. And it certainly does seem a relatively small annual number of newcomers to the profession.

The complete picture, however, is much bleaker. It is estimated that the number of students emerging each year from *all* drama schools is nearer 3,000 than 300. Some of the schools that are not part of the CDS set-up are thoroughly reputable and may be listed by the Department of Education and Science as 'efficient' to the point of giving perfectly adequate professional tuition, which lacks only the 'cachet' of the top schools.

But there are far more than these. Anyone can open a drama school or set up as a drama teacher, without licence or registration. Consequently there are dozens of these 'academies of dramatic art', some doubtless very good, others virtually useless. There are also, of course, drama courses in establishments not exclusively concerned with drama: universities, polytechnics, colleges of further education. Not all the students taking these peripheral

112

drama courses have serious professional ambitions. But a great many of them do want, at least, to 'try their luck' and it is, in fact, true to say that almost every kind of drama training has *some* representatives among the successful members of the profession.

That applies even to the 'stage schools' where the pupils are largely there not by their own choice but by that of stage-struck or money-grubbing parents. The stage schools take in children as young as eight and direct them towards acting careers in the context of a syllabus of general education the extent and quality of which is variable. I have known child actors, products of such schools, who were wholly illiterate; others who seemed education-ally in advance of children at conventional schools.

The stage school children do work quite a bit—in the regular theatre, in children's theatre, in films and television, in 'com-mercials', and on straight modelling jobs. More often than not, the school has a vested interest in seeing that they do, for it also acts as their agent, or is closely associated with an agency. Parents who send their children to such schools in the hope of a nice capital return are generally disappointed, however, and not a little sur-prised to find that the fees earned by the kids are rarely in excess of the tuition fees charged by the school. At the end of it all, these children are very often the saddest entrants to the adult acting profession: their academic qualifications probably fit them for no other career. Although they will almost certainly have been coached well enough to get through drama school auditions, they often have neither the ambition nor the interest in the theatre that are necessary if they are to survive in the professional rat-race.

Most people find it mildly mysterious that so few of even the 'stars' among child performers grow up to be successful adult actors. The reason usually is that they don't want to be. There they all are, though, at least for a time, swelling even further the numbers trying to get a foothold in this overcrowded profession—thousands of them, those who have had some form of training being joined by those who have had none at all but just seem to fancy the acting life and try to ease themselves into it via the tatterdemalion 'fringe' groups. A few hundred of them will get jobs and Equity cards. That, however, may be just the beginning of their troubles.

Getting an agent can help. Agents are not interested in actors who don't work or are unlikely to work much. So the youngster who is signed up by one of the leading agents can at least be sure that he has employment potential. That can do something for his confidence. It can also give a false sense of security. He may feel, indeed, that he can now relax a little and let the agent get busy on his behalf. Then he might consider getting his head examined.

We ought to have a look at agents.

MORE THAN
TEN PERCENTERS

12

It would be cruel to call them secret agents. But that, alas, is what too many of them are, these men and woman in whose hands actors and actresses place their careers so hopefully. Agents—or personal managers, a term preferred by those who are uneasy about the parasitical connotations of the other—take a minimum of ten per cent of their clients' fees and salaries, which may seem incentive enough to get them beavering away at the business of ensuring that their clients are kept as regularly and as gainfully employed as the exigencies of the profession permit. This is an enthusiasm that afflicts young agents, new to the game, who are collecting clients and eager to impress. They grow out of it.

On the whole, that is. They will always keep trying for their stars, their big-money players. But even with the big names the job is not in getting work for them—even if that is what most people, including newcomers to the acting profession, think. It is mostly in accepting or rejecting the offers that are made—out of the blue, *without* soliciting, because the players are in demand and they don't want the indignity of anyone out there touting on their behalf. And, if it's accepting, it's a question of negotiating the terms and drawing up the contracts. That's for the players who are in demand. Most are not. They're the ones who *could* use an agent·in the meat market to do the hustling for them. Nine times out of ten, and more often even than that, they have to get their own jobs. And, again, all the agent does is the money talk and the paper work.

Even so, when you hear people talking about the iniquity of the agency business, mostly they won't be talking about the lack of work that agents put in to get work for their clients. You get all this guff about the agents' lack of feeling for art and lack of concern for their clients' 'best interests'—how they go out grabbing lucrative film and television parts for them, when they should be developing their talents in the theatre, bringing them along with a Hamlet in Wigan or a Juliet in Wolverhampton and a long slog through a summer repertory season playing *everything*.

I saw an article just the other day which spoke seriously of a conscientious agent's dilemma over whether he should put his client in a TV commercial paying £500-plus for an appearance lasting seconds, or pass it up and send the poor devil out to tread the provincial boards for £30 a week. In a pig's eye, it's a dilemma. The agent will go for the telly spot. And not just because it's what makes him fat, but because it's what his client would do if he were handling his own affairs. The actor, after all, is getting 90 per cent of the money.

A few actors, a very few, do handle their own affairs, opting out of the system and keeping the whole one hundred per cent of their earnings, before tax, to themselves. They have to have a good head for business, a precise appreciation of their own worth, and not be shy of talking money. This is too tall an order for most actors. Frederick Jaeger is the most notable of the handful who cope with it successfully: he decided moons ago that there was nothing an agent could do for him that he couldn't do for himself, and no theoretical nonsense about his art to give him dilemmas. When, for instance, he had conflicting offers of a thirteen-episode television series and a good part in *The Merry Wives of Windsor* at the Mermaid Theatre, he didn't hesitate for an instant. 'I'd like to get back into the theatre, especially in Shakespeare,' he said, 'but I've got to think of the kids' schools fees.' Perhaps another play at the Mermaid, with the prospect of a West End transfer, might have tempted him, but he must have known that *The Merry Wives* (which was also being done by the Royal Shakespeare) had all the earmarks of a stiff. Naturally, he took the television series, negotiating his own fee and keeping it all.

It's the frequent haggles over money that discourages most actors from doing away with the services of their agents, though they have a warm respect for the few like Frederick Jaeger. I heard one of his colleagues put it to him like this:

'Look, Freddy, a TV producer that I've worked for before wants me again and rings my agent. He offers £500, which he says

116

is all the budget will allow, but it's me they want. My agent tells me. He points out that it's a couple of hundred below my rate. "Take it, take it," I say, "I need the money," and of course he will, dressing it up with a spiel about me being fairly insulted but nevertheless I'm considering it because I appreciate the producer's difficulty, but I do like working with him and I do have a couple of free weeks, so couldn't he split the difference and go to six hundred? No? Five-fifty? But the producer sticks on five hundred. He knows I need the money, he knows I'll take the part, and I do. What I'm absolutely incapable of is all the jazz before I take it, but that doesn't bother you?'

It didn't bother Jaeger. He reckons producers always know when agents are bluffing and lying, and they'd know it of him, too, so he cuts the haggle down to the token minimum. If he does work for a lower fee than he thinks the part is worth, it will only be after he has carefully weighed the matters of how much he wants to play that part and how much damage, if any, his acceptance of a lower fee will do to future prospects. He believes he is at least as capable of assessing those things as any agent, and if there have been occasions when an agent might have pushed successfully for a little more money, those benefits would have been more than cancelled out by the percentage of everything he would be losing.

Obviously, being agentless is a good deal easier for an established actor than it would be for a beginner. Managements, directors and casting directors know his work, and his name will come to mind when suitable parts are being cast. He will have to keep himself informed on who's who and what's going on. But he won't have to do all the personal 'selling', auditioning, begging and suppli- cating that beginners in the profession—and some who are far from beginners—have to do. He has one or two other useful advantages. For one thing, he will always know exactly how much money is due to him; and for another, he can be sure of getting it.

An actor with an agent may very well have these advantages, too; the chances are that he will, especially if he is with one of the big agencies which have too much to lose, and would find it too complicated, to start cheating their clients even if they should want to. But every business in which cash is being passed around has its temptations and the agency game has more than most. There's not much opportunity for simple 'fiddling' where a theatre engagement is concerned. But there certainly is in television and radio where the artists' contracts specify 'repeat' fees and 'residuals', additional payments for screenings and broadcasts in other countries and so on, and an actor has to depend on his agent (who receives the fees) to know when such fees are due and to send on the actor's percentage of them when they're received. The less scrupulous agents can be awfully forgetful about these things.

The system of fees being paid to agents, who are selling their clients' services, rather than direct to the actors who are providing the services, is a perilous one for the actors. The money an agent receives for his clients' services is legally regarded as part of his own assets, while his clients are technically his creditors for the percentage that is due to them. The actors may get their money promptly, but there are some agents who like to hang on to it for a month or two or three. If an agent uses his clients' part of the money to pay the rent, the telephone bill, the secretary or whatever, or even just for good living, he's quite within his legal rights —and an agent whose business is going badly may have to do those things. And if, notwithstanding his juggling and hustling, the business goes so badly that it ends up bankrupt, the actors whose fees have not, at that point, been passed on to them will be in the queue with the agent's other creditors for the percentage share-out of whatever funds may be in the kitty on liquidation. It does happen; not frequently, but often enough for actors to feel uneasy about the lack of protection the law provides for them if they get into the hands of a dodgy agent.

The law is generally pretty loose where agents are concerned, starting at the point where they set up shop. Virtually anyone can go into business as an agent—anyone, that is, with no criminal record—simply by advertising in the profession's weekly newspaper, *The Stage*, his or her intention to apply to the local council for an agency licence. The advertisement appears for three consecutive weeks on the leader page of *The Stage*, giving the address from which the business is to be operated, and, if no valid objections are raised , the council concerned will automatically grant the licence. It has to be renewed annually but is not likely to be revoked except, of course, on evidence of criminal malpractice, and there are opportunities enough for agents to be sharp within the law without their having recourse to actual crime.

All this may be conveying the notion that agents are a generally shifty crew. In fact, the wonder is that so many of them play it straight and can even show a kind of benevolence, generously refraining from mulcting their more lowly-paid clients of the ten per cent entitlement. The better agents will invariably skip the commission on theatre jobs paying only the Equity minimum, and some of them are prepared to hold off until the client is making over £60 a week—all in the interest of retaining the goodwill and good opinion of those they believe in. Which is not entirely altruistic. If the actor steps up, as they hope, into the high-price bracket, earning big fees in all the entertainment media, these generous gestures in the early years will pay off. An actor who is properly grateful to an agent for 'carrying' him a bit when he needed the help will not lightly desert his benefactor when he strikes it rich.

This is an important consideration, especially for a small agent, in a business where contracts between actor and agent are rarely for long periods. The usual is twelve months renewable annually, with each side having the option to cancel if notice is given up to two months before renewal is due, but there may be nothing at all in writing. 'Poaching' is rife, and an actor who is suddenly in big demand for well-paid jobs will find himself in demand among the agents as well. The less fashionable agent will have to build up quite a backlog of gratitude in such an actor if he is to hold his client in the teeth of offers from the big agencies with all sorts of international connections going for them. It's a hard thing to prove, but there is a common belief that one or two of the big boys give 'poaching' first priority: that is, they don't waste time on the chancy business of spotting promising newcomers who may never actually make it. They just wait till the actors *have* made it and then set about wooing them away from the agents who have struggled with them through the lean years.

But the big agencies themselves are frequent victims in the 'poaching' game. Many of today's independent agents were once executives of big firms. As such, they developed friendly and special relationships with the clients they were assigned to 'look after'. When an executive leaves to set up his own agency, those clients tend to go with him. There's not much the big firms can do to protect themselves against this sort of thing—the best they can usually hope for is to cut themselves in for a percentage of the breakaway executive's business for a limited period, which he may agree to under threat of litigation.

Some of the larger agencies are also cute enough to departmentalise their businesses, so that each client's theatre work, film work and television work are separately handled by different executives. The agency accepts the confusions that can thereby arise, and the difficulty of taking an overall view of a client's work opportunities, career and development, in return for the advantage that no actor is 'looked after' by one executive exclusively—something which minimises, but does not entirely obviate, the possibility of a 'walk-out and poach' operation.

That magic and much-bandied-about figure of ten per cent, by the way, is to some extent a fiction. It's the one that comes up in all the familiar jokes about agents (as in the one-liner in which the actor says that he's going to be cremated when he dies and ten per cent of the ashes will go to his agent; and in the one about the agent at the theatre grumbling about 'that ham up there getting 90 per cent of my money') but quite often it's only a basis for negotiation. As I've indicated, an agent with an eye on the future will frequently take no commission at all, or perhaps just a token five per cent, from a low-earning player; he will advise the young aspirant to spend any spare money on taking further post-drama-school acting lessons, voice and movement lessons, and on keeping decently dressed and getting good photographs to pass around. But when the money gets bigger, the agent will often be getting much *more* than that basic ten per cent.

The agent justifies this by claiming to be 'much more than an agent': he will also be his client's accountant, lawyer, psychiatrist, nanny and someone who is always there to lean on. Maybe you think a good agent should be all those things anyway, as part of being an agent and justifying even ten per cent. Not so. For taking such total charge of a client's professional affairs (and, sometimes, his private affairs as well), an agent will whip off up to 25 per cent of the incomings. The client will be generally persuaded that he's worth it. And, since there's no duress involved in these arrangements, he probably is.

Any grumbling is likely to be on the agent's side—not over the money, but when the client doesn't take his advice. If an actor is adamant about taking a part that the agent thinks is a mistake, the agent will negotiate the contract and see the show and make the right noises—but inside he'll be wincing like a fond parent watching a daughter getting into a disastrous love affair. Likening the agent–actor relationship to that of parent and child is apposite; for just as parents were young themselves once and think their children should be ready to benefit from their own experience, so a great many agents were once actors. On the whole, agents have better luck than parents in passing on the benefits of their experience.

Those that were not actors were probably accountants, and will concern themselves more with finance, putting up persuasive arguments for raising the basic ten per cent to $12\frac{1}{2}$ or 15 per cent, on the grounds that their overheads (rents, telephone, correspondence, and travelling expenses) have gone up beyond the recent increases in the salaries from which their percentage comes. There may be something to be said for their case. Not all agents are in favour since they recognise that it might be bad for their 'image' —not only with the public, but with the acting profession. It is, of course, a fact that the average income of agents is higher than the average income of actors.

Agents, like most people, are cagey about giving details of their income for publication. One reasonably successful agent told me that he'd be disappointed if he couldn't take a minimum of £10,000 a year out of his business. He estimated that his colleagues among the top 25 or 30 agents were making at least that amount, and that the top executives in the big combines (formed, over the years, by mergers) drew salaries considerably higher.

The proliferation of combines is a general source of disquiet in the theatre and the rest of the entertainment business. This disquiet increases to the extent that there are connections, through interlocking directorships and blood relationships, between the combines and the employers of actors such as theatrical managements, film and television companies. In the 1970 Report, *The Theatre Today*, initiated by the Arts Council and produced after a committee inquiry under the chairmanship of Sir William Emrys Williams, few matters were regarded with so much concern as the danger of a monopolistic situation stemming from the management–agency octopus. The Report used careful language, but the implications are clear if the reader provides his own italics and reads between the lines.

'Theatrical agents perform an important function and in this country have a high standard of integrity,' it said, throwing in some routine and creamy flattery before getting to the hard stuff:

> But dangers at once arise if a producing manager has a financial stake in an agency, for this is plainly a situation which could be exploited to the disadvantage of an artist. [Between the lines: also to his advantage and to the disadvantage of another agency's artist.] An agent's duty and loyalty should always be to his client, to advise him how to advance his career even when this could lead to disappointment on the part of a management which had different ideas on the matter. We do not know that agents in this country transgress this vital principle, but it is possible for an agent linked to a producing management to put his client's interest second and not first. Moreover however impeccably the agency is conducted at its top level [of course, of course], a subordinate in the organisation could conceivably act in a detrimental way to the client because he believed it would please his employers even though they might be unaware of action he had taken to pressurise his client. [Now how could that be? And if it could be, what would be the point of this ingratiating underling doing things to please his employers without their knowing about it?] Moreover the fact that an agency was financed or controlled by a powerful theatre management would be likely to have a bad psychological effect on artists in search of employment [yes, yes], for they might have reason to fear, justifiably or not [mm, do go on], that they might become pawns in a power game.

What this official report was stammering quite bravely to say is that a theatrical management or a film company or a television company having influentially interlocking connections with, if not outright ownership of, an artists' agency would have an advantage over other managements and companies in securing the services of that agency's artists; that such an advantage may not be to the advantage of the artists; and perhaps that, conceivably more im-

122

portantly, such an advantage is to the disadvantage of artists who do not happen to be on that agency's books. It could also have been trying guardedly to suggest that such an association is of incalculable benefit to the *agency*, not only in obtaining employment for its desirable artists (which is not a big problem) but in placing others on its books who are not sensationally in demand.

The situation that so exercised Sir William's committee altered somewhat when the Grade Organisation, which has heavy connections with the powerful EMI and all branches of show business, sold off its agency interests. It would, however, be absurd to suggest that connections no longer exist between agencies and managements—even if such connections are not directly related to the financial or executive control of either, but exist primarily in kinship, friendliness, partnership in unrelated enterprises and a showbiz equivalent of the Old Boys' Network.

Only a few years ago it was a demonstrable fact that nearly a quarter of the players in the West End were represented by agents and agencies under the aegis of the Grade Organisation. Sorry to mention *them* again, but they were the biggest beans in the bag. That cannot be said to be any longer so, if we confine ourselves to shareholdings and directorships, but I doubt whether such a wide and long-standing sphere of influence could be nullified by the stroke of a pen and the disposal of shares. It would be remarkable if it had entirely evaporated.

Quite apart from this aspect of the relationship between employers of artists and artists' agents, there is further food for thought in the fact that it is hardly unknown for agents to invest in theatrical productions; and even if this were prohibited by law as it is in the United States, I daresay that such investments would continue to be made through nominees and subsidiaries, especially by the big combine agencies. These, in any case, possess a further advantage which is apt to disturb those actors who do not happen to be on their books,

What principally disturbs these actors, I find, is the employment-by-association situation. It operates even in the case of a small agent who has the good fortune to have an in-demand actor on his books; and the bigger the agency and the more 'stars' it has, the bigger the operation. The practical effect of the mergers of agencies in recent years has been in fact to bring perhaps 80 per cent of the big box-office names within the control of a handful of big agencies.

Now any producer or casting director who wants one of those big names would be foolish if he did not look very favourably indeed upon the other artists looked after by the agents who have the disposition of the top talents in their hands; and any agent with an in-demand actor would be similarly foolish if, other things being equal, he did not at least *hint* that he had other actors worth employing. The implication would be that the greatly in-demand X would be happy to take a part if there also happened to be parts with the same company or management for Y and Z. These matters are, of course, not referred to out loud.

I have never known an agent who would admit that such practices were part of his business; and I have never known an actor who did not believe that they were. It is just possible, in fact, that they are the key to success in the agency game.

STARS IN 13
YOUR EYES

Show business tends to devalue its own verbal currency. Words like 'fabulous' and 'thriller' are the veritable half-crowns and halfpennies of the vernacular, not only devalued but meaningless in any literal or literate sense; and I'm afraid that even 'star' is nowadays bandied around so casually that its usage bears as little relation to its former meaning as a decimal pound to a gold sovereign.

It was in the cinema, rather than in the theatre, that the rot set in, in the abandonment of the old convention of reserving exclusively to 'stars' the billing space above the title. As virtual nonentities (or their agents) claimed the same billing rights as the Garbos and Gables, albeit perhaps in less eminent films, so the agents of even lesser performers with only the most tenuous of claims to 'star' status (possibly on the basis of prominent 'featured' work in those less eminent films) demanded 'star billing' for their clients.

This led, inevitably, to degrees of 'stardom' until it has become no uncommon thing to see a film poster on which two players are billed above the title; then, below it, comes the word 'starring' followed by four more names in slightly smaller type, and the words 'also starring' followed by another four names in type slightly smaller again, and the words 'and introducing' followed by another couple of names which, though taking a low place on the bill, are confusingly in the same type-size as the two above the title. The confusion might be further compounded absurdly by the presence of 'guest stars' as well—though whose guests they are, or in what sense their presence is different from that of the other players in the picture, has never been entirely clear. What *is* clear is that, in such bizarre circumstances, the word 'star' can no longer be applied definitively, while 'starlet' has become almost pejorative (though perhaps it always was).

To restore 'star' to something approaching its old par value, at least in conversation, another word is sometimes added: 'quality'. Certain performers are said to have 'star quality' and some of them unquestionably do have it, though it is an elusive attribute to catch in cold print. It may be instantly recognisable, but trying to define it is roughly as easy as trying to nail a custard pie to the wall. There are accomplished actors who never put a foot wrong—and will never have it. There are others who can fluff and stumble and practically walk through the scenery—and yet will never lose it. The late Sir Noël Coward once came up with an engaging description of this intangible in describing a fictional actress in one of his short stories:

> *Her figure and looks are little more than attractively adequate. She is not particularly intelligent. Whatever genuine emotional equipment she originally started with has long since withered in the consuming flames of her vanity. But you go in and watch her on a matinee day with a dull audience, in a bad play, and the house half full, and suddenly you are aware that you are in the presence of something very great indeed.*

The last part of that, at least, is true of every real star, and it has nothing to do with publicity, reputation, billing or age. Example: the first time I ever saw Maggie Smith was in an undergraduate revue from Oxford at a tiny London theatre club called the Watergate, now defunct. She was unknown and unheralded, but her star quality was unmistakable. They say, those who were there, that the same was true of Vivien Leigh, the first time she set foot on the London stage; and much more recently, everybody saw it in Kate Nelligan.

The quality is not, however, always so instantly recognisable, and I am not persuaded by those who claim to have seen it again and again at first sight; memories tend to be coloured by subsequent events. I may tell myself that the first time I saw Dorothy Tutin (again at a now-defunct theatre club and in a relatively small part) that I *knew*, and I may think similarly of, say, Claire Bloom and Donald Sinden and Peter O'Toole; but perhaps I was merely 'impressed' and thought them 'promising' and recollection has been amended by experience. I have also, sometimes, been misled in an eagerness to discover this 'star quality'. I thought I saw it, for instance (and even now I'm not altogether sure that I didn't), the first time I watched Ronald Pickup—in a part that was little more than a last-act walk-on in *Armstrong's Last Goodnight*, years ago at Chichester. Pickup was groomed thereafter for the great parts, since there were plainly others who shared my impression. He played most of them well. He is unquestionably one of the finest actors of his generation—certainly the most likely 'Hamlet' of his generation, though that is a part he has so far taken only in a radio production—yet it becomes increasingly difficult to claim for him the quality of the 'star'. If he showed it once, as I supposed, in that first flash of magnetism, we may see it again. Before it is universally accepted, though, the recognition of it must *be* universal—it must be evident even to those who may not especially *like* the kind of actor he is.

This last is one of the essentials. Anyone honest will concede 'star quality' even when recoiling from the kind of 'star quality' it is. I never myself particularly cared for, say, Gracie Fields. But it would be foolish to deny that she had 'star quality': she radiated it. I am not keen on the performances of Robert Morley, who seems to me to project an excessively powerful personality often to the detriment of the play he is in. Nor, should I regard him as an actor of spectacular accomplishment; yet he is, unquestionably, a 'star'. Conversely, the greatest actor I ever saw—perhaps the only *great* actor I ever saw— was the late and woefully alcoholic Wilfrid Lawson, but he was *never* a 'star'.

What I suppose I am edging around to here is a redefinition of 'star' that is more generally acceptable in terms of the contemporary theatre. And what that comes to, I think, is the 'sure-fire box-office name'. Actors and actresses who would fit that enviable description might also qualify as 'stars' in the old meaning of the word—Laurence Olivier, say, or John Gielgud or Peter O'Toole or Ingrid Bergman, none of whom is it possible to imagine failing to attract the crowds—but these are the great rarities. You get them and you're home and dried and cleaning out the feedbox, just on the 'advance'. No matter what they're in. Truth to tell, they're usually careful pickers, but they're at a stage in the game when it matters less and less at the box-office. John Gielgud packed the Royal Court (and made them money) in Edward Bond's *Bingo*, one of the great mind-numbing plays of all time and in which his own performance was one for the embalmers. Similarly Paul Scofield kept the till jingling for months at Wyndham's in a second-rate production of *The Tempest* that may not have looked so thrifty in Leeds but fitted the West End of London like a Berwick Market barrow in the food hall at Fortnums. Yet Scofield, though he has been called 'the greatest actor of his generation' is by no means sure-fire box-office.

Much commoner nowadays than these great names are those who, as far as the theatre is concerned, ascend briefly to the 'sure-fire' ranks by virtue of some popular success in television or still, perhaps, the cinema. In the case of the latter, they're usually old-timers, who may even have more pulling power in the theatre than they have retained in the cinema, because all their old fans have grown up with them and are theatregoers now: hence Ginger Rogers in *Mame*, Lauren Bacall in *Applause*, James Stewart in *Harvey*. And as for the television 'names', what else can account for the substantial London runs of an awful comedy called *Why Not Stay for Breakfast?* and a tawdrily inept 'thriller' called *Who Saw Him Die?* other than the fact that Derek Nimmo and Stratford Johns, respectively (and both featured in popular television series), were in them?

Beyond such phenomena as these, however (the proven 'star quality' players and the imports from *yesterday*'s cinema and *today*'s television), it is less and less likely that the success of a production on the West End stage can be assured merely by the popularity of the players in it. Even Brian Rix, whose reputation in farce was once (believe it or not, like it or not) good for a two-year run, could not keep *A Bit Between the Teeth* going for more than three months or so in London. The music had stopped. And the 'names' from *today*'s cinema and *yesterday*'s television don't have the magic, either: David Hemmings 'died' in *Jeeves* in a matter of weeks; Honor Blackman (once a certain theatre 'draw' on the heels of her stint in *The Avengers*) couldn't save *The Exorcism*.

The best success combination nowadays is a good play with players of proven merit if not necessarily 'star quality'. People who are just occasional theatregoers may still tend to ask 'Who's in it?' and to regard the presence of Tom Courtenay or Michael Crawford or Diana Rigg or Sheila Hancock (to mention an assorted quartet at random) as an additional inducement to come up with the admission money. But the key word there is 'additional': what they primarily wish to be assured of is that the play itself—so far as it can be taken from the reviews or from word-of-mouth recommendation—is worthwhile.

Of course, there are still remnants of the old 'star sytem' as it used to be called, a system under which the 'star' became the dominant influence in the commercial theatre. Owners and lessees of theatres in the West End are still influenced by what they think are box-office 'names'—so that when, for example, the film star, Gayle Hunnicutt, dropped out of the cast of a play being 'tried out' at Guildford, the West End theatres that had been ready to take it in promptly lost interest. But producers, on the whole, nowadays put the play before the players. Perhaps they always did try to put the good plays and the good 'names' together; the difference now is that, if the good 'names' happen so much the better, but they aren't the primary consideration any more. In any case, the director will want them to be 'right' for the play. The 'stars' are clearly still helpful; very few of them are quite the wreckers they used to be.

They used to be wreckers in *two* senses. In the first, they lent their box-office appeal to rubbish, which happens less and less—partly because they and the managements have better taste and know the difference, and partly because they're aware that the public's taste is better. If they get themselves into bad plays or flops or both it's because of genuine errors of judgment. In the second sense, in the old days, too, they could be wreckers because of what their often miscast personalities did to good plays. They can still be temperamental, prima-donna-ish; they can still steal scenes in which they're supposed to be subordinate; they can still kill laughs for lesser members of the cast; they can still work their little up-staging tricks—not, perhaps, as obviously as once upon a time, but you see a 'star' doing the merest bit of 'business' during somebody else's 'moment' and you are looking at a 'star' who is hell to work with. They can still come on altogether too strong. But directors are less and less prepared to let them get away with it.

129

The money they get, these 'stars', is not nearly as high as most people probably imagine. Certainly the really big ones—the ones justifiably describable as *international* stars—will be on a four-figure weekly take. These however are few—and that sort of money is outside the budgets of all but the wealthiest managements. Most of the top 'names' in the West End nowadays are prepared to work for £200 or £300 a week *plus* (and that 'plus' explains the low 'basic') a percentage of the box-office. This can be pretty lucrative for them. It can even actually get them into (or pretty close to) that four-figure bracket if they're in a winner. The percentage is variable between two and four per cent, but can go higher: those sturdy knights, John Gielgud and Ralph Richardson, for example, when starring in *No Man's Land*—a National Theatre production that transferred to Wyndham's and also to New York —were each taking ten per cent, which is quite a bite. Even a percentage of that order, however, for that sort of name, is not disagreeable to a management. The stars are taking a lot. They're also pulling in a lot. And in a way, it does cut the initial risk capital.

TAKE IT 14
FROM ME

The man (or, occasionally, woman) whose word ultimately goes is the director. Once the stake money is in the kitty, getting a new play on a stage is a three-handed collaboration—author, players, director. But only one can play God. And the director is the one. Usually. For better or worse.

This is not to minimise the author's contribution. It's *his* play, and he is its first begetter, though not necessarily its only begetter. His is the foundation on which they're all building. And, to hang on to the metaphor, he's the architect and the draughtsman as well. The players, above the level of the mere journeymen, add something as the building comes off the ground—perhaps nothing more than incidental decoration, but sometimes, with the sort of thoughtful, analytical actors there are around these days, something more fundamental.

The director, though, is the more likely instigator of any really important text changes: he may well have been working closely with the author from a fairly early stage. But, regardless of whether or not he has had an influence in the writing prior to the start of active production, from that time on he has to have his eye, always, on both ground plan and structure. How it will all look on opening night is his responsibility.

Everybody has to trust the director and his instincts. With the odd, embarrassing exception they all do. The exception is the 'personality star'—with whom no director with a care for his own reputation will get involved, other than inadvertently, because no director is ever going to influence him, or, more often, her. Sure, she'll *listen*, darling, if the token ear she lends is capable of it, but she *knows*; from the start she knows; she'll do her own thing, she'll give the performance she came along to give because that's the one her public expects of her, which is fortunate because it's the only one she *can* give; and if the production ends in total disaster because of that very performance, the chances are better than six-to-five that the reviewers will give her sympathetic credit for her valiant efforts in trying to save it. What can the director do but cut his wrists?

More rubbish is written by reviewers about the functions and achievements of directors than about almost any other aspect of the theatre. 'Well directed', 'imaginatively directed', 'inventively directed', 'plausibly directed', 'tautly directed', 'reverently directed' etcetera, etcetera. The dutiful little compliments trip off the typewriter airily enough. And sometimes a reviewer—emboldened to a confidence of which I stand in awe, although more often aghast—will elaborate his adjectives, going into all manner of detail about the director's contribution to a production.

This is, more often than not, a subject for groping conjecture—especially where successful productions are concerned. The unsuccessful ones are sometimes easier, for it is often evident enough that if this or that had been done or not done, some dramatic effect would have been advantageously heightened, some important climax achieved, some clarifying emphasis given; but even this can take a shrewd and practised eye. In the case of a production where everything goes as smoothly as could possibly be imagined, when no nuance of the author's lines is lost and all his themes and purposes lucidly communicated and helpfully illuminated, in such a case I daresay it can be safely said that the play has not been badly directed, even that it has been well directed; but precisely how far that praise of the director can fairly be taken is hard to say. Usually only he, and his author and his players, can know.

Can anyone who hasn't actually read the script (and it is rarely that even reviewers have read the script of a new play) be certain that the author himself has not provided the precise blueprint which the director has merely 'stage managed'? Can anyone who has not been present at the rehearsals be certain that the praise accorded the director does not properly belong to the players (though I suspect the contrary is more often the case)?

I shall not plead too much ignorance. Sometimes certainty, with experience as its handmaiden, is possible. For everyone; not just

132

reviewers. You won't pick up the fine detail of what a director does, but you've probably seen the players before and can roughly assess what they're capable of without directorial inspiration; and you've seen the director's work before, too, and when you've seen it a lot you'll learn to recognise the kind of influence he brings to bear on a play and whether he is at his best in exploring emotional or intellectual content, and perhaps whether he is likely to have concerned himself more with arranging the stage than with specifically directing the actors.

I've been talking about *new* plays. With an old one it is, to some extent if not totally, possible for us on the outside to know what the director has been up to. Simply by comparison: we've seen the play before and we are aware that it is now being done differently, and better, or worse. But there will still be that area of conjecture as regards the performances, and sometimes everybody can get it very wrong.

There was a production not so long ago of *The Importance of Being Earnest* in which Lady Bracknell was played as a matron of Middle European origin. The director was Jonathan Miller, and since Dr Miller is generally notorious for the novelty, not to say eccentricity, of his interpretations, this was regarded by all as his idea. Miller has stated frankly that he recognises no particular obligation to a dead author whose work is in the public domain, that he likes directing the plays of authors who *are* dead because they can't give him an argument. So it seemed clear that in the case of *The Importance* he had just sat down and taken the play apart in a search for some starting point for an entirely fresh interpretation. Well, as to Lady Bracknell, even before her entrance, there is a reference to her ringing the doorbell in a 'Wagnerian manner', and does not her daughter, Gwendolen, at one point decline to give way to 'German scepticism'? These are thin reasons for concluding that Lady Bracknell could reasonably be played as an immigrant (even granting that Wilde was no longer on hand to give Miller an argument), but they seemed no thinner than the reasons behind previous Miller fancies. I don't think the reviewers could be blamed for concentrating on Miller in discussing, on the whole pretty caustically, this curious view of a lady hitherto regarded as a formidable example of the traditional English aristocrat of stage comedy.

133

In fact, it wasn't Miller's idea at all. What had happened, apparently, was that the actress playing Lady Bracknell, Irene Handl, came into the rehearsals fresh from a television series in which she was using a German accent. She began reading the Bracknell part in the same accent—not really seriously, just for a gag. Everybody fell about. It was good rehearsal fun. Miller thought it was so funny that he decided to use it for real, but it was never one of those things he'd carefully worked out in advance, as everybody, excusably in the light of his record, thought.

Even so, however mistaken we might have been about the source of that particular idea—and were thus misled into all manner of quaint theorising about why it was there—there was nothing unjust in hanging it on Miller. If he hadn't wanted it in the show, he could have thrown it out. The director is the man who always has to carry that responsibility—and, in this case, the can. It's the sort of thing that's got to make you wonder, though, just how many 'revolutionary' or otherwise bizarre productions come about as a result of casual fortuity rather than intellectual theory.

In that regard, I'd give most directors the benefit of the doubt—if there *is* a doubt, and if there is a benefit. They know what they're doing, even if I don't like what they're doing. There are more (many more) bad directors than good ones. But perhaps there are only a few dangerously egomaniacal ones who have let the power of 'playing God' go to their heads and give a bad name to what is sometimes called 'directors' theatre'. It's the classical repertoire that tends to bring out the worst in the egomaniacs, for the classics they deem to be fair game for their 'interpretative' fancies—though not many are as frank about it as Jonathan Miller; mostly they put up an elaborate pretence of really *caring* about a dead author's work and 'intentions' which have never been fully recognised until this moment when their own baby hands fell upon the stuff. Plays whose value, importance and distinction are firmly established can doubtless survive whatever disrespectful indignities and whatever 'look-at-me-I'm-directing' conceits are visited upon them; it is when the adulation of fashionable directors of this showy kind leads to similar attitudes being taken towards new plays that we're in bad trouble.

The playwrights who make it, and can hold out for the directors they want, generally try to stick with the ones they know and trust. They need the reassurance of the rapport, and sometimes they need a creative working relationship with a director who knows what they want to say and helps them to say it. David Storey has it with Lindsay Anderson, Peter Nichols has it with Michael Blakemore, Harold Pinter with Peter Hall, Edward Bond with William Gaskill, Peter Shaffer with John Dexter. John Osborne had it with Anthony Page; and Alan Ayckbourn has got it going with Eric Thompson, as has Tom Stoppard with Peter Wood, who directed his *Jumpers* for the National Theatre and his *Travesties* for the Royal Shakespeare Company.

Every one of these names, authors and directors, will be well-known to keen or regular playgoers. But I suspect that people with no particular interest in the theatre will have heard of only two of the directors—Lindsay Anderson and Peter Hall, the former because of his work as a *film* director, the latter because he is the head man at the National Theatre. Directors of plays are little in the public eye *as such*. It's not an invariable rule, of course, but it does strike me that mostly the directors who achieve 'stardom' are bad directors—at least, they are in my book, in the sense of being bad for drama and the theatre. They're the 'look-at-me-I'm-directing' directors, projecting their own personalities and building reputations on the ruins of the plays they lay waste.

This, regrettably I feel, is a minority view. It has to be, or the reputations would never be achieved. Ostentatious directors collect good notices the way bees collect pollen. They have talent, of course. Often they're bursting with it, and they know it, and, knowing it, they're agog to share the knowledge. The sort of recognition they are after is not to be fostered by going modestly about the job of presenting the work of an author as he himself might have visualised it; for to do merely that would not bring the sweet massage of praise and applause to their tumescent egos. It would also be to concede the superiority of the author, and that is not the 'star' director's game. Authors, like players, are his puppets, and everything they do must be seen to be at his behest. He usurps the creative function—creating, if not plays, what he will call 'new theatrical experiences' which, in the case of the familiar old classics, seems to be exactly what the critics are after.

Don't hold that too hard against the critics. *You* may see any

135

given classic only once in a lifetime; the professional reviewer sees it again and again, and becomes more and more inured to its impact. Thus, in a review of almost any Shakespeare production, the most damning word in the reviewer's vocabulary is 'conventional'—which means that all he has been impertinently invited to see is Shakespeare's play. He has seen it before. God, how often he has seen it before. It may be *As You Like It*, but it is not as *he* likes it. Let's get it into drag, and we may be getting somewhere.

Clifford Williams did just that in a production of *As You Like It* for the National Theatre he took over, and oh my, what larks they had, with the enterprise copiously, carefully, though conflictingly, 'rationalised' in pages of bizarre programme notes. Here, on the one hand, were quotes from the eccentric Professor Jan Kott, lining out the theory that boys playing girls—especially boys playing girls who were pretending to be boys—add an extra dimension of eroticism to the proceedings. And here, on the other hand, was Williams explaining his own intentions which seemed to be almost exactly the opposite—that, in fact, he was employing an all-male cast in order to get rid of the eroticism, to kick the surface sexuality out of the play in 'an atmosphere of spiritual purity' that would ensure that we did not 'miss the interior truth'. Whatever hopes he may have had in that regard had little relevance to anything that appeared on the stage. In that bright plastic setting (including a greenwood tree like a pipe organ in perspex), futuristic and antiseptic, I don't think any sexual innuendo was missed. The show impressed the critics no end. They'd been seeing *As You Like It* as a play an average of once a year since they left school. And now here it was as a 'new theatrical experience'. It also impressed Kenneth Tynan, who was the National Theatre's literary manager at the time: he later got Williams to direct *Soldiers* and *Oh! Calcutta!* and *Carte Blanche* for him.

Whatever he may have done with *As You Like It*, the reference to Clifford Williams here has been somewhat out of context, for he is not one of our 'egomaniacal' directors. He serves playwrights well, whether they're alive or dead, and the drag adventure seems to have been a temporary aberration. I like to think he'll have a chuckle (and a blush) at those programme notes in his old age.

The man to bring up at this point is obviously Peter Brook, the great standard-bearer of 'director's theatre'. People don't come out of a Peter Brook show talking about the play or the author, they come out talking about Peter Brook—not necessarily politely, until they read the papers next morning and find out how wonderful it all was. The famous production of *A Midsummer Night's Dream* done first at Stratford-upon-Avon, later in London, New York and all around the world, is one in which Shakespeare gets barely token recognition. To all, it is 'Brook's *Dream*'—the supreme achievement, the highest accolade and, of course, the ultimate condemnation. (More of 'Brook's *Dream*' in the chapter on Shakespeare and the Royal Shakespeare Company.*) He is not, clearly, a man with too much regard for words; he would seem to care how they *sound*, but is not much taken by their meaning and doubtless enjoyed few things as much as his extravagant staging of *Orghast* at Persepolis, for which the text was especially written in an entirely new language, thus making absolutely certain that *no one* would understand a word of it.

Not that Brook is short on words himself when it comes to rationalising and explaining what he does. And he is taken very seriously indeed by lovers of the Higher Bosh. The players with whom he works only briefly sometimes find this all a little trying, since they are quite aware that they are simply being directed in pursuit of some whimsical visual effect beyond their comprehension. Most of those involved at the National Theatre in his notorious production of Seneca's *Oedipus* in 1968 could probably be placed in this category, with the exception of Irene Worth (who played Jocasta and is devoted to Brook both as director and 'thinker'), and possibly of Sir John Gielgud (Oedipus) who was there to give the proceedings some veneer of respectability and who rendered the speeches with noble dignity and otherwise seemed aloof from the general razzmatazz, although I cannot help thinking he surveyed it all with some distaste. Brook's production was all surface dazzle, the intellectual and emotional content of the play subordinated to 'the need for ritual' and 'the theatre of cruelty'. Loyalty to the stoical notions of Seneca was wholly and orgiastically abandoned at the end of the performance when, the stuff of tragedy having been cleared away, the cast hauled on, under gaudy wraps, a formidable and explicitly sculptured gold phallus, some ten feet tall, which was erected and left alone,

* See page 83.

137

centre-stage, in what might at first have been supposed to be their rebellious and ribald comment on the production. Staring at the thing naturally palled after a time, however, and at the performance I attended the audience concluded that there was nothing else doing and began to drift out . . . only to be met by the cast, now changed into golden robes and masks, streaming back through all doors to comport themselves wildly in the auditorium and on the stage around the phallus, led by a lively Dixieland band playing 'Yes, We Have No Bananas'.

This is what I should regard as the worst of 'director's theatre', and while the *Dream* and the *Oedipus* may be the most extreme examples of Brook's 'art' to have been seen in Britain (he is said to be discovering new horizons of extremity in his International Centre of Theatre Research, founded in Paris, though the production of *The Ik*, which he brought to the Round House in 1976 was no more than a glum bore), they demonstrate why he is the most famous director we have. Or, perhaps, one of the two most famous.

The other would be Miss Joan Littlewood, who built such an extravagant reputation for herself in the late 1950s and early 1960s that it has survived all these years between, even though her work since then has been sporadic, at best, and tends nowadays to be approached with a sort of apologetic surprise by the reviewers who once lauded her but have now outgrown her.

There are points of similarity between Brook and Miss Littlewood, although the end-products of their methods are often greatly different. Both are much dedicated to improvisation, but under Miss Littlewood's direction it seems far more haphazard. Brook imposes a discipline upon his actors that Miss Littlewood would perhaps regard as an intolerable restriction upon their freedom. This may be why she is generally spoken of as 'well-loved' by those who have worked for her Theatre Workshop in the East End, which is something I have no reason at all to doubt, although there are some actors (those, perhaps, who feel a positive need for discipline) who, while continuing to think of her as 'lovable', have nevertheless taken their leave of her company in some relief.

There was a time when I confess I thought Joan Littlewood the most dangerous director in the theatre. This, I think, was

138

because, unlike most of the showy directors who generally use the classics as the raw material for their creations, she worked a great deal with new plays and budding writers at a crucial stage of their development. In the cases of some she was unquestionably responsible for their success—I think of Brendan Behan, Shelagh Delaney, Stephen Lewis—but I'm not sure that, in the long-term, her influence was ultimately good for any of their talents.

It might well be argued that her promotion of Brendan Behan alone was justification enough for her methods. But I have never ceased to wonder whether that wayward Irish genius would not have achieved considerably more if, instead of taking the untidy and palpably unfinished script of *The Hostage* and by dint of her own emendations, improvisations and exuberant direction making a wild commercial success of it, she had returned it to him for the further hard work it undoubtedly needed. Behan, more than most writers, was in need of a rigorous discipline if he was ever to become a genuine professional. Joan Littlewood, with the best of intentions, made it all too easy for him; she made him money for his amateurism when, as it turned out, just about the last things he needed were, first, the idea that anything he cared to scribble in a relatively sober moment would serve, and second, the easy money supply that bought him the drink that ruined and ultimately killed him.

It could have happened anyway. The fact stands, however, that Behan wrote nothing else of consequence, and it is significant that no new writing talent nurtured by Miss Littlewood's Theatre Workshop has ever notably flourished elsewhere. Miss Littlewood herself, come to that, has never flourished other than with her own company and she has never wanted to—apart from the débâcle of the West End musical, *Twang*. Her kind of theatre is not my kind of theatre, but what is undeniable is that she has always been totally dedicated to it. Even in her heyest day, her name was not to be found on other managements' playbills. Offers there may have been from the trendier West End impresarios, but she never sought them.

She may not be entirely unique in that. But she is unusual. Most directors, even though particularly associated with one specific theatre or company (and nearly every subsidised theatre, for instance, is under the control of a director), will take whatever

139

opportunities may be going to do an 'outside' job. It's a game much subject to the vicissitudes of fashion, and even the top directors can rarely count on making a lifetime career of it, so they're wise to capitalise on whatever demand they may be in.

What they will also do, if they can, is to work for a piece of the action—say, two-and-a-half per cent of the gross. (Directors' percentages can be as low as one per cent or as much as five per cent for someone in high demand.) Working for a straight fee is obviously more advantageous in the case of a flop—but they don't knowingly get involved with flops, and simple arithmetic shows that a play filling an average-sized theatre for two or three months and taking £50,000 to £60,000 at the box-office will, in that time, return a two-and-a-half per cent director £1,250 to £1,500 which would be generous fees to directors on West End productions. A director in demand and working on percentage might easily have two or three of his productions running concurrently in London and would be beginning to make a respectable living. The gamble, therefore, is always worth taking if the chance is there, since a fee man is going to have to work very hard indeed—and be given the *opportunity* to work very hard indeed, getting several commissions in the course of a year—in order to make that respectable living. Except for those contracted to the larger subsidised theatres, less than a dozen directors could count on that. The others would be lucky to knock up a couple of thousand a year, and outside the West End mainstream—in 'fringe' theatres, club theatres and repertory theatres—the fees come so low (£75 to £150 a production) that a director with no other source of income could hardly survive.

At the top end of the percentage scale, of course, it can be quite a gravy train. The few weeks' initial work on a production can bring an income for years, with no further effort beyond the occasional sharpening rehearsal, understudy rehearsal or cast-change rehearsal. Peter Cotes, the original director of *The Mouse-trap* in 1952, is usually quoted as the supreme example of a director's luck with a percentage; and rightly so. On a straight fee at the time he might have got about £350. After a few years of the run, the manager, Peter Saunders, tried to buy out his per-centage contract for £2,000, but Cotes wisely hung on and must, by now, be running up to £30,000 on the job, even though *The Mousetrap* has never been in a large theatre.

Though lucky in regard to that particular play, Cotes has been generally unlucky in other respects, suffering more than most from the spins of the wheel of 'fashionableness'. Like Joan Littlewood (though wholly *unlike* her as a director), he has always been happiest working with his own group of actors and running his own theatre. But his indifference to trendiness, perhaps coupled with his solid experience, has made him an unlikely candidate for the Arts Council grants that seem to be necessary in such enterprises nowadays. At the same time he has generally displayed too independent a temperament to ingratiate himself with vitally important managements: his insistence on sticking to the terms of his original contract for *The Mousetrap*, for instance, brought about a rift with Saunders (always a hard bargainer in money matters), who was to become President of the Society of West End Theatre Managers, and he had also antagonised the late Hugh Beaumont* of H M Tennent Ltd, when Tennents were the management that dominated the commercial theatre. This has meant that Cotes, though among the best directors we have for certain types of drama. (Ibsen, Strindberg and the psychological thriller have seemed to me his particular specialities), has been obliged in recent years to work largely under his own management.

In fact, of the directors who were in demand at the time of *The Mousetrap*, very few are represented in the West End even occasionally today. Frith Banbury continues to work intermittently, usually under his own management. Peter Glenville has for some years worked mainly in America. John Fernald was, for a time, principal of the Royal Academy of Dramatic Art, later ran a university theatre and theatre school in America and, since his return, seems to have directed mainly in Scandinavia. The rest have slipped into oblivion.

It may be hard to imagine that today's top directors—men, for example, like Peter Wood, William Gaskill, Michael Blakemore, John Dexter, Ronald Eyre and even Peter Hall—who have already had some years at the top, will have vanished from the scene altogether in another ten or fifteen years. But, on the record of the past, that is their likely fate. Their distinguished contemporaries

* See page 156.

among actors will simply have graduated to playing older roles, and their distinguished contemporaries in other professions will be judges, consultants, chairmen of boards and cabinet ministers, or will perhaps have retired with lavish pensions. The directors will not even be collecting royalties from the sales of acting texts and the performances of plays on which they may have originally collaborated considerably in the writing, or at least have offered the ideas and suggestions that led to the plays' successes, for such copyrights belong to the playwrights. Very few playwrights indeed acknowledge contractually the help they get from directors. It's a tough life. Tough and short.

WORDS IN 15
THEIR MOUTHS

The late William Shakespeare probably got about a tenner for *Hamlet*. And any successful dramatist of his day who hadn't been able to cut himself in for a share of the box-office would have made little more—probably even less—from writing a play. Today, an Alan Ayckbourn piece on a three-year run, would net its author upwards of £100,000 for starters. And, to go right up to the top money-spinner of them all, when a new comedy by Neil Simon rolls out of his typewriter at least a million dollars is lined up to slip into his bank account.

The difference that 400 years have made in the earnings of top dramatists is only minutely attributable to the diminishing value of money. The big change came about with the establishment of the royalty system. The progress to that position was gradual, beginning with a seventeenth-century arrangement whereby authors were paid the profits (that is, the box-office takings *less* the theatre's running costs) from three performances of their plays—usually, the third, sixth and ninth. In those days, the sum might be as much as £50 or as little as £5 a night. Things had picked up somewhat by the latter part of the eighteenth century, when the author of a hit staged by David Garrick at Drury Lane could get as much as £1,000. But that was *it*. There were no subsequent payments, no recognition of further rights even for provincial performances. And, when the Copyright Act of the 1830s at last arrived, it took some decades to have beneficial effectiveness.

The position until virtually the dawn of our own century, when a royalty system became generally accepted, was that successful playwrights received considerably less than the successful actors who needed the playwrights' work in order to be successful themselves. Nowadays, the reverse is true; which seems as it should be.

In the West End, the playwright begins with a five per cent share of the box-office gross, rising to seven-and-a-half and ten per cent when the takings pass an agreed figure. With a successful play, the dramatist's income from that source—according to the capacity of the theatre and the volume of business—could run anywhere from £1,000 to £10,000 per week. And that is just the beginning. There are additional prospects.

There will, for instance, be the continuing royalties on repertory and amateur productions once the play is released for general performance. Even at an average of only £50 a week, these could add up to a few thousand. There is also the chance of a New York run, which would earn the dramatist as much as the London run, even if it were only half as long; followed by the back-up of American touring and amateur rights, which would produce five to ten times the income from those sources in Britain.

Other foreign rights—and there is a healthy market on the continent for British successes—could add another £5,000 a year for a few years, and the film rights could be sold for anything from £5,000 (unusually low for a *successful* play) to £75,000. There are also the royalties from publication of the play, which would bring only a few hundred pounds—unless there is a US publication as well, and especially if the play should be adopted as a set text in schools. Robert Bolt's *A Man for All Seasons* for example, has sold well over half a million copies—but that *is* unusual. One way and another, the author of a hit play with everything going for it could run up a quarter of a million pounds.

There are, of course, outgoings as well. Taxes, naturally, would skim off a lot. The writer's agent will take ten per cent of the earnings, pre-tax; the West End management that originally staged the play and set it on the road to the bonanza will also have a whole string of percentages contractually due to them (20 per cent of anything from television or the cinema, and $33\frac{1}{3}$ per cent of repertory royalties are usual); and the New York management will be in for an even higher cut of subsidiary benefits over there. Even so, the amount remaining to the dramatist is not hay. And, since a successful dramatist tends not to have only single successes, he is likely to build up, over the years, a repertoire of continuing earners keeping him in the 'millionaire class' without actually being Neil Simon.

144

There is a false impression abroad that even successful plays do not bring an author as much money as film scripts. I had this impression myself and remember innocently asking Christopher Fry how much more, proportionately, he had received for writing the screenplays of such epics as *Ben Hur, Barabbas* and *The Bible* than he had had from a play such as *The Lady's Not For Burning*. I had put the question the wrong way around: the play had been much more lucrative.

So why the perpetual complaint from writers that the theatre doesn't provide a decent living, and that they cannot therefore be blamed for writing instead for films and television? The answer to that is that the complaint doesn't come from *successful* stage dramatists, of whom there are relatively few. There could be a hundred British plays a year staged in the West End (far fewer than that recently). But only a small handful of them could be regarded as anywhere near as successful as the hypothetical example I have been going on about. Counting the repertories of the National and Royal Shakespeare, but not the 'fringe', there are, at the moment of writing (early 1977), 35 non-musical plays available in London. Subtracting the revivals and the importations from Europe and America, 16 are British originals, of which no more than eight are in the hit category with prospects of a two-year run—if they haven't achieved it already, as, indeed, four of them have. Eight playwrights with prospects of making fortunes.

There are riches at the top, and there's always room up there. But not many make it. And a play that runs for only a few weeks, or perhaps a month of two, is unlikely to attract the fringe benefits of repertory, amateur, foreign, film and television productions, so the author would be fortunate to get as much as £1,000 for his work, most of it made up of his option money and various advances on other rights that, in the circumstances of West End failure, will lead to nothing more. He could get as much for a one-hour, one-off television play, and earn ten times as much from film-scripting, although neither of these markets is any easier for a beginner to break into.

Honest theatrical managers, who recognise that the continuing health of the theatre must depend ultimately on its attracting and keeping the best writing talents available, will admit that playwrights, below the hit level, have a poor deal. In the case of playwrights struggling to get established there is a strong argument—which many managers would support—for upping the 'advance', and compensating by keeping the royalty percentage at five per cent up to a higher gross before graduating to seven-and-a-half and ten per cent. This would ensure that a writer whose work was deemed to be worth putting on did get a respectable sum for it, even if, in the event, it wasn't a commercial success. Under the present system, the production of a play could be capitalised at around £45,000, of which the writer receives only a few hundred pounds and is thus obliged, willy-nilly, to share in the management's gamble.

Not many playwrights hit the jackpot first time, or even have the opportunity of doing so. It is hard to say how many who have a potentially valuable talent are discouraged from trying again because of the economic pressure. If I think that there are fewer who are so discouraged than is commonly suggested by those agitating for a better deal for playwrights, that is not because I want to deny them a better deal, but because I do not believe there is all that much valuable talent about.

The Royal Court—which might be generally thought to represent the best chance a new writer has of getting a play staged—has 600 or 700 scripts a year submitted for consideration. Perhaps a dozen of them are staged, and I'm not being wilfully spiky in saying that, judging from the ones we actually see, the hundreds turned down by presumably sound play-readers must be pretty ghastly. Commercial managements are similarly inundated with scripts, and only rarely are any found from new writers to merit serious consideration for production; although some show sufficient promise to warrant helpful letters being despatched to their authors urging them to try again. The work of new playwrights that does get produced has usually come about as a result of such encouraging noises from managements and their play-readers. A major management puts a submitted script through three readers. The good opinion of two of them would mean the boss himself taking a look, and in the first place the play has probably come through an agent who may also have done some encouraging of the aspiring dramatist.

If you think you're a playwright, the best thing to do is to get an agent—or try to. A play submitted by an agent whose judgment

146

is respected gets more careful consideration—naturally enough, since it is assumed that some sorting out has already been done, that the chaff has been dispensed with and all that remains is to assess the quality of the wheat. If a good agent (Margaret Ramsay is universally regarded as the best) is prepared to take you on and submit your work, you're almost home and dried; so it follows that getting a top agent to handle your play is just as difficult as getting a top management to produce it.

None of it is easy. I am not sure that any playwright of conse-quence in recent years has sailed straight into the West End with a first play, although Peter Shaffer may have done it with *Five Finger Exercise*. In the case of most, it is a progression through radio and television, or possibly through provincial theatres or the 'fringe'. Robert Bolt, Harold Pinter and John Arden are among those who wrote first for radio; Peter Nichols, Tom Stoppard and David Mercer had plays on television long before their work was produced on the stage; Christopher Hampton, who 'took off' while still at university, had his first play, *When Did You Last See My Mother?*, done at Oxford (subsequently at the Royal Court in 1964); David Hare and Trevor Griffiths arrived via 'fringe' theatres; Arnold Wesker's first plays were staged at the Belgrade, Coventry; Alan Ayckbourn's early work was produced 'in-the-round' at Scarborough (where, indeed, most of it still is, initially). Indeed Ayckbourn's first play in London, *Mr Whatnot*, was a dud that got no further than a bleak week or two at the Arts. So Ayckbourn is the most striking example of that rarity, a talent that wasn't immediately evident to either London reviewers or the West End public, and he was so depressed by his *Mr Whatnot* experience that he thinks he would have abandoned writing but for the encouragement of Margaret Ramsay and his initial mentor, the late Stephen Joseph, at Scarborough. But look at him now: his big subsequent successes have been in an entirely different vein from that twee early piece, he's had as many as five plays in the West End at the same time and has only sniffed failure in the case of the 'book' for the musical, *Jeeves*.

So, aspiring playwright, keep plugging away, even if they *don't* raise the option money: the jackpot can be like winning the pools (except for the taxes). The only thing to beware of, then, is an agent who also handles actors and directors: he'll be tempted to tie

147

those other clients of his into a package deal for a management, and they may not be strictly to the advantage of your play. In which case, you'll have to help him to resist the temptation. Come to think of it, you'll be big enough, then, to *insist*. Or if there's some small print you hadn't noticed, you could try breaking his arm.

THE CASTING 16
COUCHES

I shouldn't be surprised if this were a very short chapter. Well, come *on* now—you didn't think I was going to name names, did you? Everybody, not only in show business but in show business especially, is frank to the point of embarrassment about their sex lives these days. And if people are shacked up without benefit of clergy, as the old term was, it's rarely a public secret let alone a private one. Only the gossip columns still indulge in such hinty euphemisms as 'her very close friend'—and that, presumably, is just to excite the prurient conjecture of their country readers, and not, usually, because the very close friends would mind a more explicit turn of phrase. Suddenly it's all an open book. That is when the relationship is just for fun. When it might be considered that on one side it's for profit, that's different. And if I don't take cognisance of that difference I'm going to be the lawyers' favourite writer.

That's one reason why this is a short chapter. Another is that, really, the casting couch just isn't as busy—or, rather, it isn't as decisive—as it used to be. This is partly the result of the climate of the times, which might be called permissive or dissolute according to your point of view, and the old saw about not buying a cow when milk is so cheap applies. It is also partly because nowadays authors and directors are greatly more concerned about the quality of performance on the stage rather than the quality of performance in bed.

It was very different once upon a high old time in the earlier days of Hollywood, when the purity imposed so laughably upon the moving pictures by the Hays Office Code and assorted Leagues of Decency was lavishly counterpointed off-screen in the orgiastic party revels in all those mink-lined mansions that sprang up around the film capital. In those days, though, acting talent was almost the last thing a girl needed to get into movies—even to become a star. Somehow people didn't notice, or didn't care, that the standard of actual *acting* by the goddesses of the silver screen was abysmal, but nowadays when those antique reels are run on late-night television it is impossible *not* to notice.

Films were shot in non-sequential 'takes' whose direction was counted in seconds rather than minutes, each one of them done scores of times and the finished product pieced together from those that produced the fewest winces in the editing room. I'm not much of a film buff and I'm not sure when all this began to change. But there is plainly a connecting link between the extended duration of 'takes', the economies that restricted the number of times they could be done, the consequential need for more identifiable acting talent—and the phasing out of the influence of the casting couch.

In the theatre, though less strikingly, there is a similar contrast between 'then' and 'now', the necessity for talent being generally imposed by Equity rules that have the effect of restricting casual entry into the profession, and a keener public appreciation of good acting. It would be naïve to pretend that there are no actresses around who didn't get there through being generously accommodating. It still happens. I do know of one willowy blonde who was starred in a terrible Shaftesbury Avenue comedy only a year or two ago entirely because she was the current mistress of the show's principal backer, a sporty gentleman of wealth and title who, in fact, kept the play on with transfusions of money on her behalf until it eventually became a moderate success. Nevertheless, since the arrangement was fairly well-known in theatrical circles at the time, it probably did the young woman more harm than good— for her sponsor has since moved on to another girl friend (not in show business) and our 'star' has found it tough to come by any further work. Now, if she had played it straight, the chances are that she would be working as regularly as she had been before on the more modest level to which her talent fitted her.

It is common enough to hear the bitchy speculation that so-and-so *must* be sleeping with somebody important to account for her success. In the theatre at least (I speak not of television) it is rarely true in such blatantly business-deal terms as were alluded to in the previous paragraph. There are a great many cases in which actresses have close relationships with the directors and producers who employ them or the playwrights who write for them, but in nearly all the cases that occur to me, the relationship has developed from the professional association rather than inspired it. A young actress who hits the top with what seems suspicious speed, has more likely just had some good luck going for her; and if she stays there, she has talent going for her as well.

More often than not, anyway, the more scurrilous stories have no foundation other than in the jealous imaginations of the people who spread them around. Show business is notorious for both its jealousies and its bitchiness, and this is one of the areas where these two peevish attributes get slanderously together. No one without a close eye to bedroom keyholes can be positive about these matters. And, if I say that the stories are most likely to be true where they concern, on the one hand, producers and directors whose professional achievements are less than distinguished, and on the other, actresses who are clearly destined for swift oblivion, someone is sure to come up with an apparently authentic anecdote in contradiction.

It so happens, for instance, that one of the young actresses who has made the greatest impact on the British theatre in the last few years, makes no secret of her sexual availability, It further happens —and this is a report that comes from too many people close to the source to be doubted—that a girl who has become one of the biggest Hollywood 'names' of the decade, left her East Coast acting school with the coolly confident announcement to her classmates, 'I'm going to be a *star*, and I don't care who I have to fuck to do it.'

The point is, though, that both these girls happen to be very good actresses indeed. There are hundreds of others who are as promiscuous as the one or share the cynical view of the other. But in these two cases, it wasn't sex but talent that got them there. Or, anyway, keeps them there.

MADLY 17
GAY

If you don't mind an old joke, or a familiar quotation . . . well, it *is* about the best on this particular subject . . .

Squelching a young actress who purported to be outraged by the attachment of an elderly actor to the young leading-man in their company, the devastating Mrs Patrick Campbell is reputed to have said: 'Does it *really matter* what they do—so long as they don't do it in the street and frighten the horses?'

And, in most respects, of course, it doesn't matter in the least in the theatre. Even the general public, except in especially cloistered villages, seem to care little or nothing about whether a man or woman is a homosexual, unless, perhaps, when they are startled by the sudden public admission that someone previously thought to be no end of a masculine fellow is, in fact, a man's man —as it were.

When a well-known store arbitrarily sacked a shop manager who had been reckless, or frank, enough to admit in a television programme that he was a homosexual, the 'gay people' organised a picketing of that store. And public sympathy, as far as I could divine, was with the victimised employee. The Campaign for Homosexual Equality probably has the support of most people, however certain its parliamentary candidates may be of losing their deposits.

What I find curious about the CHE, though, is that there are so many show-business names listed on its notepaper. If there is one area of life in which homosexuals achieved equality—to say the very least—long, long ago, it is surely show business. Homosexuality never held anyone back as actor or writer, director or designer or dancer. Rather, as a matter of fact, the contrary. And *that* may give some cause for alarm. Especially to the extent to which it is often so vociferously denied: whether it is the Shakespearian scholar, Dr A L Rowse writing an article for *The Times* contending that 'there is no homosexuality in Shakespeare whatever', or the lengths to which certain actors, and even convincing female impersonators (who are homosexuals almost to a man, or whatever), will go to conceal their proclivities from the public.

This is so even among the young and supposedly 'enlightened' generation of entertainers: a couple of male rock singers who spring readily to mind make a great point on the stage of sexual ambiguity, and are clearly the sort of chaps who give coots such a bad name. But off-stage for public consumption, they take care to be seen and photographed as often as possible with *girls*. Evidently they have no great faith in the changed climate of public opinion since the days when it would have been virtual professional suicide for, say, Ivor Novello to have told the truth about himself.

It is just *possible* that they may be right. For this reason I shall have to pick on dead people for any names I may name here: there may no longer be obloquy attaching to homosexuality, but if anyone chooses to deny it and I don't happen actually to have the pictures (which, of course, I don't, any more than I have, or would want to have, in respect of *anyone's* private life), the published statement of it might very likely be held by a jury to be libellous and could cost me an arm and a leg. It's probably significant that *politicians* don't admit it—not, anyway, until it becomes public knowledge, when they quickly sign up in support of the CHE. So we'd best stick to Ivor Novello, and Proust and Gide, and Hugh Beaumont and Noël Coward.

The last-named pair died in 1973, and though it could hardly be said that their deaths brought the edifice of homosexual domination of the British theatre tumbling down, the loss of these two pillars of it inevitably made the structure look a little less secure. The influence wielded by the two men, the man of acumen and the man of talent, did not at all accord with their public reputations and was, it must be said at once, of different kind.

Hugh 'Binkie' Beaumont and Noël Coward were friends of long standing, professionally associated for over 30 years, moving in the same show-biz circles and within the network of homosexuality that covers so much of theatrical life. Coward's last

154

'public' appearance in London was at one of Binkie's parties (one of those gatherings of which it might be said that there were more fag ends walking around the room than there were in the ashtrays). And they died within a few days of each other. But to link them beyond those superficial facts, as was done at the time, would be to invite misleading inferences.

Coward's influence, from the point of view of his homosexuality, was indirect; so far as it existed at all, inadvertent; no more than an aura. He was a public figure who flaunted his personality and gave prodigally of his wit, and whose influence stemmed entirely from his talent, Though a great deal of wrist-flapping went on around him, and rather more mincing than you'd see in a day at a hamburger factory, and though there were 'boy friends' (one, of course, in particular) who figured in his shows, their presence was incidental and the 'casting couch' was never the seedy factor it was in his era with many heterosexual producers. Coward was too much, and too instinctively, the professional. The public did not, in any case, know of his homosexuality. And most would even have doubted it. Furthermore, that element of his personality did not pervade his work, nor greatly impinge upon it: the 'sex' situations in his plays were convincing enough, and although nearly all of them could be played quite as plausibly as homosexual situations, the same might easily be said of many plays written by heterosexuals.

The public knew Beaumont hardly at all. His name never appeared on playbills and rarely in the press. But in the business his shrewdness was legendary, his suavity unrufflable—and his influence, not all of it bad, pervasive. He was the managing director of H M Tennent Ltd, sat on the boards of other managements who owned theatres and presented plays. Moreover, for a lengthy period after the second world war, he came closer than anyone—before or since—to establishing a theatrical monopoly in the West End, not only by the number of theatres directly or indirectly within his control but by the number of important authors, directors, actors and actresses under contract to him. His power was immense, and for that reason—for that reason only—his homosexuality was important.

In a book about Broadway,* William Goldman wrote baldly

* *The Season* (Harcourt Brace, 1969).

that 'Arthur Miller is the only major American playwright since World War II who has not been associated with homosexuality.' In England we might make more exceptions (though I suppose only their hairdressers would know for sure). But that may be simply because we have had more major playwrights. Much the same might be said of directors and actors. At theatrical parties it isn't only the girls who call each other 'darling'. Inevitably the off-stage ambience has been reflected on the stage.

The majority of the directors employed by Beaumont were homosexuals, and the majority of the actors they picked were homosexuals also. There were, of course, notable exceptions. One of them was the director, Tyrone Guthrie, who put on record the crucial fact which everyone else knew but no one else had said: 'More than any other single individual he [Beaumont] can make or break the career of almost any worker in the British professional theatre.' Workers in the theatre sometimes found out with mind-numbing speed the truth of that 'make or break' contention. One young director, not a homosexual but nevertheless engaged to direct a Tennent production, had a disagreement over interpretation on the second day of rehearsals with the leading actor (who *was* a homosexual); within hours the director was taken off the production, being politely told that his approach was 'unsuitable'. Youthful, reckless and angry, he was incautious enough to argue the point with Beaumont with special reference to his inability to direct a 'pouf' production of an ostensibly virile play; whereat he was told, equally politely, that he would never work in London again, and indeed he had great difficulty in ever doing so. Regarded at the time as an up-and-coming man, he abruptly stopped coming up.

As Guthrie also said, 'The iron fist was wrapped in fifteen pastel-shaded velvet gloves, but no one who has known Binkie can for a moment fail to realise that there is an iron fist.' Beaumont was always polite. The smile never left his grey eyes when he blandly told one actress, who had withdrawn from a Tennent production on a point of principle, 'My dear, the last actress who opposed me like this has not worked in London since.' It was a threat he was fond of making; the number of occasions on which it was carried out can be only a matter of conjecture. But Binkie was always capable, by nature and by influence, of making it stick.

156

It is irksome to discuss homosexuality in the theatre. It seems so, well, I mean, *illiberal*. There is no reason why a homosexual should not be as good an actor—and that, after all, is what would seem most to matter—as one who has women lining up down the street. But rampant homosexuality in the upper echelons of the theatrical 'establishment' is certainly of concern to actors who don't happen to be inclined in that direction. At the height of the Beaumont influence, many a young actor eager to get on pretended to be 'bent' even when he wasn't. Beaumont's theatre auditions (not to mention the unofficial 'auditions' at the London house in Lord North Street, where Binkie held court reclining in pastel pyjamas in black silk bed sheets) were famous for young things hopefully camping it up. One of the more familiar stories was of a good-looking young actor, 'up' for a juvenile role, who completed a successful audition, much approved by the watchers in the stalls, but felt constrained when the lights went up to step down to the footlights and say cheekily, 'I think I ought to tell you, Mr Beaumont, that I'm not queer—but it doesn't show from the front.'

The yarn is probably apocryphal, but the fact that it was so long in circulation was indicative of the general feeling about those auditions, although actually, except in really blatantly 'gay' cases, it *doesn't* 'show from the front' one way or the other. This makes it hard to say, other than from personal acquaintance and informed report, whether the incidence of real and counterfeit homosexuality in the theatre is in decline, now that the condition has fewer advantages. It so happens that one of the most successful theatrical managements of the post-Beaumont era is presided over by a homosexual. But there is no evidence that either the plays he presents or the actors presented in them are predominantly homosexual. And this, of course, is the only aspect of the matter that is of public concern.

Looking back on his earliest days in the theatre, John Osborne wrote:[*]

> *The first thing that struck me about working in the theatre was the equality between the sexes: equal pay, billing, and no favours asked, expenses shared. The other was the universal*

[*] *The Observer*, February 6, 1977.

domination at every level by poufs. It certainly hasn't changed much in this respect. I have been hag-ridden by these treacherous monsters ever since.

That is one man's experience which I am bound to note. It is incontrovertible that the theatre, for one reason or another, attracts more homosexual males than other areas of life. Some think this is because of the opportunity for feminine-type exhibitionism, others feel it to be because the precariousness of the employment does not appeal to, or retain its hold upon, men with girls to woo, marry and support. But my impression is that the proportion is marginally diminishing and certainly that homosexuality, real or counterfeit, is no longer so essential to 'getting on'. The younger actors rising to the top seem to be as masculine, on the whole, as their predecessors appeared to be in the eyes of their innocent admirers.

This could well be because the most important of the younger playwrights are heterosexual and are able to write about man–woman relationships other than from hearsay, and the situations and characters demand to be played with the same accuracy. There is still the occasional play in which women are depicted with that peculiarly vicious bitchiness of which only the shoulder-chipped, disaffected invert is capable. But homosexual playwrights are free, since the abolition in 1968 of play censorship, to write frankly of homosexual relationships, and homosexual actors are free to appear in them. Both do. Things seem generally to be moving in the right directions. At least we are getting to know where we're at.

THE LOVED 18
ONES

On the Sunday before the Royal Shakespeare Company's production of *Hedda Gabler*, with Glenda Jackson in the title-role, opened in London in 1975, the principal 'arts' feature in *The Observer* was a full-page interview/article by John Heilpern headed, 'The Magic of Glenda May'. ('May' is Miss Jackson's middle name.) The stunning effect of the 'magic' on Heilpern was occasionally to fracture his syntax but he was, nevertheless, able to set down all the received facts:

> *What's so fascinating about Glenda Jackson is that she explodes so many sides of the conventional image. Almost everything about her contradicts the popular idea of what a modern actress should be. It seems that she's totally without vanity or pretension. And something equally rare among actors: totally unsentimental. Her two Oscars and more than 40 other awards don't seem to matter a damn to her. She's been called fearsome and cold; very ambitious. But in truth acting is far from essential to her life . . . Yet she's become a star capable of filling any theatre or raising vast amounts of finance to back new films . . . but* the finest actress of her generation *has an apparent ordinariness so strong that it seems to fly in the face of her talent . . .*

The finest actress of her generation? The phrase leaps out of the page as any opinion stated as a fact always will for the reader sensitive to such infiltrations; and yet Heilpern's opinion *is* taken as fact in many places; among the public; among the reviewers. Never mind that her performances do not necessarily accord with the opinion-fact. When *Hedda Gabler* came up for review, opinions were, in fact, mixed:

> . . . *this interpretation makes Hedda's drama one fought out mainly with herself. It is her own womb that she loathes, not her suburban companions. This gives Miss Jackson outstanding opportunities. She walks restlessly up and down the stage, on the edge of vomiting almost the entire evening. It is a memorable vision.*
>
> (*Harold Hobson*, Sunday Times)

> *This charmless Hedda is an unlikely lure for three men and a sad companion for the audience.*
>
> (*Robert Cushman*, The Observer)

> *Miss Jackson looks solid and sensible, although when alone she groans and grunts from frustration. Hedda's sardonic sense of humour is given full rein; indeed I have never known this play to yield so many laughs.*
>
> (*Frank Marcus*, Sunday Telegraph)

> *Glenda Jackson . . . has given Hedda a cold, reptilian quality which is almost clammy to watch . . . Meeting each crisis with twitching facial expressions, flashing smiles as welcoming as an Exit sign, impatiently drumming her fingers as she tries to suppress her permanent boredom, she seems as cosy as the hostess of a concentration camp. As a technical achievement it is certainly interesting, but it removes from Hedda that sensitivity and fastidiousness which make her conduct justifiable.*
>
> (*Milton Shulman*, Evening Standard)

> *The clue to Miss Jackson's heroine is that General Gabler wanted a boy. In gait and voice she is a mannish creature . . . The great question for any actress is to reveal the private workings of Hedda's mind . . . Miss Jackson's approach is to play the character on a gradually rising wave of nausea . . .*
>
> (*Irving Wardle*, The Times)

160

What, however, makes the reading so original is that Miss Jackson gives us not a woman driven to suicide by her stifling provincial environment but a cowardly bungler whose few positive acts always misfire . . . It is an astonishing performance . . .

(*Michael Billington*, The Guardian)

Let me confess to bitter disappointment in Glenda Jackson's Hedda Gabler . . . One of the great female roles, it demands an actress who can suggest the intense inner life of a suppressed hysteric . . . Miss Jackson has something of Hedda's aristocratic hauteur, but otherwise relies on a compendium of tricks . . .

(*John Barber*, Daily Telegraph)

To some extent these reviewers might be thought to be describing different plays and different performances, and while cynical and cursory readers of reviews may believe that this is the usual thing, it is not, in my experience, so. Strikingly disparate reactions of this kind only occur in these specific circumstances, when the reviewers are confronted by an actor or actress of great though mysterious reputation (which they have themselves, at least partly, created), and who therefore impels their respectful attention for an interpretation of a major role that is at odds with their previous view of it.

I do not altogether agree with the last of my quotations, John Barber's comment, but I find it the most understandable. Barber at least gives an impression of knowing what *Hedda Gabler* is about, while some of the others seem to be groping for some way of justifying an extraordinary performance which, because it is given by this woman of reputation ('the finest actress of her generation'), has to be seriously considered. I think Barber is wrong in attributing to Miss Jackson 'a compendium of tricks', but it is interesting that he was 'disappointed'. Disappointment follows expectation, and even he, it seems, had so accepted the general view of Miss Jackson that he had expected her to be able to play 'one of the great female roles'.

What Miss Jackson actually *does* is rarely related to what she is expected to do (which is to be sensationally good) or to what she

161

is later reputed to have done (which is to have *been* sensationally good). Her reputation as a 'great actress' is now so unshakeably established as opinion-fact that it no longer matters whether she is or not. Reviewers approach her performances with the opinion-fact as their basic assumption and write about her in the light of this received hypothesis.

The public, guided by the written word, do not question it—anymore than they would dispute that the Post Office Tower is a tall building—and she is, therefore, a box-office magnet. Impresarios, putting the written word and the consequential commercial appeal together like two and two, go right along. Thus, less than a couple of weeks after the 'mixed' reception of Miss Jackson's Hedda Gabler in London (which had followed a similarly 'mixed' reception in the United States), Philip Oakes in the *Sunday Times* was quoting the film producer, Richard Fleischer, talking about the picture he was about to make of the life of Sarah Bernhardt:

> *The challenge of the film is that it's about the greatest actress who ever lived* [another opinion-fact, by the way, which is now part of theatrical mythology, though no longer demonstrable one way or the other] *and to convince an audience you have to produce the greatest actress now living ... With Glenda in the film I feel quite secure.*

When reviewers, public, producers and accountants are all in such accord, there is no way in which Miss Jackson's status can be seriously questioned. To offer a dissenting opinion might even be thought to be gratuitously insulting. My own view of Glenda Jackson as an actress—when, making a monumental attempt at objectivity, I close ears and eyes to the chorus of acclamation—is that she is no more, if certainly no less, than ordinarily competent. Why is the general view so different?

I'm not sure that I can give a convincing answer to that. But I think it has been helpful to her career—in an age in which commentators have been generally 'anti-glamour-girl'—that she is neither pretty nor beautiful and has not pretended to be either. Almost inevitably she played Elizabeth I, a part in which no plain actress can fail, and she played it on television to audiences of

162

millions. (What I should regard as her failure in *Hedda Gabler* was due, at least in part, to the fact that she was palpably miscast as a woman who, in any plausible reading of the play, is an absolute stunner.)

She is also singularly intelligent, which is also helpful in an age in which the trendier pundits of the media have been eager to promote ladies who are something more than 'sex symbols'. When Miss Jackson talks to interviewers of press or television she eschews actressy airs and talks as a woman whose opinions are worth listening to—which, considering what the interviewers usually run into, rather bowls them over. She has cultivated the impression of seeming aloof from the commercial aspects and fruits of success—which is quite a trick when you nip about in a Mercedes rather than a Mini. Further, her dedication to her profession has been backed by a shrewdness of choice—in the years since she has been able to be choosy—in the parts she plays and the people she works with. Sometimes, nowadays, she is wrong, but at this stage, so long as she is not wrong too often, it no longer matters. For Glenda Jackson, partly because of what she is and partly because of what has been written about her, is one of 'the loved ones'.

She is, indeed, the major example of 'the loved one' that the business currently has to offer, which is why I have gone on about her at somewhat inordinate length. There are others, of course: those about whom there are received opinion-facts which have little to do with what they do or have done. They get good notices most of the time and never actually get bad ones, although sometimes surprise may be expressed that they are not as good as they are supposed and expected to be. Even when disenchantment sets in, as in the case of the director, Joan Littlewood (a 'loved one' from way back), the unfavourable notices will be edged with regret that such a great talent should have come to this.

Vanessa Redgrave and Maggie Smith—to name two stars who are better actresses than any of the loved ones but are not themselves, in this context, loved ones—get good and bad notices as they deserve them. Helen Mirren, on the other hand, does not get bad notices: the standard opinion-fact about her is that she is the irresistibly voluptuous sex-pot of classical drama whose radiation can melt a man at twenty paces; she endeared herself to reviewers when one of their number, who had approached her in an hotel room after one of her earliest sexy roles at Stratford-upon-Avon, returned to the foyer clutching a hard-kicked crotch; some time later she proved herself brave enough, independent enough and literate enough to write a letter to *The Guardian* attacking the spendthrift policies of the Royal Shakespeare Company which employed her; since then, at least, and forever, Helen Mirren is 'a loved one'.

Similarly Vivien Merchant: who is supposed to have very sexy eyes, very sexy legs, very sexy everything. Her manner of acting is, with these striking advantages, a model of restraint. Miss Merchant's art is all tiny, studied gestures and mysterious glances; for her to cross or uncross her legs is an action so significant that it apparently has her admirers leaping in their seats like trout. A cool customer, than whom marble is not more arch, she is usually said to exude a 'veiled sensuality'. I feel miserably deprived, because from me it couldn't be more veiled if she were exuding it in a closed tent, but she has most of the reviewers going for her. I cannot recall that she has ever had a bad notice. Vivien Merchant is a 'loved one'. She and Miss Jackson and Miss Mirren must come very close to being the reviewers' favourite actresses.

It may be, indeed most certainly is, because most reviewers are men that most of 'the loved ones' are women; but not all of them are. A few actors qualify as well, perhaps most notably Robert Morley, whose performances—for reviewers as well as for the public—transcend almost anything he happens to be in; and the same might be said, I think, of Leonard Rossiter. Ever since Rossiter's storming performance in *Arturo Ui*, in which his full repertoire of manic eye-rollings and mouth-twitchings was turned on in a character supposed to be a caricature of Adolf Hitler, reviewers have been extraordinarily pre-disposed in his favour. I cannot imagine that the 1976–77 double-bill of revivals under the title *Frontiers of Farce*—which had first a season at the Old Vic and was then brought into the Criterion—would have been especially well received with anyone but Rossiter in its showiest roles: the works themselves were thin and not very funny (sub-standard pieces by Feydeau and Wedekind), but the reviews went on at such length and so ecstatically about the actor that the in-different quality of the scripts seemed of little consequence. This

164

is very good for Leonard Rossiter who—though the limited and idiosyncratic nature of his performances does not make him easy to cast—is continuously in demand; and it is generally very good for the box-office, as all 'the loved ones' are; but whether it is good for the overall quality of theatre is a different question.

That question, to return to the starting point and Glenda Jackson, was very tellingly dealt with by that splendid actor, Timothy West, when he got back from the world tour with *Hedda Gabler*, in which he played Brack. In an interview with Michael Owen of the London *Evening Standard*, West said:

> '*It's a funny thing going abroad with a play that has one big star like Glenda. The rest of us did tend to be treated like also-rans by the press and public, especially in America. It gets a bit tedious after a time. There was such a rush to the No 1 dressing room. I suppose it's silly in a way, but it does get boring.*
> '*Then the notices arrive and there are four paragraphs about Glenda and possibly one about the rest of us. What I really object to is that it affects people's attitudes to the play.*'

That is about all anyone could object to when confronted with the phenomena of 'the loved ones'. But it is a large and important objection. Reviewers should perhaps be rather more circumspect in the distribution of their affections. There are, of course, more things than that to say about reviewers. What they write is what most people know about the theatre. They really need a longish chapter to themselves.

MATTERS OF 19
OPINION

I'd better watch my words here or I'll lose any chance of getting respectable reviews for this little book. Theatre books are invariably reviewed by theatre reviewers, who tend not to be ruled, on the whole, by the late George Jean Nathan's dictum that people in the brick-throwing business should expect to be hit by a brick or two. Not, as a matter of fact, that I feel there is much need for brick-throwing at reviewers. They seem to me, on the contrary, much under-appreciated, and have reason for their sensitivity. Kind words are not penned about them. They are the people who usually get the blame.

If a play flops, neither the creative people nor the associated business people are going to blame themselves, and probably not each other. The handiest scapegoats are the reviewers. They killed it. Even when they praise, though the plaudits are avidly fallen upon and ransacked for advertising 'quotes', they praise, it is held, for the wrong reasons. They are accused of misunderstanding what authors are trying to say, of paying too much attention to stars and of having no idea what a director does—let alone of whether he has done it well or badly. They are assailed for their lack of 'technical' knowledge, accused of 'writing for effect' and of sacrificing an honest opinion to a smart line, and regarded generally with contempt by nearly everyone in the business, even when this contempt, for politic reasons, may not be publicly expressed.

Some of these complaints may, in some cases, be justified. Most are not, and some are irrelevant, if not downright foolish. 'Technical' knowledge, for example, is no business of reviewers (you don't, as the familiar phrase goes, have to be a chef to judge the quality of a meal), and the one or two who have it and display it are

167

the dullest reviewers. And, if they don't always 'write for effect', I should hope that at least they try—since their first priority is to be read (by others, that is, than those they are writing *about*, who will read them, anyway, whatever they say and however they say it). As for their honesty and integrity, by their lights, I do not believe that any unfavourable opinions (and it is these that people seem to worry about) are ever dishonest, and the so-called 'smart lines' are only likely to occur to the reviewer in the context of the opinion he has already and honestly formed. Occasionally, a *favourable* notice might excite my suspicions—but perhaps unfairly, for no reviewers, to my knowledge, can be bought for money, and probably not many of them for love.

Reviewers who are known to be on friendly terms with players or playwrights sometimes, indeed, go out of their way to treat those friends more harshly than others. This is tough to do and accounts for another of the late George Jean Nathan's famous dicta: 'Show me a critic with a quorum of artists as bosom friends and I will show you a critic who is a hypocrite and a liar.'

But the word I have been using myself is 'reviewer'. They are more usually called critics—theatre critics, drama critics and even dramatic critics (the last inexplicably, for they are rarely in the least dramatic). The work of the critic, however, has always seemed to me a much loftier business than that of the reviewer. Criticism is important stuff, usually found in learned quarterlies and books from university presses, and more often than not unconscionably dull. Reviewing is immediate, a series of impressions, reactions, opinions, often instant and with no great depth, but not, in the case of any reputable reviewer, ill-considered. Criticism is for posterity as much as for today's reader or play-goer; highly detailed, it has wider terms of reference, relating a play to the drama of its time and the life of its time, and these, in turn and by extension, to the drama of all time. Not much of drama, at *any* time, demands or deserves that kind of study. Reviewers perhaps recognise the drama that does; and they will, in writing of it, touch the fringes of criticism, which is as much as their readers ask of them.

Even so, they themselves would seem to prefer to be known as critics, and their professional association is called the Critics' Circle. Founded in 1913 this is a body with no particular power, though it offers some point of contact between theatre managements and the press where agreement can be reached on irksomely trifling matters such as the supply of free programmes to reviewers (as well as the free seats that are traditional). It is also as a result of agreement between the Critics' Circle and theatre managements, and agreement among members of the Critics' Circle themselves, that productions are now attended and reviewed on arbitrary *press nights* and not, as of yore and as news editors would prefer, on *first nights*. There are very few 'first nights' in the old sense in London nowadays, when the first performance is the one that will be reviewed in the next day's newspapers. With the disappearance of so many provincial theatres and the consequent impossibility of 'touring till ready', the first performance is merely the first of a series of 'previews'.

Occasionally, the Critics' Circle is prepared to use a little muscle, as when, for example, a reviewer is arbitrarily removed from a management's invitation list because of his real or imagined hostility. But, except in the case of theatres supported by public money, that is fairly shaky ground for the Critics' Circle, for it is only by traditional privilege, and not as a right, that reviewers attend as guests rather than as paying customers.

There being rarely anything of consequence to discuss, meetings of the Critics' Circle tend to be dreary affairs of the recording of minutes and the deaths of members, the making of plans for the Circle's occasional functions (wine-and-cheese get-togethers or dinners for theatrical personalities), and the trivia of accountancy. They are otherwise largely addressed at length by Ossia Trilling, who writes mainly for European newspapers, is evidently a considerable linguist and greatly interested in the international aspects of theatre, and is forever either suggesting, arranging or attending international critical symposia and conferences, matters which can be depended upon to bore the ears off the rest of the membership. You may be surprised, not to say alarmed, to know that there are over 200 members of the Critics' Circle, of whom about 80 are in the drama section. You have never heard of most of them (*I* have never heard of *some* of them, though I have been around the theatre and its reviewers for some decades now). I suppose only about two dozen of them would have any important influence on either the theatre as an art form or the theatre at the box-office.

169

Influence? Kenneth Tynan has averred that he had more real influence on the theatre while Literary Manager at the National Theatre and adviser to Laurence Olivier than he ever had as a reviewer. I am inclined to doubt that. I think reviewers do have influence of a sort. Even authors and players and directors and managements, who detest as well as despise them, know that; which is probably why they detest them, and why they are invited. Their opinions, if not respected, are wanted. Managements would rather risk bad notices than get none at all. There were a few weeks in the 1950s when the newspapers were on strike and everything that opened in the West End during that period flopped—which was clearly more than a coincidence. Even a bad notice contains the news that the show is on—as Paul Raymond discovered when having seen his *Pyjama Tops* run for six or seven years after getting a unanimous panning, he concluded that he could dispense with the masochism of inviting the reviewers, only to see its successor, *Snatch 69*, flop forthwith. Managements go to great lengths to avoid 'clashes'—two plays opening on the same night—because even those papers that have more than one reviewer usually have space for only one substantial review. In any case, every management wants the paper's Number One reviewer, and few things open in London when the top men are away in Edinburgh for the Festival or in Dublin for the booze. Second-string reviewers are doom, disaster and sudden death. This is not to say they are dishonest, but they are not predisposed to like, and their hostility will be more sharply expressed, for they are usually young, and desperate to make an impression, which is more easily made with pans than with praises.

An exception to this generalisation is, of course, Eric Shorter of the *Daily Telegraph*, who is second-string to John Barber, as he was to Barber's predecessor, W A Darlington, and, as well as offering the shrewd judgments of experience, is more good-natured than anyone has a right to be who spends most of his nights slogging round the provinces. There is not, in fact, much doing for Shorter in London, since, even when there *is* a clash of dates, it is Barber's frequent habit to take in a preview of one of them. This unflagging pair cover lunchtime theatres and 'fringe' activities as well. In the circumstances, it would scarcely be expected that their reviews would be notable for sparkling prose.

But their enthusiasm seems indomitable (anyone who doesn't regard that as a compliment and a tribute should try sitting through a couple of hundred plays a year, most of them rubbish, and see how much enthusiasm survives. Both Barber and Shorter write lucid, down-to-earth, sober notices that I take to be exactly attuned to the *Telegraph* readership.

The *Daily Telegraph* would be regarded as a paper greatly conscious of some strange comprehensive responsibility towards the arts. I am inclined to doubt whether the range of its coverage is nowadays justifiable in terms of reader interest, and I am absolutely certain that the coverage by *The Times* is *not*. It is a question of space and balance. The *Telegraph*, as far as the theatre is concerned, probably covers more things but the space accorded each is in some approximate proportion to the number of its readers likely to be interested in it.

This is hardly true of *The Times*, whose principal critic, Irving Wardle, is quite likely to write as lengthily—I forbear to say as boringly—about some glum lunchtime play in the back-room of some obscure public house on the outskirts of London (where not one in a hundred thousand of *Times* readers is likely to be found dead or alive) as he does about a new production in the commercial West End theatre. It often appears that Wardle's mission in life is entirely to change the lifestyle of *The Times*'s readership in regard to theatregoing. He will not withhold his praise from a play in the commercial theatre that has entertained him. I cannot, however, help feeling that such entertainment comes as a surprise to him. When he describes a piece as 'a typical Shaftesbury Avenue comedy' it is clear that the words are intended to sound pejorative.

This is not to say that Wardle is a bad reviewer. I could wish, myself, that, whatever his views, he were a livelier writer, and displayed more sense of humour—but his style in that respect may be deliberately calculated, for the generality of readers tend to take more seriously a reviewer who writes soberly than one who prefers to inform his criticism with a genial sense of humour and a texture of wit.

Irving Wardle, I find, is the most respected of the reviewers among other reviewers. He is literate and thoughtful. Where his colleagues may be observed jotting only notes during a performance,

Wardle often seems to be writing carefully composed sentences—and paragraphs. And he can be depended upon to turn in a review-essay of up to a thousand words between the fall of a curtain and eleven o'clock. Moreover, he projects his own positive view of the theatre and what it should be. It is not mine, and I suspect it of being a minority view, expressed for and appreciated by only a tiny proportion of *Times* readers—who are themselves, of course, a small enough minority in total.

The complaint is frequently heard among theatre people, by the way, that the newspapers devote a miserably inadequate amount of space to theatre reviews. The opposite opinion is, in fact, the more persuasive. Even the popular tabloids, among whose millions of readers London theatregoers must be an infinitesimal minority, find a few inches to review new productions in the West End. Among the more serious papers, from the *Daily Mail* on up, I have no doubt at all that the number of column inches devoted to the theatre, compared with the number accorded television and the cinema, is entirely disproportionate (to the theatre's advantage) to the comparative reader-interest. Believing as I do that the theatre is more vital, more important and more usefully creative than other media of entertainment, I applaud the fact that the newspapers continue to take the same view. I am not sure, though, how long this position can be maintained and for how long the drama critic of a newspaper will be regarded (as he is) as the most respected and senior man in the reviewing hierarchy, It must be mystifying to the majority of readers, especially those in the provinces, to see his comments given pride of place in the arts or show business pages.

If this situation changes, some of the reviewers themselves will have made a large contribution to their own downfall. In terms of the real or potential audiences for the works they review, it makes absolutely no sense whatever for them to go on about esoteric and coterie entertainments in attics and cellars and pubs and clubs at such inordinate length. It is almost as though a newspaper's principal sports columnist were to lavish his space upon some local badminton tournament, to the neglect of international football, a state of affairs that would not long be tolerated by either his editors or his readers.

Irving Wardle, as I have mentioned, is one offender in this

regard, but there are others among his colleagues—perhaps notably those on the principal Sunday papers, the *Sunday Times*, the *Sunday Telegraph* and *The Observer*—who could be similarly charged. It may seem premature to put the *Sunday Times* man, Bernard Levin, in this category, for he only took over the job in October 1976—to the general consternation of theatre people, recalling, with a retrospective shudder, his days as reviewer for the *Daily Express* when he and Robert Muller, who performed the same chore at the *Daily Mail*, were known jocularly along Shaftesbury Avenue as the two kosher butchers. And Levin's acceptance of the appointment was probably surprising to nearly everyone, for it was hard to imagine why, having once made his escape, he should wish to return to an occupation that had previously seemed to bring him no great joy.

In his *Express* (and, later, *Mail*) days, Levin had confined himself largely to major London productions—as is the way of the popular papers—but at the *Sunday Times* he has been doggedly trekking around the 'fringe' and out to the provinces and suburbs, and to lunchtime pub shows as well. This is doubtless a tribute to the conscientiousness of a man who could easily get away with reviewing one play a week rather than four or five. But even if the sheer drudgery of it doesn't take the edge off his lively style, his readers will surely begin to question why he should be so persistently trying to interest them in minute and localised places of entertainment which they have no opportunity to visit—even if he should recommend them to do so.

Harold Hobson, whom Levin succeeded at the *Sunday Times*, had had the job since 1947, when he inherited it from the late James Agate. He was often spoken of as the doyen of the profession and, soon after his retirement, was given a knighthood. Though he had the misfortune to be crippled, he made light of his disability, was indefatigable in his theatregoing and was not even discouraged by the Royal Court's Theatre Upstairs, the flights of steep stone steps to which might sap the enthusiasm of many a younger and nimbler auditor.

Hobson is a cultured, courteous man but became a little infatuated, I think, with his position. There seems no question but that, if I may risk heaving a stone from a glass house, he went on too long. In the later years he had seemed to strive for a perversity of opinion that made his notices something of a joke in theatrical circles. It was almost invariable that he took an emphatically unfavourable line on Sundays with productions that he deemed to have been over-praised in the daily press during the week. Conversely, he sought something to praise in the things his confrères had roundly condemned.

It was in the latter cases that he touched, in the general view, the most extravagant foolishness, and his own self-justification—that, once upon a time, he praised a play by Harold Pinter, *The Birthday Party*, that was otherwise mercilessly flayed—was wearing a trifle thin towards the end. Though it is on the cards that, by the law of averages alone, he might again have stood alone in defence of some play that will be ultimately recognised as having greater merit than was at first commonly supposed, the frequency with which he attempted the trick was itself a factor militating against its successful accomplishment. Nevertheless, he kept it up to the end, suggesting that Pinter could have taught Shakespeare a thing or two, acclaiming the works of William Douglas Home in terms that might seem extravagant if applied to those of George Bernard Shaw and delighting us all by praising an almost incredibly boring play called *Dimetos* on grounds that no one else, conceivably including the author, had noticed.

In the matter, however, of his discovery of superior talents, dramatists of genius and assorted masterpieces almost every other week, one would have to take a very high and optimistic view indeed of the gifts and intelligences presently deployed in the contemporary theatre to have believed him to have been right even *half* the time. I am not sure that he was right even about *The Birthday Party*, though he is welcome to the pleasure he takes in having seen so many converted over the years to his opinion of this work. This is one of a number of occasions in theatrical history when just one critic—by beating his drum hard enough and often enough—has 'made' a play almost single-handed. As Hobson did in the case of the Pinter play, so his predecessor at the *Sunday Times*, Agate, did in the case of *Journey's End*, and so did Kenneth Tynan, when the reviewer of *The Observer*, in the case of John Osborne's *Look Back in Anger*.

These are instances of the power of newspaper reviewers to influence success. But such power and influence seem to me to be

174

declining—conceivably, though I would not go so far as to say necessarily, because of the gulf that may be opening up between the tastes of theatregoers and the view of the theatre taken by some of the leading reviewers. There is a tendency on their part to adopt authoritarian airs and to imply, if not explicitly to say, that their readers damn well ought to see and to like certain works because they will be good for their minds or their souls or both. In cases like that, a whole sheaf of good notices won't guarantee success. On the other hand it is rare that a play can succeed in the teeth of universally bad notices. Except in the case of some of the sex farces and sex revues (when bad notices are not taken seriously but are regarded by the public as proof of their suspicion that 'critics' are an ascetic and high-minded lot, to whom such things are always 'boring'), achieving box-office success after a set of bad notices is a hard trick to turn—or, at least, an expensive one, entailing sitting out the period until the notices are forgotten, advertising confidently and using up an awful lot of money, and still having no guarantee that it will eventually come back.

The conclusion from all of this may seem to be that the reviewers' influence is more likely to be negative than positive. But I have been talking only of the extreme cases. There is a vast middle ground where the reviews are crucial. In this area different reviewers and newspapers will, of course, have influence at different levels. In the case of a play with any pretensions to seriousness, a management will want to have going for it a majority of the 'quality' Sundays and the *Daily Telegraph*, *Evening Standard* and *Financial Times*; and perhaps *The Times* and *The Guardian* as well, although the public for the West End theatre, at least, is more suspicious of the opinions of Wardle and Michael Billington (once Wardle's deputy but now with *The Guardian*) than they ever were of their predecessors, respectively A V Cookman and Philip Hope-Wallace. In the case of more 'popular' shows, it is still hard to do without the approval of the *Daily Telegraph* and *Evening Standard*. But the *Daily Mail*, *Daily Express*, *Evening News* and even *The Sun* and the *Daily Mirror* have real influence at this end of the market.

Among the weeklies, *What's On In London* and, in the case of the 'fringe', *Time Out*, are useful allies, since their readers are mostly specifically *looking* for some kind of entertainment. Even so, their effect on the total box-office is marginal rather than decisive.

175

The 'serious' weeklies have no box-office influence at all, although their reviewers have usually been respected. *The Spectator* has had no particular consistency in regard to the theatre and its reviewer from 1970 to 1976 was notoriously wayward and plainly far too frivolous for the company he kept; but the *New Statesman* employs the estimable Benedict Nightingale, who is insistently readable and might justifiably have felt aggrieved at not being appointed to succeed Hobson at the *Sunday Times*. Nightingale seems to have been writing mainly about the theatre for most of his working life, being different in that respect from most of his colleagues who, in the main, drifted into their jobs fortuitously from other branches of journalism—although, for all I know, theatre reviewing may always have been their long-term objective.

Kenneth Tynan was one who made it his *short-term* objective, prefacing a book of reviews he wrote,* before getting regular employment, with the declaration that, 'When maturity overtakes me, I shall have a great many less important but weightier things to do than sit trembling in theatres.' As it happened, what he had to do was sit *counting* in theatres (the box-office takings at *Oh! Calcutta!*) but that is by the way. Tynan was unquestionably the most notable theatre reviewer in this country since Shaw, and by far the most valuable—not because of any particular confidence I would repose in his judgment, but simply because of the irresistible sprightliness of his style, which got people reading and talking about the theatre again at a time when very few were doing either. Whatever his opinions, agree with him or not, Tynan in *The Observer* was required reading every Sunday, and it had been a long time since anything of that sort could accurately have been said about a reviewer of anything. When he departed for a rather less distinguished career as the National Theatre's first 'literary manager' (Laurence Olivier is said to have engaged him in that capacity chiefly to ensure that he would not have to endure the wounds of his written criticism), and later to make his fortune (notoriously) by putting together *Oh! Calcutta!* (a grievously witless mélange which I suspect he would, as a reviewer, have mercilessly flayed), a gap was left in the reviewing ranks that has not yet been filled. Even so, the present man at *The Observer*, Robert Cushman, is the best in today's line-up.

* *He That Plays the King* (Longmans, 1950).

Best? I do not mean that his opinions are the most reliable, for that would be merely to say that they coincided with my own and on that basis every one of the reviewers would be the 'best' for some people—that is, if they are taken entirely as a guide to what to see and what to miss. I apply my tendentious superlative to Cushman because I think that he is the most pleasurably readable of the reviewers, that his judgments are founded in an attentive experience of the theatre. He has, in fact, much of the 'technical knowledge' that theatre people seem to think reviewers should have, but he does not brandish it tediously over the heads of his non-technical readers. And, in a civilised view of life, he argues engaging cases even for judgments that are at variance with my own, and—while he does not have Tynan's old command of the penetratingly accurate phrase or the precisely evocative simile—his writing has a keen wit and a humour that is subtle without being esoterically donnish.

Cushman is, of course, a Sunday reviewer and might thereby be thought to have an advantage over the daily appraisers, in regard to both style and judgment. Oddly enough, if this *is* an advantage it is not one that is envied by the men whose notices have to be in their newspapers on the 'morning after'. *Drama*, the quarterly theatre magazine, conducted a survey on this point not long ago. Ten daily reviewers were asked to complete a questionnaire on their working conditions. The magazine was trying to build a case for a general twenty-four-hours' delay in the publication of reviews. The reviewers themselves turned out to be better satisfied with things as they are.

This surprised me as much as it did the magazine. Important plays are tending to become more and more complex in their themes and arguments. I should therefore have thought that most men, charged with giving a fairly detailed opinion that may prove to have vital consequences both in the commercial sense, as well as in regard to a dramatist's reputation and future prospects, would feel that an opportunity to 'sleep on' such a work was highly desirable. Attentive theatre buffs will doubtless have noticed that, in cases where a play offers, or seems to offer, a profound intellectual challenge, the opinions of reviewers in the Sunday and weekly press are often sharply opposed to those in the dailies. Even in the case of trivia, I had thought that a reviewer—although he may be

quite positive in his view as soon as the final curtain is down—
would appreciate the chance to transcribe his quick notes during
the following day, to think of more telling phrases, to shape his
sentences and paragraphs with more stylistic care, and to take the
finished piece along to his office and remain to check the proofs.

Not so, apparently. He likes things the way they are: the
scribbled notes in the dark, the improvisation on the telephone,
the misprints. In general, he doesn't admit to having second
thoughts that are different from his first thoughts, and contends
that much of the criticism levelled at him (such as that he has
overvalued or undervalued plays or players) is not a consequence of
haste and might be levelled with equal force at weekly reviewers.
He may sometimes regret having to leave a performance before the
final curtain in order to meet a deadline (*Hamlet*, invariably), but
his preferred solution to that problem would not be to delay his
comment but for the play to begin earlier (as many now indeed do
on press nights).

'Does the knowledge of having to write at curtain-fall interfere
with your concentration?' *Drama* asked the daily reviewers and
received in reply an almost unanimous 'No'. The reviewers spoke
of the urgency of their employment as being helpful, improving or
intensifying concentration, sharpening the faculties, stimulating
the intellect. If these answers were honest, it might seem that
the daily reviewers' opinions are the most reliable of all—which
means throwing out of the window the apparently logical notion
that a judgment is likely to be better if it is reached after a period of
reflection. I daresay the answers *were* honest. But I cannot help
thinking that maybe they were influenced just a little, even if
subconsciously, by the respondents' reluctance to prolong their
working hours. Better to sleep on a play, worry about it and spend
the next day carefully writing about it? Or better to get it all over
with by midnight at the latest, have a leisurely late supper, sleep till
noon and not start work again till seven-thirty?

The latter would be the more tempting way of life, but it would
be misleading to suggest that it is widely followed. Most of the
theatre reviewers are busy on other things during the day. Some
review films as well as plays. Others busy themselves writing other
articles or books or in trying to write plays of their own. And others
have additional editorial responsibilities with their newspapers.

For, just in case you were wondering, no one makes much of a living simply from reviewing plays. A salary of £5,000 a year would be thought reasonable for the work—and only the best are getting more.

In the light of that, it is surprising that reviewers have been tending to stick at the trade for such long periods. The line-up has not really changed much in the past 20 years, although there have been exceptions—such as Peter Lewis, who reviewed for the *Daily Mail* for only five years before handing over the job to Jack Tinker. I once asked Lewis why he had given it up. There were, he said, two reasons. One was that he was offered a job that paid more money (he became the *Mail*'s literary editor). The other was simply that he didn't think the reviewing job was one he wanted to grow old in. 'I used to look down the aisle night after night,' he said, 'and see the backs of the same old heads—A who was incredibly old, B who was deaf, C who was probably blind, D who was just interested in the boys, E who was asleep, F who was drunk—and I felt I was getting confined in an enclosed society. It was claustrophobic and it was a relief to escape. Shaw said that no one should do the job for more than three years. He then did four. I thought that five was the limit.'

There are public misconceptions about nearly every aspect of the theatre. But I doubt if any of them are wilder than those about press agents—not just *agents*, whom we've already dealt with, but *press* agents, publicists. The man in the street, if he thinks of them at all, settles for the handy fiction provided by vague memories of old motion pictures about Broadway shows in which the press agent seemed to be the livest backstage wire around, a man with nothing much rattling about in his head except ideas for getting the show mentioned in the public prints, preferably with pictures. His day was spent badgering columnists, news editors and picture editors—on the telephone or in person. If there was nothing especially newsworthy about his show or the people in it, he invented it.

This picturesque 'image' is so well established that it is accepted even by those of the theatrical profession itself—at least up to the moment when they come face to face with the discouraging reality. I have known newcomers even to the ranks of the impresarios who have been startled to discover that their press agent or publicity man does not regard himself in that sort of light at all.

He does not, indeed, even call himself a press agent or publicity man as he used to. Now he is a press officer, a press representative, or, I'm afraid, a public relations officer. Des Wilson, formerly of Shelter, introduced a nice variant when for a time he took over the relevant department at the Royal Shakespeare Theatre and adopted the title, Head of Public Affairs.

Public relations officer is, however, the preferred term: it is fashionable, and it sounds at once glamorous and respectable, where press agent has a mild touch of the vulgar. Ask a press agent his job and the chances are he'll say he's 'in PR.' He isn't, of course. But he has as much claim to the term as most who sail under that flag, having as little general contact with the public with whom they're supposed to be having a relationship as the average advertising agent.

There is, it occurs to me, another similarity between advertising agents and press representatives: the ones in favour are subject to constant change, and there are occasional amalgamations as well. Trying to recall, offhand, the theatre publicists that were prominently active about 20 years ago, I could think of only some half-dozen who were still noticeably in business, and two pairs of those had formed partnerships with each other; of the rest, a few have died or retired, while the others seem to have gravitated to other divisions of the PR game. On the whole it seems a profession in which experience is rarely the desirable attribute, and life at the top is generally as short as it is for professional sportsmen.

No ready explanation for this comes to mind, since today's lot are not essentially any better than yesterday's. Some of the changes, though, are certainly due to the fact that many publicists' fortunes are tied to those of particular managements. Others, I suspect, are due to the constant though vain search of impresarios to find one who will accord with their preconceived—but erroneous —notion of what their press agent will do for them.

The best theatre press agent I ever knew was John Carlsen, or perhaps I only judge him the best because I liked him the best. I thought him wholly and persistently likeable, which is probably a good thing for a press agent to be. But I can't say that Carlsen was anywhere near the most successful. That, I should judge, is because he cut himself off from the part of the business in which he was most at home—music-hall, variety, vaudeville: not one of my own great enthusiasms, but certainly his. He was the press man for Moss Empires in the 1940s and 1950s, and thus for the London Palladium (part of that group) during its great days; but with the contraction of the Moss empire, as the rise of television brought the downfall of the music-hall, Carlsen found himself in a dying business and saw no alternative but to cut himself loose. After that, he concentrated largely on personal publicity. The trouble in taking this line is that far fewer artists than you may think actually employ a personal press agent. That is because the theatre management or film or television studio for which they

182

happen to be working will have its own publicity department and most artists are content to leave it at that. Carlsen later worked for a time as the press man at Sadler's Wells, but his enthusiasm was evidently considered not compensation enough for his lack of basic knowledge of opera, and he was axed. As far as I know, the only other staff job he had was a temporary one at the National Theatre, where he filled in for a few months after the rather abrupt departure from that organisation of Virginia Fairweather. But it was made clear to Carlsen that the job *was* only temporary—regardless of how efficiently he might handle it—presumably because he was by then fiftyish, and it was a time when youth was so much in the ascendant as to be a cult. John Carlsen died, suddenly, early in 1975 with no more than a few lines of report in a couple of newspapers to mark his passing. There was no reason, probably, why there should have been more; for publicists do not publicise themselves, and to the public at large their names are generally unknown.

I mention him here, partly as a small tribute, but partly also to observe that a press agent, no matter what his enthusiasm, energy and likeability, will only be really successful when he has a total love for, belief in and knowledge of whatever he happens to be pushing—as John Carlsen had in the case of the music-hall. He was never as successful as he was then, and it was his misfortune that he came to that business in what were its last days.

It should be mentioned at this point that very few press agents work exclusively for one theatrical management. The subsidised London houses—the National Theatre, the Aldwych, the Royal Court and the Mermaid—all have their own people, who don't officially work for other managements, and Delfont shows are handled from the press office of EMI; the London Palladium has always had its own man, who is also responsible for whatever provincial activities Moss Empires may still be operating. But none of the other commercial managements tie up their press agents on exclusive contracts, so most of them work on a freelance basis, receiving a set fee from each production. This fee doesn't vary a lot, being usually about £40 a week (though I hesitate to give a figure that is subject, as much as any other, to our inflationary times). A 'fashionable' press agent will probably be handling five or six productions on this basis, and since—subtracting the handful of theatres with exclusive press agents—there are less than forty productions to go round, plus, at most, a dozen others on the road prior to a projected West End run, there plainly isn't room for many of them to be 'fashionable', or even to make a decent living.

I have so far been using the pronoun 'he' about press agents. This is, in fact, more than a little misleading. One of the results of the high incidence of change in the line-up of the principal press agents is that the profession has reflected more than most the abandonment of sex discrimination. Looking at the list of the principal press agents in the theatre at the time of writing, compared with a similar list of those of a quarter of a century ago, the most striking feature—apart from the fact that the two lists are almost completely different—is the number of ladies in the business today. In immediately post-war days there was only one, Miss Vivienne Byerley, who, for so many years until her retirement in 1973, was the press representative of the H M Tennent organisation, once by far the most successful commercial management in the country. I daresay it was the high regard in which Miss Byerley was held at Tennents that had much to do with encouraging other managements to employ women.

There was another woman, too, whose influence may have been even greater in some respects. This was Suzanne Warner, and she, I would say, came closer than anyone else to conforming to the 'image' of the press agent. An American, she came to London first to promote the Jane Russell film, *The Outlaw*, and anyone who was around at the time will remember what a successful and gaudy promotion job that was. Looking around at the state of the publicity game in Britain, Miss Warner could not help but notice its general air of casual lethargy and somnolence, and conclude that anyone with her zip and flair could revolutionise it. To the consternation of the theatre publicists, it was the theatre on which she decided to concentrate her attention.

Miss Warner beavered and hustled, she made stories and she made shows, pushing her clients' interests with tough, driving energy. Newspapers and magazines that had become accustomed to getting only a dull cyclostyled hand-out about a forthcoming production (and a picture if they asked for one) suddenly found that she was giving them a whole showbiz news service that they could not ignore. No doubt, also, she pushed the advantages of her methods among theatrical managements; they could not ignore her either, and she got business. The local men, alive to the threat, formed themselves into a kind of union—the Association of London Theatre Press Representatives—which may have had many high-sounding objectives on paper, but seemed to have as its principal practical purpose resistance to Suzanne Warner. Either by her own decision (because she could not conform to the rules), or because the rules were framed to exclude her, she was not a member, and an agreement was reached with the theatre managements whereby only members of the ALTPR could be employed as press representatives. I doubt if the Association's bargaining position was ever compellingly strong, and I'm not sure how the battle between Miss Warner and its members would have turned out. What happened, as I remember, is that she bought herself into commercial television, which was just then getting off the ground, turned her attentions and energy to that, stepped out of the theatre publicity business and made a fortune.

The Association of London Theatre Press Representatives, its chief *raison d'être* having disappeared from the scene, fell into moribundity. It still nominally exists, but has no particular function and none of the newer press agents are members of it—if, indeed, they have even heard of it. The girls among them are not in the Suzanne Warner league, though they are pleasant enough and lose nothing by comparison with their male rivals. Part of the reason why they succeed, though, may be wrapped up in the very fact that they *are* girls and are more persuasive with male columnists and are more convincing liars, this being a very vital part of a press agent's function. Some of them have worked as assistants to senior press agents before branching out on their own, but others seem to take up the business on a whim or by accident. The best of them is probably Gloria Taylor, who is a former fashion designer. She became a press representative at the Royal Court simply because she was asked whether she would like to try her hand at it and because she wasn't doing anything else at the time. She spent several years at the Royal Court and then took off on her own as a freelance.

I said that press agents had to be good liars. This is because they often have to spend at least as much time keeping things out of the papers as they do on trying to get things in. And most of the things they keep out are true. No production, for example, is ever doing bad business or in danger of closing until the 'notices' go up—and even then it is preferred that the matter does not become public knowledge, lest it further damage what little remains of the business during the final days of the run. If a star player, considered important to the box-office, falls ill, the press must not be told—nor the public either, until they get to the theatre and find that 'owing to the indisposition of . . .'—unless the star's absence is protracted, when a replacement of comparable stature, rather than merely the understudy, will take over and be publicised. But when a star of the first magnitude actually leaves a show, having agreed only to play for a limited period anyway, the replacement will be very lucky indeed—or have an agent with a tough negotiating line—if any announcement is made and if the press agent is not under direct instruction to soft-pedal the star's departure.

The private lives of the personnel in a show are also a headache to press agents. Weddings and births are good news, but affairs, estrangements and untidy divorces can be poison. Animosity between members of a cast can be worse. In one Shaftesbury Avenue comedy a year or two ago, the leading lady discovered the infidelity of the leading man, who was her husband. She declined to go on the stage 'until that man gets out of my house and out of this play'. Eventually he did both, but meanwhile no word of the trouble reached the papers, and columnists who heard of the lady's absence from the cast and inquired of the press agent were fobbed off with bland murmurs about some trivial indisposition.

Few press agents have had a more nerve-racking time on that 'private life' part of the job than Virginia Fairweather, who was Laurence Olivier's press agent at the time when his marriage to the late Vivien Leigh was breaking up because of his love for Joan Plowright, his present wife, whom he met when she played his daughter in *The Entertainer*. It was a time when gossip columnists were even more importunate and even less inhibited in their invasion of privacy than they are now, and Mrs Fairweather— with the job of protecting the privacy, the interests and the public 'images' of all parties involved—spent her days and nights at first

186

denying all the burgeoning rumours of a rift between 'Larry and Viv' and later, when that possibility was no longer credibly open to her, denying all knowledge of the whereabouts of her clients, with whom, of course, she was in constant touch.

Mrs Fairweather, a former actress and revue artist (she was Virginia Winter before her marriage to David Fairweather, also a theatre publicist), was the National Theatre's first press agent, she and her husband, either separately or together, having represented Laurence Olivier and his companies and productions in that capacity for some time previously, and the move with him to the Old Vic from the beginnings of the operation at the Chichester Festival being a natural one. David Fairweather, in fact, remained at Chichester (and stayed on through the Sir John Clements regime there, too), while his wife took on the National Theatre press job. After she was summarily sacked she wrote a book about her experiences* which I always felt could have justifiably bared a little more claw; even so, the book blew more of the gaff about a press agent's work in the theatre than has elsewhere been revealed so frankly. It also, incidentally, provided evidence enough for the proposition that keeping things out of the papers makes heftier demands than getting things in.

A press agent's work is curiously dichotomised. The conflict isn't always as obvious—and at once as vital and as trivial—as that which confronted Virginia Fairweather in the Olivier-Leigh-Plowright situation I've referred to, when her attitude, as she knew, was plainly doing her no good at all in her relationship with the pressmen and yet had to be maintained in loyalty to her employers. The press agent's relationship with the press is always a knife-edge business. On the one hand the work depends on a happy, trusting collaboration between the two; on the other, the very fact of putting the client's interests first—once it is decided what the client's interests actually *are*—means a head-on collision with the journalist's interests, and the press agent is bound to come out looking more obstructive than cooperative, and at the end of the day will be wiping the yolk out of his eyes.

The object of the press agent, engaged to represent any production, is to get that production mentioned in the editorial columns of as many newspapers, and as favourably, as possible. Let's take

* *Cry God for Larry* (Calder and Boyars, 1969).

an easy one: a play by a well-known author with a cast headed by a couple of well-known stars. The news of the production is sure to make a paragraph, perhaps even a decent headline, in every paper. The press agent would settle for that for starters. But is he going to be allowed to? When play-casting is going on, a lot of people know about it and talk about it; and when well-known names go on dotted lines, somebody is sure to think it worthwhile mentioning to a newspaper columnist.

So a couple of weeks, say, before the announcement is to go out in a general statement—or press release—to all the papers, the press agent gets a call from somebody on one of the important columns seeking confirmation of its details. The call will only come if the columnist is dubious about the authenticity of his tip-off; if he is certain of his facts, he won't call, because what he will get will be either a flat denial (not really likely, but possible, depending on circumstances), or a guarded confirmation (with the press agent saying that he's heard something of it, is awaiting more details and will call the columnist back with the full, definite story). In the latter case, the press agent is playing for time. He may want to consult the management; in any case he has to decide himself whether to let the columnist have his 'scoop' (which will mean that none of the other papers is likely to make anything of the story) or whether he can get away with a call back to the columnist, followed instantly by calls to as many other papers as he can contact before the first one is in print. This would hardly be ethical and would not go over big with the columnist. What the press agent has to decide is whether his relations with one columnist are so important that he cannot afford to jeopardise them even at the risk of alienating all the other papers (perhaps he can mollify him or them with subsidiary 'exclusives' later), and where the best interests of the management reside.

This is a decision that exercises him all the way, in some sense, with every story he has to handle, and especially in the case of productions that do not have very newsworthy names associated with them. As far as theatre stories are concerned—other than those that are in some degree scandalous—news editors can be said to cloak their enthusiasm under a persuasive show of apathy. So Jack Whosit and Jane Whatsername are opening on the 25th in a new play by Sam Nobody, so who cares? The information may be conveyed to attentive readers in a filler paragraph, bottom of column 3, page 7. And in a case like this, the press agent may think that just one reasonably prominent story will be worth more than any number of mere 'mentions', in which event he will be prepared to give one of the columnists a tip all to himself—for an 'exclusive', about however trivial a matter, does interest columnists and news editors.

Here again, though, unless he has been in the business long enough to be seen to have shared such items around the papers impartially, it's a procedure that entails the risk of antagonising more papers. How much is that one item worth if it upsets the press not only in regard to the one particular production, but in regard to others he may subsequently or concurrently be handling?

That, plus a certain amount of sheer laziness, is why most press agents tend to go for the routine of playing safe: the same stories in the same words—the unembroidered facts, set down with neither sparkle nor imagination—go out to everybody at the same time. Received in the newspaper offices they land on the desks of the 'theatre correspondent' or 'arts reporter' or 'diary editor', these journalists being, on the whole, as idle and unenterprising as the press agents themselves, and a mutually satisfactory arrangement is established: the press agents settle for getting their drearily humdrum hand-outs into print. The journalists oblige them and hope to kid their editors that they've been out and about getting news. Some of the hacks go so far as to slap in the hand-outs under their own by-lines without giving the material even the most cursory re-write job. For this ludicrously undemanding kind of activity, they are paid more money than coal miners and should probably be getting less than street sweepers.

As far as the press agents are concerned, one other duty actually imposed upon them is to see that review tickets get sent out to the critics, to greet the critics when they arrive at the theatre (always assuming they recognise them, which isn't always so) and perhaps give them free programmes. They might also, in the case of critics who have to telephone their reviews, arrange some telephone facilities. Subsequently, it may be part of their job to circularise various organisations, clubs and such that may be likely to make party bookings. This sort of 'public relations' work apart, once the show is launched they are required only to provide any liaison

189

that may be required between management and press, answering such inquiries as they can, providing photographs and setting-up interviews.

Some press agents, usually when they're new to the business, work reasonably hard on the picture and interview angles. They do their best to think up valid reasons for asking newspapers and magazines to publish pictures of people connected with the productions they're publicising, and they try to persuade feature editors and the producers of radio and television chat shows that their people are worth interviewing. Persistence pays off in these fields, for the media people need a constant flow of ideas. There are too many press agents, though, who regard such pushiness as irksome, disagreeable, fatiguing and furthermore beneath their dignity.

Only a few years ago, any book about the theatre in Britain would have been bound to include a hefty chunk about the 'fringe'. Maybe no one would have read it. But it would still have been there. Sometimes the theatre seemed almost like some unfortunate island with the tide coming in, inexorably, from all directions—the surrounding waters with their threatening defiance of the laws of nature being the 'fringe'.

It was everywhere—and growing, as anyone with a spare attic, cellar or warehouse, a group of like-minded cronies who persuaded each other they had talent, and the nerve to badger the Arts Council into giving them a hand-out, set up shop as a theatre. Some of the operators, of course, did have talent and the critics were obliged to give the movement serious attention lest they be caught missing something vital stirring in the undergrowth—or the 'underground', as it was often called.

These days the picture has somewhat changed. The tiny rebels are still tumbling about in their playpens. But no one to speak of is watching them anymore. A few intellectualising reviewers still go along to see what they're up to. Even so, the truth must be beginning to dawn that they're not going to be up to anything much. A great fiction has evolved that holds that the 'fringe' in its heyday was nurturing the talents that the theatre needed to survive. In fact, this was never the case. Experiment they did, certainly, but very little came of it.

The few worthwhile talents that worked in the 'fringe' theatres graduated at early opportunities to 'establishment' theatres—even if only, so as not to feel entirely respectable, to the experimental sections of the Royal Court, the Royal Shakespeare and the National Theatres, where no doubt they sometimes contribute valuably to the creative processes. Left behind in the padded cellars are the dregs, the actors who could never be bothered to learn technique (and sometimes not even lines, since 'improvisation' is the preferred working method in many instances), the writers who decline to accept the formal disciplines of the craft. The 'fringe' was always overloaded with this anti-talent; now it is swamped by it.

I confess to have paid only minimal attention to the 'fringe' even when it was being hailed as the salvation of the theatre as a whole. My feelings about experimental theatre are much the same as my feelings about experimental medicine: that is to say, it is sometimes comforting to know that it is all going on out there, and that every now and then the processes of trial and error may result in something wonderful. But my own eagerness to be one of the guinea pigs, as patient or audience, is not marked. It is an attitude that may seem a touch irresponsible, but indeed, in regard to the 'fringe', nothing wonderful has come out of it, and my experiences, whenever I did venture into it were persistently unfortunate.

It was not that I went out looking for disaster. There was a week, about 1971, for example, when I really did resolve to try to come to terms with the 'fringe' and I examined the possibilities of the week, reading carefully all the blurbs that solicited my attendance. One of them read:

> *A multi-octave sound-picture of Man's evolution, through constant organisation—explosion—reorganisation, in search of a creed to contain evolving individuals. When the singer learns that all history is present in total self-awareness, competitive conflict dies. Self-control, self-reverence remain. The dreamed-of synthesis of singer and songs become embodied.*

I didn't go. I mean, would you? I picked the Arts Lab instead. It was one of the more highly regarded outfits and was in the midst of an 'International Alternative Theatre Season', putting on different shows at 7.30 and 10 of an evening. I reckoned to catch the two latest on the same night and duly presented myself at the Arts Lab's new headquarters which appeared to be a converted (but not *too* converted) warehouse. The early show was to be *Party*

192

Without a Host, a piece written and directed by a Jacqueline Skarvellis, and while I waited for it to begin I read that Miss Skarvellis was an actress working in *Oh! Calcutta!* Also about her play:

> *Five people, products of a sick society, are invited by a stranger to a party: a homosexual, an alcoholic without morals, a hippy and a young girl obsessed by religion and spiritualism through drugs, are led by Dante, the fifth guest, into a cycle of primitive rites and slaughter.*

I felt some unease right there. Perhaps I should have read all that before I arrived; somehow it didn't sound quite my, or anyone's, kind of party. I was worrying unnecessarily, though, for not only was there no host, there was no audience, either—apart, that is, from me and another guest of the management—and in the circumstances, the company decided to call it off. By then, I'm afraid, my enthusiasm for that evening had cooled and I had no heart for hanging around to discover whether the late show (a programme of readings by a Mr Harvey Matusow including, among other delicacies, 'The Saga of John Sadballs') would be more lavishly supported. I suspected not. Indeed, the experience reinforced my conviction that very few people apart from actual participants were interested in 'fringe' theatre.

The discouragements of that evening were by no means unique. I remember a lunch-time show at the King's Head, a pub at Islington which serves meals with theatre. This was a piece called *Spider Rabbit* in which the big moment came when one character spooned out the brains of another character and ate them. A lot of food seemed to be getting left on the plates, and nowadays the King's Head—though technically of the 'fringe'—puts on a rather more conventional form of entertainment. Worthwhile things are often seen there; as they are also at such places as the Hampstead Theatre Club where they always have an eye on the possibilities of a transfer to the West End.

That is the way the 'fringe' used to be, before it was called the 'fringe'. It used to be made up of small, mainly club theatres, which existed partly to circumvent censorship restrictions but also to provide a platform for work on which commercial managements

193

were reluctant to take a chance until its appeal had been demonstrated one way or the other. The Mercury at Notting Hill was one of the more distinguished of the little off-West End theatres in those days, and it was where the postwar revival of verse drama (T S Eliot, Christopher Fry and Ronald Duncan being the leading practitioners) first burgeoned. When I went back to the Mercury in the early 1970s, I found it occupied by a troupe named Bird in Hand, founded in New York City in 1968 (a circular informed me) by Josephine Sacabo (who turned out to be the leading lady of the evening) and Dalt Wonk (the leading man and also the author) who was said to have been 'nominated Best Playwright off-Off-Broadway'.

That sounded promising. Their play was called *To the Hot Toe*, described as a comedy with music. It was a little late in starting—due, I fear, as at the Arts Lab, to some feeling among the company of five that it would be improper to begin while they outnumbered the audience. But, once the thing was under way, it was quickly established that the performers had little to commend them beyond their supernaturally cheerful gameness; that the comedy would require a degree of indulgence such as it is given to few of us to offer; and that, despite a beguiling reference to some innocent form of foot fetishism, I would never be able to relate the action to the title.

Such things, if you will spare me from submitting further evidence, the recollection of which can only revive the memory of past pain, are typical of much that has been going on around the 'fringe' since it proliferated in the late 1960s. The wonder is that it did not discourage more people more quickly, and especially more critics. The latter have seemed uncommonly eager to give the benefit of the doubt even to impenetrable obscurity, perhaps feeling that something important was being said just over their heads. Having confessed total bafflement, a reviewer of this ilk is likely to conclude:

> *Yet the inconsequentiality had a certain weight of consequentiality about it. It could be a fraud, but I suspect this author is too clever to have perpetrated a fraud.*

You think I'm making it up. It is actually a quote from the

194

former *New York Times* reviewer Clives Barnes on an Off-Broadway drama, in which he appeared to be saying that if the Emperor is said to be wearing a robe by Cardin then he, for one, is going to have a hard time believing he's wearing no clothes. Tender reviewing of this order, rather than the quality of the talents involved, has been largely responsible for the survival of the 'fringe'; that and the generosity of the Arts Council, which has taken a similar view. But the situation may be, in fact most probably is, changing. The last Arts Council report, when published late in 1976, was accompanied by a statement by the then chairman, Lord Gibson, who said, *inter alia*:

> *The attitude of those people in the art world who say that no artistic judgments are possible about contemporary art, and that the function of those who present it is simply 'to reflect what is going on', is totally unacceptable to the Council. As long as the arts are free and vital, mistakes are inevitable. But before the activity is grant-aided, the Council's advisers . . . must be of the opinion that what is proposed contains an element of vision, creative imagination or insight which validates it as an attempt to create a work of art.*

If that view is taken, as we may hope, by the holders of the purse-strings of subsidy in regard to the theatre, the 'fringe', as we have known it, is close to the end of the line. Which is a good reason why this chapter is much briefer than it would have been five years ago. The tides are receding.

FUTURE 22
INDEFINITE

There it is, then: the present state of play in the playhouse, and the present state of health of the 'fabulous invalid', the theatre that is perennially said to be dying but for which the obsequies have always to be postponed. I hopefully suspect that they will continue to be.

Fears of imminent death continue, of course, to be voiced. Currently they would seem to be focused upon the condition of the *commercial* theatre. My own greater concern, oddly enough, is for the subsidised theatre.

Subsidy has polarised the theatre much as it has polarised opinion; the middle ground has virtually disappeared from both, and I am disturbed that it has become so largely a political question. It is as inconceivable that a play taking even a mildly conservative position should be staged in a subsidised theatre, as it is that the radical left should concede that the business of subsidy has got somewhat out of hand.

For most people, today, the principle of public patronage is readily conceded *per se*; but it is a principle that rests essentially on such beliefs as that, firstly, it is only the best and worthiest that are and deserve to be subsidised, and secondly that, since the money is public money, it should be used to bring the best of theatre within the reach of as large a section of the public as possible. It is impossible to feel confident that either of these conditions is actually being fulfilled. Granted that we are in the realm of opinion rather than fact, it has become too easy to argue that it is often the worst rather than the best that is subsidised, and that, so far from extending its audience, the theatre is cutting itself off from its potential public because subsidy is allocated to the arrogantly self-indulgent who care not whom they please or displease so long as they please themselves.

I have concern even for the big fellows, the Royal Shakespeare and the National, sitting on top of the heap. The National Theatre, especially, gives cause for alarm: as the heaviest spender, it comes under the closest scrutiny and under the most persistent pressure to justify itself. Perhaps it will do so; if it does not, its shortcomings will become more evident as the building itself loses its novelty value as a tourist attraction. In those circumstances it is possible that not all future Governments and Arts Councils will take as generous a view as has so far been displayed. This, indeed, is a possibility that all recipients of subsidies might advantageously bear in mind.

As to the commercial sector, I do not wish to minimise its problems. They are real enough. That theatre management is not the plum and the jam-making opportunity it once was is evidenced by the facts that some of the shrewdest operators in the game have in recent years off-loaded their interests in the ownership of theatres and theatre leases. To take a specific instance, there has been no stampede to take on the lease of the old Playhouse Theatre since the BBC relinquished it and the Westminster City Council put it up for grabs. Again, to allow production managements to pay higher rents (to help theatre lessees) and have better chances of profitability (to help themselves), seat prices should go up; but they can't go up much more—and certainly not to an extent that would bring them in line with the inflation-struck costs of everything else—without, very likely, losing audiences who have enough to cope with in the high cost of non-luxury items. It would obviously help if VAT came off the tickets—not to make them cheaper, which would not happen, but so that the managements themselves could pocket the tax money instead of turning it over to the Customs and Excise. With all of that, nevertheless, however, notwithstanding and who cares, there is still good business in show business.

It may not be the best kind of business, but that depends on your lights. When I hear people saying earnestly that the commercial theatre is wasting away, I think they mean essentially that the opportunities for presenting 'serious' plays commercially are drying up, and that we'll be stuck with the trivia—the sex comedies and farces, the musicals and murder plays. There is a danger of that. But it seems to me—strictly on the record and by direct

198

comparison—that the deterioration hasn't been criminally notice-able over the last 20 or even 40 years. When good plays come along, they get put on, and furthermore succeed. At least I have no evidence to the contrary; only demonstrable evidence that there is a shortage of good plays—as, indeed, there always is. They're not easy to write. Contrary to the mythology that consoles the writers, promoters and backers of stiffs, plays usually fail because people don't want to see them, and people usually don't want to see them because they are bad. The time really to worry is when good plays, attracting good houses, can't keep running because expenditure is leaping ahead of receipts. The time may come. It isn't here yet.

Commercially managers have a more legitimate grouse when they complain that the major subsidised theatres are command-eering too much of the talent. The prestige of having a play done by the Royal Shakespeare or the National Theatre, or of acting or directing there, has an appeal—to say nothing of a security—that the commercial sector cannot altogether match. I think, though, that that appeal is not what it was, and there are not many talents entirely cut off from the commercial theatre when the deal is right. Commercial managers who get their hands on a good play will have no difficulty in getting the financial backing for it, and little more difficulty in getting a good director to direct it and good actors for him to direct. The good show is the fundamental requirement, as it always was: a good farce, a good comedy, a good musical, a good thriller, a good 'serious' play. Get one, and you're in business.

Now that's a word I've used a lot: 'business'. Sorry if you think it barbaric of me. But while I appreciate the theatre as an art, I also enjoy it as show business. The occasions on which these elements merge may be quite rare; but I should not care to see either sub-merged by the other. Until that happens I shall continue going to the theatre. So I hope, will you.

GLOSSARY
Some theatrical terms

Alienation effect: Much associated with Bertolt Brecht, it involves the use of playwriting and acting devices by which the audience is discouraged from emotional involvement and identification with characters and situation, being constantly aware and reminded that they are watching a theatrical performance.

Angel: A backer; one who invests money in a theatrical production. Sixty per cent of the profits, if any, are shared among the backers in proportion to their investment.

Apron stage: An extension of the stage playing area beyond the proscenium arch into the auditorium.

ASM: Assistant stage manager. In small companies, especially in repertory, he or she is also a junior member of the acting company.

Audition: A reading for a part in a play, or for a place in a permanent company, usually competitive.

Backing: (1) Angels' money. (2) The backing to the scenery that, say, blocks off fireplace openings or shows the landscape seen through a window.

Billing: The advertisements for a production, and especially the prominence given in them to individual players, author and director.

Bit player: One who plays very small parts.

Blood: Stage 'blood' is usually made with cochineal and glycerine.

Boat truck: A low platform on wheels for moving heavy sections of scenery into position. Newer theatres have more sophisticated arrangements.

Book: The script of a play, and the spoken dialogue of a musical.

Box set: A plain, and usually unattractive, stage setting for an interior: no alcoves, recesses, staircases, etc.—in effect, three sides of a box.

Business: (1) Preceded by the definite article, it means the theatre as a whole, which is referred to as 'The business', whereas the cinema is referred to as 'The industry'. (2) Without the article, it means the things

201

an actor does which are not essentially included in the script, the actions that keep him occupied when not actually speaking, designed either to establish character or to add additional comedy.

Call: (1) Notice of an engagement for an actor, the time he has to report for rehearsal or performance. (2) 'Taking a bow' at the end of a performance; the way and the order in which members of the cast take their 'call' is as carefully rehearsed as the performance itself.

Call-boy: The person, not usually a boy and the term is becoming obsolete, who lets the players know how much time they have before they're required on-stage.

Catharsis: Aristotelian term for the purging of the emotions by tragedy.

Censorship: Non-existent now, but prior to 1968 a function of the Lord Chamberlain, to whom all scripts were required to be submitted in order to be licensed for public performance; and if he refused a licence, or insisted on deletions or amendments as a condition of granting one, there was no 'Court of Appeal' in which he could be challenged.

Clear (as in 'Clear, please!'): The instruction, from stage manager or ASM, for everyone not involved in the opening scene to leave the stage before the rise of the curtain.

Close: Verb applied to the end of a run: 'Closing on Saturday'. It is less common than 'fold' nowadays.

Closet drama: Plays written (not always intentionally) to be read rather than acted.

Cue: The last words spoken by one player that indicate to another that it is his turn to speak. An actor may have a 'cue sheet', which is a script containing only his own part and the end-of-sentence cues to him from the other parts.

Curtain: The one-word instruction usually given in a script to indicate the end of a scene, or of the whole play, when the curtain comes down. The curtain itself is usually referred to as 'it', as in 'Take it up' (raise the curtain) or 'I thought it would never come down.'

Cyclorama: A backcloth (usually sky) tightly stretched on a semi-circular frame from top to bottom and across the back of the stage.

Decor: The scenery, or the design thereof.

Dock doors: High doors through which the scenery is taken into or out of a theatre.

Dresser: The person who helps a player to dress for the stage, and with costume changes.

Dressing a set: Adding the curtains, pictures, furniture etc to the basic scenery.

202

Dry: Verb meaning to forget the lines. Experienced players can often cover up such forgetfulness with 'business', and can help another's forgetfulness by a quick rearrangement of dialogue. The technological age has enabled a few players, of advanced years and failing memories, to have ear microphones through which they can be prompted.

Emergency understudy: Someone who is able to go on in the emergency of neither the player cast nor the regular deputy being available.

Expressionism: Theatrical method of writing and production in which psychological states are more prominently mirrored than physical situations and actions; sometimes the mingling of reality and fantasy. Greatly prevalent in the German drama of the 1920s.

Feed line: A line of dialogue with the sole purpose of eliciting a funny reply; imported into 'straight' drama from the music hall stage on which a comedian and his partner usually work in this way.

Fit-up: A travelling show, playing in non-theatres, halls or even outdoors, where everything from the proscenium arch, if required, to the scenery has to be fitted up by the company before the performance can be given.

Flats: The individual sections of a set that make up into the complete scene.

Flies: The section of the stage above the players, with a grid from which scenery is suspended (or 'flown'). The gallery high on the side wall, from which 'flyropes' are operated, is the 'fly rail' or 'the flies', and stagehands doing the operating are 'flymen'.

Floats: Footlights; deriving from the days when these were provided by lighted wicks threaded through corks that floated in oil troughs.

Follow-spot: A spotlight focused on a performer that moves with him around the stage.

Fourth wall: The non-existent fourth wall of a room, represented only by the proscenium arch; the players, at least in naturalistic drama, assume it to be there, and the audience assume it has been removed so that they can see the action in the room.

Front of house: Usually the auditorium lighting system focusing on the stage area.

Front of the house: The foyer or foyers, or, sometimes, the Business Manager. 'House' is the general word for the theatre building, or for an audience (as in 'Was it a good house?').

Get-in: The bringing of the scenery, etc., into a theatre. At the end of the run comes the 'get-out', but . . .

Get-out: Also a term used for the minimum sum that can be taken at the box-office for the management to break even on the week.

Ghost walks: The paying-out of weekly salaries to a theatrical company: usually on Fridays—morning on tour, evening in the West End.

Going on cold: Reading a part at an audition without having had an opportunity to study it.

Half: 'The half' is half an hour before the commencement of a performance, and it is indicated to the players by the 'callboy', who also calls 'the quarter', 'five minutes' or 'two minutes' and, finally, 'overture and beginners'.

Holding the book: The function of the prompter, who is 'on the book' or 'holds the book' during the performance and is able to supply the memory-jogging words when a player 'dries'.

Kill: Verb meaning to extinguish ('Kill that spot') or remove ('Kill that chair'), or to come in so quickly on cue that no audience reaction to the previous speech is possible ('He killed my laugh').

Legit: Or 'legitimate': Americanism for the non-musical stage.

Lines: (1) The words of a player's part. (2) The ropes used on a stage for raising and lowering scenery.

Notices: (1) Reviews. (2) The announcement posted on the back-stage noticeboard by the management informing the cast that the show is to close ('The notices went up last week').

Open stage: A stage with no proscenium, often extended as an apron stage with the audience on three sides of the action, and sometimes on all four sides ('in the round').

Opening cold: Opening in the West End without the benefit of a try-out tour or public previews; it is extremely rare.

Paper: Complimentary tickets ('The house was all paper'). To 'paper the house' is to give away tickets when business is bad, which is more encouraging to actors than playing to the Wood Family (*q.v.*) and gives the impression to any paying customers there may be that the show is doing better than it actually is.

Pass door: The door from the auditorium to the stage or back-stage, never used during a performance by anyone, and only used by members of the audience when escorted (as VIPs may be, as an alternative to using the stage-door to 'go back' or 'go behind' to see members of the cast).

Pilot light: Or 'working light'; a single naked light used at early rehearsals. Not until the 'lighting rehearsals' and 'dress rehearsals' is the stage fully lit.

Plot: (1) The story of a play. (2) Any list or schedule detailing stage particulars, as in 'lighting plot', 'property plot', 'effects plot', etc.

Prompter: The person who 'holds the book' (*q.v.*). 'OP' means 'opposite prompt', always to the players' right. 'PS' is the 'prompt side', to his left.

Props: An abbreviation of 'properties'; all the articles used in 'dressing a set' (*q.v.*) or taken on-stage by players. The latter are either 'hand props' to be carried (and ready to hand on the 'props table') or 'personal props' which are attached to the player or in his pockets (spectacles, cigarettes, stage money, etc.). The word 'props' is also used to refer to the room where they are kept, and to the person responsible for them.

Pros: An abbreviation of 'proscenium' or 'proscenium arch', the frame separating the stage from the auditorium (which open stages do not have).

Rake: The angle of incline of the house seating or, sometimes, of the stage itself.

Rep: An abbreviation of 'repertory'.

Returns: (1) The account of the money taken at the box office. (2) Tickets returned for re-sale.

Revolve: A revolving part of the stage, electrically operated, enabling a quick change from one set to another, the two being constructed on either side of the revolve.

Scene dock: The place at the back or side of the stage where the 'flats' (*q.v.*) are stacked.

Set: A stage setting or the scenery for it.

Sight lines: The lines of vision from all the seats in the auditorium, which should be taken into account when the set is designed and the action is staged so that everything essential can be seen by everyone in the audience (often impossible in the older theatres).

SM: Stage Manager; the person responsible to the director for seeing that everything required for the performance is ready and working.

Stage wait: Any delay in the rise of the curtain, or any unprepared pause in the performance (as might be caused if a player 'dries' or misses his entrance).

Strike: Apart from its ordinary meanings, also a verb meaning to take down the scenery.

Supers: An abbreviation of 'supernumeraries'; players needed in the action but with no lines to speak.

Tabs: Curtains. 'Front tabs': the main curtain; 'running tabs': the curtains drawn mid-stage across the set.

Upstage: Verb. To 'upstage' an actor is to cause him to turn away from the audience, a ploy improperly resorted to by another actor who deliberately takes attention by moving to the back of the stage so that the others have to turn round to address him.

Wings: The 'flats' masking the side areas of the stage from the audience, hence the use of the word to describe also the areas just off-stage at each side.

Wood Family: Unoccupied seats, if they outnumber the occupied ones. A show doing bad business 'plays to the Wood Family' if the management has not bothered, or is unable, to 'paper the house' (*q.v.*).

INDEX

208

212

213